THE SKIERS

Also by Jen Craven

Best Years of Your Life
The Baby Left Behind
Her Daughter
The Day She Vanished

THE SKIERS

Jen Craven

ISBN: 979-8-9863116-2-3

www.jencraven.com
@jencravenauthor

For Dad
Thank you for always dropping me at the sandbar.

Witness #1 Statement

I saw it happen. And believe it or not, I wasn't all that surprised. I mean, those two had it out for each other since childhood. The media didn't help anything, always pitting them against one another. Poor girls. They were in a lose-lose situation. Everyone's saying it was an accident, but I know one thing for sure: boats don't just explode on their own.

Chapter 1

NOW
March

The thing about friends is they want to see you succeed, just never more than them. This truth had been ingrained in Sadie Norcross for twenty-eight years—how to be gracious on the outside, and ruthless on the inside. It's what set her apart. What led to her being the face of an otherwise unknown sport.

"I don't understand why this has to be a joint interview," Deb Norcross said, standing next to her daughter, one hand on her hip, the other holding a white tumbler printed with Romans 8:31 in small script font. *If God is for us, who can be against us?* She tapped a heeled boot on the hotel's hardwood floor. A few staff members peeked out from around the corner, hoping to get a glimpse of the skiing stars, only to be disappointed to find much of the camera equipment and umbrella studio lights blocking their view. "Just because you're the two biggest names, doesn't mean you always have to be paired together like some sort of package. She's not your friend, Sadie. She's the competition. This is *People* magazine we're talking about. It should have been *your* interview, *your* moment."

Sadie blinked away the puff of powder that billowed from the makeup artist's brush. She shrugged. "It is what it is."

She had to be careful what she said, had to calculate her response to appease her "momager." The truth was, Sadie had woken with butterflies in her stomach that morning, knowing she'd be sitting side-by-side with Willa again. Sure, they saw each other at every competition, spent the last eighteen summers trying to one-up each other, but the once childhood friendship faded a long time ago when adult things entered their young lives. As it turned out, neither got to be a kid for long.

Sadie picked a piece of dry skin from her bottom lip. Would she have chosen for this to be a joint interview? No—especially not with Willa. But then again, Sadie probably would have preferred no interview at all if she'd had her way.

If only she had that much control over her own life.

"Well, I think this is bullshit," Deb said with a huff. "It's not what we originally agreed to, and they shouldn't have sprung this change at the last—"

"Mom," Sadie said with a pointed look. "Please. Drop it."

If it had been a smaller outlet, Deb probably would have canceled the whole thing. But this was *People*, and the cover story to boot. Deb had remarked more than once that *she* had never made the cover of *People* during *her* heyday.

Despite her reluctance, Sadie recognized a big deal when she saw one. Even Baz, her husband, had seemed impressed. This was a major publication. These people had connections. And connections were what had secured the Goode sponsorship last year. Not just any ski brand—the best. With a name like Norcross, Deb reminded Sadie daily, they were entitled to the best.

Sadie yanked the paper collar protector from her shirt. "I think we're good here." Too much makeup—she never wore more than waterproof mascara and lip balm. She tossed her glossy blonde hair behind her shoulders, not used to the way it felt after being blown out by a professional. Not even her mom got dolled up regularly. In their world, sunscreen replaced foundation, and swimwear counted as clothing.

"You don't want the earrings?" Deb said, holding up a pair of sparkly gold hoops to which Sadie crinkled her nose. If she was going to be on the cover of a magazine, she wanted to look like herself. Fresh-faced. Natural.

Mother and daughter made their way across the room to where the interview had been set up. Two oversized arm chairs were positioned side by side, with a third facing them, a small table and vase of splashy flowers in the middle. The interviewer, a staff writer from the magazine Sadie had learned once wrote a feature on Simone Biles, sat with her legs crossed, reviewing notecards on her lap.

Deb leaned in close to her daughter. "It'll be the standard questions. How you're feeling about the season, your goals, all the usual stuff. I'm sure they'll want to talk about Baz. Shame he isn't feeling well. Stomach flu, you said?"

"Mmmm," Sadie acknowledged.

"Of course, on the day of your biggest interview. Imagine how much better it would have been if it had been you and Baz on the cover. Oh well. We'll make the best of it." Deb smoothed a wrinkle from Sadie's shirt, pulled the cross necklace out so it was more visible. "Since it's Willa instead, I'm sure they'll try to draw comparisons. You know how the media loves a friendly rivalry. But don't worry—it'll be good for us. You've always been better with the press. Just be yourself."

Yourself. Such a seemingly simple concept.

At the exact moment Sadie pondered the comment, the door opened and everyone turned. Willa Betts came through, dark hair trailing like Black Beauty's mane. She'd mastered the sporty chic look the stylist had requested—jeans and a quarter-zip with sharp, neon trim. Those in the room couldn't help but gawk at Sadie and Willa, the visual of them outside their signature swimsuits completely odd. Sort of like running into a college professor wearing sweatpants on the weekend. Sometimes it's easy to forget that even recognizable figures are still just regular people.

"Ah, welcome, Willa," the interviewer said, covering the ground to shake Willa's hand, and then turning to her coach, Roxanne, who followed closely behind. Willa returned the greeting with a polite smile and a hello. "Such a pleasure to meet you. Come on in. We're just about ready to get started. You're going to be here, the chair on the right."

Willa and Roxanne continued, passing where Deb Norcross stood against the wall, skinny jeans as tight as her scowl. Sadie couldn't be sure, but she felt the room's temperature dip at that very second.

Willa took her seat as instructed, and a makeup artist swooped in to do her magic. She patted tan powder—two shades darker than Sadie's—onto Willa's nose. "Gets rid of the shine," she said with a smile. Satisfied, she replaced the compact and touched up Willa's hair, brushing it off her face. "Oh. You want me to...?" She held up a small bottle of concealer and gestured to Willa's forehead.

"No. Just leave it," Willa said, well-versed in accepting the scar that bothered others far more than it bothered her. In her teenage years, she'd worn sideswept bangs to cover it, but that was ages ago. She no longer cared. The makeup artist nodded, gave Willa one last look, and moved out of camera shot.

Sadie sat, instinctively crossing her ankles like she'd always been taught. Her grandfather was a stickler for manners. She snuck a quick glance at Willa. The two didn't see each other like this often, all polished with blush and blowouts. It was usually more like soaking wet French braids and SPF. This felt foreign, and in the truest sense of the phrase, they really were fish out of water.

The air buzzed with anticipation. Having two big sports stars together made everyone giddy—all except Deb and Roxanne who had planted on opposite sides of the room and avoided eye contact at all costs. The two interview subjects sat awkwardly close, so close their elbows touched. Both equally striking, but whose looks were so diametric, it was as if they stemmed from different halves of the equator. So much history between them. So many confused emotions.

How much they each wanted to turn to the other, to impart a warm smile, to giggle at the memories of those early years on the lakes together. No one on the planet knew them better than each other. But things were different now, time and age and circumstances pulling them apart for reasons that should have brought them together.

Sadie pressed her hands in her lap. She cleared her throat and prayed this would be over quickly. After what felt like hours, the interviewer took a seat opposite the women. Sadie and Willa put on their best smiles.

"Ladies, thank you so much for taking the time today to talk with me. We at *People* have loved reporting on your careers, and we're just thrilled to have you both on the May cover to kick off the season. What a treat for our readers! Okay, let's get started. This first question is for you, Sadie…"

Chapter 2

Willa's blood boiled a little at that. Sadie first. Always Sadie first. Sadie got the louder cheers. Sadie made it to the top of the podium even if it was only by an inch. Sometimes Willa swore the judges were intimidated by the legendary Norcross name, by her grandfather, afraid they'd get blacklisted from the sport if they didn't score Sadie's runs the highest.

Willa wasn't a jealous person by nature—as an only child, it wasn't like she had siblings to squabble with—but even the most confident person can be rubbed wrong from time to time. Mention Sadie, and Willa was liable to become raw. And yet...that same person filled up more of Willa's fond memories than any other. Affection and envy in equal measure.

When *People* had reached out for the interview, Roxanne, as Willa's coach, agreed on the spot.

"Seriously?" Willa had said. "That's amazing!"

"Yes! But... there's more. It's with Sadie."

Willa's shoulders had dropped.

"Don't give me that look," Roxanne had said. "It's good PR. Drumming up hype for the season. You know this year's going to be a big one. You guys are at the top of your games. Our sport is finally getting the attention and coverage it deserves thanks to you."

She hadn't added *and Sadie*, and even though Willa knew it was true, she'd been grateful. For once it was nice not to hear their names together.

Willa had brushed off any residual annoyance. She was a pro at putting on a good face. Avoid and deflect, tactics she perfected growing up under a roof with parents who preferred the bottle over her. *Everything's fine. We're all fine. I'm fine.* Things at home had been complicated, dysfunctional. So in a way, Willa clung to Roxanne as a mother-figure for any semblance of normalcy, even if it meant doing joint interviews with her biggest rival. Children—and adults—desperate for love will do those things.

The interviewer tapped her pen against the typed cards on her lap and addressed Sadie. "The season opens with the Swiss Pro on May 1st. Are you ready?" From the shadows came a stifled laugh—Deb. Sadie lowered her chin, looked up through her lashes, giving the interviewer a look that said *Really?* The signature eye sparkle made her a media magnet. Willa grinded her teeth.

The woman laughed. "Right, right. Of course you're ready. Sadie Norcross is always ready to compete."

Willa made her best effort at a chuckle. Better to be in on the joke instead of on the outskirts. She poised herself for the same question—*And you, Willa, are you ready?*—but the interviewer continued with Sadie.

"Events only take up about half the year. What's your off-season like? What have you been doing since we last saw you?"

"Well," Sadie said, "it's not much of an off-season, really. I mean, I ski nearly every day. It's just not in the public eye. No competitions. But behind the scenes, I'm always training."

"I can imagine it would be hard to take too much time off."

"Skiing is my passion; I can never stay away long." The response came out robotic, like a factory setting programmed into a control panel in her back. Willa caught a glimpse of Sadie from the corner of her eye. *Is it?*

she wanted to ask. *Or is it your family's passion?* Somewhere in the room, she sensed Deb Norcross beaming.

"Does this upcoming season feel different? You're twenty-eight now, the height of your career, but there are others who are younger." She let the question linger, not quite stating what it implied.

Willa twisted the hem of her shirt, feeling annoyed and impatient. Why the hell was she even here if all the questions were going to Sadie?

"If you're asking if I'm threatened by my competition, the answer is no." Sadie stared straight ahead, and Willa felt herself flush at the boldness. She could read between the lines—Sadie's response had clearly meant *her.* Willa flexed her toes in her sneakers. *Not threatened? Okay, we'll see about that.*

"Speaking of competition," the interviewer said, pivoting her gaze. Willa straightened, shoulders back. *Finally.* "Willa, you've been skiing against Sadie your whole career. The two of you have had quite the matchups over the years, but at the end of the day, you're friends, right?"

Willa cracked a knuckle, sending out a *pop* louder than she'd anticipated. "I, uh...I mean, sure. Sadie and I have known each other since we were nine years old skiing in junior events. In a sense, we grew up together." Willa's mind traveled back, flashes of memories dancing across her conscience. Such a different time. What happened to those two little girls? She blinked, staying in the present. "But we're both serious competitors and serious competitors want to win, right?" A light laughter circled the room, though the meaning felt deeper than the words.

"Of course. You probably drive each other."

"Drive each other crazy, you mean?" Sadie interrupted, and the room erupted in real laughter that time. There she was again, the star of the show. People couldn't help but flock to her. Willa gave a pinched-mouth smile. Wouldn't want to come off less than good-humored. She wondered if Sadie wished the interview were over as much as she did. The two of them still hadn't made real eye contact.

"Willa," the interviewer continued, "it's no secret you've dealt with tragedy in your life. Loss at such a young age. How do you keep moving forward?"

Willa swallowed hard, the question catching her off guard. She breathed from her belly, trying not to let the panic show. *Keep to your script, give the same responses you've been giving for sixteen years.* "Everything disappears when I'm on the water," she said. "My past doesn't follow me out there." It was the answer everyone wanted to hear—the one where a child overcomes adversity and trauma. Only one other person knew the truth, and he was married to the woman sitting next to her.

The interviewer pivoted back to Sadie, and Willa let herself breathe again. "Can we expect to see your husband front and center at tournaments this year? We were sorry he wasn't able to participate in this interview today. You three were something of a trio growing up, right?"

Sadie touched the princess-cut diamond on her left hand. "Oh yes. Baz is my biggest supporter. He's really completed me as a person."

Willa bit her tongue.

"Such a disappointing turn of events for him," the interviewer said.

The crash that blew out Baz Tanner's shoulder and ended his skiing career happened mid-way through the season two years prior. Willa remembered it all like it was yesterday. The overwhelming urge to swim out to him, to hug him once they'd pulled him back to shore. Baz was never the same after that, and he never put a ski on again.

"Very disappointing," Sadie replied, with a quick glance toward her mother. Deb tapped her chest and mouthed something to Sadie, who in turn touched the cross necklace that hung around her neck. "But God works in mysterious ways, and we just have to keep the faith. Baz's injury has been a challenge, but I'm thrilled to have him out there supporting me."

The interviewer tilted her head, appearing so moved she might tear up. "An honorary Norcross."

"Yes."

Both Sadie and Willa looked down. Willa tried not to throw up in her mouth.

***

Finally, the whole uncomfortable thing came to a close.

"That was great," the interviewer said. "We're just going to snap a couple pictures for possible cover images. Okay?"

Sadie and Willa made their way to the other side of the room, which had been transformed into a photo set, complete with an erected white backdrop held up with poles and clips.

"Right there in the middle," the photographer said, pointing to two small Xs taped on the ground. "Willa, you on the right, and Sadie on the left. Uh huh, good. Yes, back-to-back. Now, look over your shoulders at me." They were almost the same height, but Sadie's lean limbs made her appear taller than she was. She craned her neck like a swan, delicate yet powerful. Willa pressed her shoulders back to match Sadie's stance. She might never have the slenderness, might always have more power in her thighs, but Willa's dark beauty was an unmatched trait. They were complete contrasts of each other.

The photographer peered into his lens, paused, then lowered the camera. "Maybe we should switch sides."

"Why?" Willa asked.

"Your, uh...your..." He pointed to his forehead, drawing an invisible diagonal line. "You don't want that showing in the picture, do you? If you trade places, we'll get the other side of your face." *The unblemished side.*

Willa's jaw clenched. "My scar doesn't bother me. If people don't like it, that's their issue."

"Oh, right, of course," he backtracked. "No problem. Stay right like that then."

Willa made a quick glance at Sadie, and it was then the two women's eyes locked for real. For the briefest moment she could hear them both saying the same thing: *This is all so silly. It doesn't have to be like this. We used to be friends.* But as fast as the thought came, it vanished, and they looked away.

"Right here," the photographer said, and the athletes smiled at the camera. Click. Click, click, click. "Perfect. Now one with the skis." Deb and Roxanne appeared and handed Sadie and Willa each a single ski. The smooth board felt like a third limb in Willa's arms, a piece of her soul. So habitual, she often found skiing more natural than walking.

The women stood their skis on end, clasping a hand around the beveled edges. Competing brand names flashed from the lacquered surface in big, bold letters, another thing to add to their list of oppositions. Rival skiers, rival sponsors. Inside, they were so much alike, those two. They could have let those similarities shine outward too if higher forces hadn't thrust a wedge where it needn't be. Now it felt too late to take it all back. Their paths were set. Only one could be the greatest.

The photographer snapped away, taking more than enough shots for a single cover image, along with one or two to accompany the article. "Aaaaand, done," he said, with a final click. Willa and Sadie exhaled.

They didn't know it at the time, but the magazine would choose a sober shot for the cover—one of the images where both women stared straight into the camera, mouths set in lines, determined eyes. It wasn't an intentional take, just one of those in-between clicks, but the deputy editor would choose it anyway, and accompany it with a headline that read "Rival on the Water," again perpetuating a narrative neither woman set out for.

Willa and Sadie retreated to their respective corners, as the crew began to disassemble the set.

"Nice job," Roxanne whispered to Willa, giving her an affectionate pat on the butt. "You're better than her."

On the other side of the room, Deb Norcross leaned into her daughter's ear. "Well played. Don't you forget, you're better than her."

Chapter 3

THEN
Summer 2004

The wind had picked up that morning, not enough for the average person to notice, but enough for a water skier—even a ten-year-old water skier. Tiny ripples crawled across the surface of Chaste Lake. Anything other than glass was less than ideal. But they'd trained for all conditions. Those girls had skied far rougher waters than this. A competition was a competition, and both Sadie Norcross and Willa Betts were ready.

Sort of.

"Sadie, what are you doing? I told you to put the dolls away. You're up next." Deb Norcross, hands on her hips, approached where the girls were playing on the grassy bank. Her blue eyes matched the claw clip holding up her blonde hair, the same icy locks that flowed from Sadie's head.

Sadie jumped at her mother's words and extended the Barbie to Willa. "Here, keep it."

"Really?" Willa's eyes grew wide.

"Sadie," Deb said with a disapproving look. She'd just got her daughter that water ski Barbie—and all the accessories—for her birthday.

Sadie lowered her eyes then smiled and reassured her friend. "It's fine." What she didn't add was that she'd rather decorate Barbie's dreamhouse than zoom the toy around on an imaginary lake. What was one less doll anyway? Sadie wouldn't even miss her. Plus, now she and Willa could play with them together. Their dolls could be sisters—Sadie's would give them matching pink rooms in their mansion, and Willa's could take care of winning all the ski events.

"Come on," Deb said, putting a hand on Sadie's back to lead her away.

"Good luck!" Willa called, clutching the Barbie.

Sadie waved a gangly arm. "You too!"

* * *

A few yards away, Baz Tanner pretended to focus on his Nintendo DS. The toy made a noise, a sad *womp-womp-womp*, indicating his player had died. No surprise—he'd been paying more attention to the girls than the game. Something about those two fascinated him. And for as much as he loved to ski, it was goofing around with Sadie and Willa at events that he most looked forward to. He'd play with them when it was things like tag or when Sadie got her new Tamagotchi. But Barbies? He drew the line there. Most of the time they just hung out, three kids doing kid things, waiting for their turn to ski. Always together, never far apart.

Today, he hung back, wishing they could wander the banks counting lily pads. Instead, the girls had chosen dolls. Bor-ing! Maybe after the first round was over he'd suggest hide and seek amongst the tents and cars. Willa was always down to play. Sadie, too—if she was allowed. To him, they were sort of like the Three Musketeers—but he wouldn't say that out loud. Not to *girls*. Still, even without the label, the friendship was a given.

Just last year, they'd sat on the ground together, butts becoming soaked from the morning dew, and put their hands on top of one another.

"A pact," Sadie had said. Willa nodded, happy to follow along with anything.

"For what?" Baz replied.

"Friends forever."

Their hands did a little dip, and then they released them into the air in a collective shout. "Friends forever!"

* * *

Deb and Sadie made their way toward the Nautique tied to the wide, wooden dock. Sadie hopped on.

"Careful," her mother said, as if it was Sadie's first time around a boat instead of having spent the entirety of her life in one. Sadie knew just about everything there was to know about boating, including how to pull a skier at exactly thirty-four miles per hour and how to effectively snap all twelve snaps on a boat cover before a raincloud unleashed a downpour.

"Ready, champ?" her grandfather said, coming onto the dock.

Sadie nodded. She loved and hated his nickname for her—both an honor and an impossible goal coming from one of the most celebrated slalom skiers in recent history. Bill "Leather" Norcross was the only man in the fifty-plus age group to successfully complete a full slalom course at the max speed and shortest rope length. His whole existence revolved around water and sun, a lifestyle that garnered him his aptly-fit moniker by the time he hit forty. The man never wore sunscreen a day in his life. It was a wonder he wasn't covered in skin cancer.

He may not have been a walking case for proper skincare, but Leather was a legend in the sport and an icon in the Church. Which made it only fitting that his offspring, and their offspring, would follow suit. Deb was ranked as the top female slalom skier in the world for nearly fifteen years. So storied was the Norcross name that Deb kept it when she married Mark, and they even agreed to use it for their children. Long live the greatest waterski family ever to grace the water. Good, faithful Christians, who happened to possess an incredible athletic gene. How much more perfect could they get? At ten, Sadie idolized them.

"Don't forget," Deb said. "Lean into the turn, arms straight. No yanking. Nice and smooth." She sliced her hand through the air, mimicking the curves. All those old medals and plaques at home didn't mean much to Sadie—her mother might have been a world champion, but to a kid, a mom is just a mom.

"I got it," Sadie said, not even looking her way.

"Yeah, Mom, she's got it," Leather echoed.

Deb raised her hands in playful fashion. *Fine, sorry for offering any tips.* There was no sense trying to coach her daughter—ten was basically thirteen, which was basically sixteen, which meant there were plenty of rolling eyes and I-know-more-than-you attitude. And anyway, Leather took the lead in the coaching department. The Norcrosses were big personalities, and poor Mark often took a backseat to his wife, father-in-law, and now daughter. It was probably why, after retiring from skiing, he'd taken a job that had nothing to do with water. Something with computer software—Sadie wasn't too sure.

Deb leaned down. "Let me pin you." She reached to pin Sadie's number on the back of her vest, careful not to cover up the sponsor logo. It was a low-name sportswear brand, but a sponsorship was a sponsorship. They didn't need the money. It was more about the prestige. Someday, her daughter would get the big ones: Goode, MasterCraft, Radar.

From under a tent along the bank, the broadcaster announced Sadie's name, and a round of applause chorused across the bleachers. One of the biggest races of the season, the Junior U.S. Open just outside Mobile,

Alabama drew crowds into the hundreds. Sadie's family had made the six-hour drive from Florida the previous day. All those spectator eyes made Sadie's insides twist. It was a lot of people. But she reminded herself she loved it—the thrill, the challenge, the finish. The approval.

You love this sport. You love this sport.

The more she said it, the easier it was to believe.

"For any newbies in the crowd today," the announcer boomed into the microphone, "here's how this works. Skiers will attempt the course starting at a rope length of fourteen meters. With each subsequent pass, the rope length will shorten, making it more difficult. There are six buoys, or balls, the skiers will attempt to round. Points will be given for full, half and quarter buoys. The skier with the most points at the shortest rope length will be the winner!"

Sadie tightened her boot bindings and fastened the Velcro on her gloves.

"All right, kiddo. You've got this. Watch your cuts; there's a little wind today." Leather put both hands on her shoulders. "Remember, this is supposed to be fun...but winning is great too." He winked, then gave Sadie a final high-five and stood back as the official race driver put the boat in gear. Sadie perched on the edge of the dock, ski firmly on her feet, and long blonde braid falling over her vest. By this time of the year, her hair had been so kissed by the sun, it was practically white.

Sadie peeked back to where her mom and grandpa stood. Binoculars hung around Deb's neck. Leather, stopwatch ready.

No pressure, kid.

Along the bank, the other skiers watched—sizing up the competition. Not everyone drew the same attention Sadie did, but between her name and Willa's talent, there were no shortage of crowds. Skiing wasn't a hugely popular sport, but according to her mom and grandfather, Sadie had the power to change all that.

Sadie grabbed the rope handle, then scooted off the edge into the warm water. She let out a little hum. This was so much better than skiing in the early spring or late fall, when that first splashdown took her breath away and brought goosebumps to her body. July was her favorite weather month.

The boat idled ahead, taking up slack in the rope until it was square with the course. Sadie released a long exhale, balancing herself as best as possible. Then, with a commanding voice, she shouted the same two words she'd said thousands of times: "Hit it!"

The boat roared forward, its nose rising out of the water. Sadie stayed in her ball, knees tight, letting the motion pop her up with ease. "It's just like standing up from a chair," Leather used to say to four-year-old Sadie when she was first learning. But that was combo skis—two instead of one. Slalom was a bit different, not as easy to "just stand up" with one foot in front of the other on a 7-inch-wide composite plank.

That was years ago. Now, she crested the surface in a breeze. She resisted picking the wedgie of her suit bottom, which she knew her mom would spot and scold her for. No time for focusing on anything but the course. If she was too worried about hair in her face or a swimsuit creeping up her backside, she'd miss the first ball.

Within seconds, the boat flew through the starting gate. Sadie leaned to pull herself outside the right-hand wake. The buoy approached. She released an arm, extending her body out as far as it would go. She rounded it, shifting her weight to the inside edge to send an arc of water spraying into the air. The crowd roared. But there was no time to celebrate.

She flew across the wake at lightning speed and did the same thing on the other side, catching the two ball. Leaning, spraying. Back and forth. Three buoys, four, then five, and finally six. All in a matter of thirty seconds.

Sadie didn't miss a single one.

She tossed the handle and dropped into the water, immediately kicking off her ski and ripping open her gloves.

When she got back to the starting line, she could see Leather on the dock, wearing a grin from ear to ear. "Nice run, champ!" he called.

"Thanks, Pops!" Sadie's heart raced and she took slow, deep breaths to conserve energy. Within two minutes, her score flashed across the board: six buoys at fourteen meters—or as race insiders would shorten to 6@14. This was the easy part. The first run always had the longest rope. Now to go back and do it all again at a shorter length. Sadie got in position, yelled "hit it" and skied.

Two runs later, and the round was finished. Sadie received 3@12—a score that would be tough to beat.

Deb gave a dripping Sadie a side hug. "Nice run, Sade. A little close on number three, though. You almost nicked it."

Sadie nodded, still catching her breath.

"That could have been a half-buoy," Leather added.

Sadie nodded again. She'd do better next time, she promised.

She slipped off her vest and wrapped a towel around her shoulders. Even in eighty-degree weather, little body fat meant she was prone to a chill. She was, after all, no more than seventy pounds soaking wet.

Sadie sat on the ground, prickling with a wash of relief. She'd done okay. And now she wouldn't have to perform for another couple of weeks. The feeling brought temporary comfort—not that she'd ever say so aloud.

She watched other skiers take their turns—girls and boys in varying age categories and skill levels. None as good as her.

None, until Willa Betts.

Chapter 4

THEN
Summer 2004

"Bet on Betts" was the slogan Roxanne came up with. The fans loved it. The media loved it. Here was a freak athlete child, destined for stardom. And now people were encouraged to bet on her success. Clever and fun, sure—but a lot for a ten-year-old to carry.

Unlike Sadie who descended from a skiing family, Willa's talent came as a surprise after a day at the lake with friends prompted a then-second-grade Willa to say, "Sure, I'll try that." Tried it and mastered it is what she did. There was just one problem: Willa's parents could barely keep their own life together let alone focus on cultivating the natural ability of an exceptional child. She'd been adulting since she was old enough to put her drunk parents to bed at the age of six. Knew enough to hide the liquor bottles strewn around the living room when someone came to the door.

The road to high achievement wasn't in Willa's cards. Nor was the money to get there. That was, until Roxanne Hill spotted young Willa that summer two years prior. The same Roxanne Hill who'd won the

American Cup against Deb Norcross a decade before and who'd recently set her sights on coaching. It was as though the stars aligned. Everything changed for Willa after that. Everything except the absent parents who still showed little interest. They remained the same.

Today's race was a big one, and Willa was ready. Sadie had just completed an impressive run, and while she was happy for her friend, something flicked against her ribcage.

She pulled her thick dark hair into a ponytail, as Roxanne tied the line off at fourteen meters. A little gust of wind gave her a shiver. Willa snuck a peek back at the shore to see if she could spot Baz. Was he watching her? She hoped so. Instead, she saw Sadie wrapped in a towel, and waved.

Roxanne handed Willa the rope handle at the end of the dock. "Hey, focus. First run. You ready?"

"Uh-huh." Willa tightened her gloves and gave her vest a tug down to cover the little bulge of skin atop her bikini bottom. It was a hand-me-down suit and the elastic was starting to wear. If she could pull off a win today, she'd ask her parents if she could use some of the cash prize to upgrade. Maybe they'd remember this time.

Roxanne tipped her chin up and closed her eyes. "Wind's out of the west. Careful on your starboard cuts. Damnit, I hate when it's not glass. But don't worry, you got this." She reached out and ran a hand down the back of Willa's head, then gave her nose a little, affectionate poke. Willa smiled, her insides warm.

The water definitely could have been smoother, Willa thought, but then again, she'd skied worse. The course should be a piece of cake. She'd watched Sadie finish moments ago—good, but not perfect—and knew she could beat it. This was her chance to take the lead.

"Up next, number 303, Willa Betts!" the announcer called. A round of applause. Then the familiar chant, first soft, then louder: "Bet on Betts! Bet on Betts!" Roxanne clapped above her head, egging on the crowd.

Willa's heart swelled. Nowhere else in her life did she get this sort of praise. Prone to Cs in school—not for lack of trying—she never got stickers on the top of her assignments. School wasn't a safe place. Girls snickered at her faded shirts, and boys whispered about her defective parents. An academic future seemed like a pipe dream, and since she had few other interests, Willa poured her soul into skiing.

In many ways, it—and Roxanne—had saved her.

Willa hopped in the water, arm through the triangle handle. She adjusted her ski underwater. The wind, which had seemingly increased with each passing minute, whipped tiny splashes into her face. Though she'd done it countless times before, she hated skiing when it was windy; it threw off her balance. *Breathe*, she told herself. *It's just like training.*

"Go get 'em, kiddo!" Roxanne called.

After making it to the starting gate and getting in position, Willa yelled, "Hit it!" and the boat took off. Up on plane, Willa shook her head to clear her vision, setting her eyes on the first ball. She left the wake, pulling hard, rounded the orange buoy, then shot back across the wake for the other side. Two down, four to go. Her ski bounced as it sliced through the choppy water. She tightened her grip and bent her knees, letting her legs absorb the rollers. Water sprayed into her mouth, and she spit it out, determined not to let anything ruin her run.

Back out to the right, the third ball. Starboard—the ones Roxanne warned about. Swoosh, slice. Rounded, no problem. *I've got this.* Four ball—yes! Two more to go. Willa flew across the wake, face pinched, vision focused. But at the same time she was about to lean into the next turn, a strong gust came from the left side of the lake. A ripple caught her edge, and suddenly she'd lost control. Her ski wobbled, her body following suit, and that millisecond was enough to throw her off course. Willa slammed into the buoy, the force causing her to lurch forward, dropping the rope and crashing into the front of her ski. Her forehead hit the top edge and a searing pain shot through her skull. Under the water, she let out a bubble of air—maybe it was a scream—and then the only thought was getting to the surface. But which way was up? She was completely disoriented.

When she finally popped up, instinct drew a hand to her forehead. She looked at her blood-covered glove and tears came to her eyes. Where was her ski? She looked around. There it was, now ten feet away. The world spun. She felt woozy. Her first run of the day and she'd crashed. The odds were inconceivable. This was supposed to be the easiest of her runs.

The boat came flying back. "You good?" the driver yelled, standing up from her seat. There'd been plenty of falls over the years, but once the middle-aged woman in a ball cap saw Willa's face, her expression registered alarm. "Oh my god."

"Hit my ski," Willa sputtered, on the edge of consciousness. "Is it bad?" It was hard to tell—once blood touches water, it spreads two-fold.

"It's bad. Get in. We need the paramedics."

And that's how Willa Betts got the scar that runs from hairline to the bridge of her nose, never quite healing as well as a laceration that gets proper care. How can anyone expect ten staples not to leave residual effects? And a plastic surgeon? No money for that. Sure, those staples left a permanent mark on Willa Betts' pretty round face, but the true scar was much deeper than that. That incident, those aftershocks, and the scar as a visible reminder set Willa Betts and Sadie Norcross on a collision course twenty years in the making. One where rivalry and friendship blurred together, and where outside accolades never quite made up for what mattered most.

Chapter 5

NOW

Sadie's chest burned every time she came home to find Baz playing on his stupid Xbox. Between the guns and the gore and the sound effects, it was enough to shut her in her room for the night with her sketchpad. Sure, there were times back in the early years when they'd played together—Mario Kart and Madden NFL—but that hobby passed for Sadie by the time she hit twenty. Video games were for kids, not almost-thirty-year-olds. Especially thirty-year-olds who were currently unemployed. *Sebastian,* she felt like saying, using his full name in a disciplinary tone.

There was hardly a point.

"Hi," she said, dropping her purse on the gray marble counter. Their Jacksonville apartment had floor to ceiling windows looking out over the St. Johns River from the fifth floor—high enough to avoid nosy paparazzi. Beautiful, solid furniture filled each room, and every surface displayed the perfect assortment of decor—a ceramic vase here, antique candlesticks there. Built-in bookshelves showcased gilded picture frames of happy times, scattered amongst thick coffee table books on interior design and style. Their place was high end, and while Sadie loved it—she'd decorated it herself—she'd always looked forward to owning a house outside the city. Some place quieter, with fewer people. That had been the plan at one time: to start a family and move to the suburbs. It's what her parents did, so it's what she and Baz would do.

Yet here they were. In limbo, dreams stalled.

"Helloooo," she said again a bit louder, and Baz turned, lifting a headphone from his ear.

"Oh, hey. Didn't hear you come in." They stayed like that—her, hand on hip, him wanting to get back to his game—for an awkward second. Like all observant husbands, Baz could quickly tell he was missing something. It took a minute and then hit him. "How was the interview?" *Whew*, not a birthday, not an anniversary. He left the headphones off, but returned his eyes to the screen and jabbed at the buttons on the controller to keep playing.

Sadie looped her thumbs through the thumbholes on her jacket, then tucked her hands into her armpits. "Good. Typical. Same questions as always." It had been one of those unsaid things where he hadn't volunteered to tag along, and she hadn't asked him to. But that kind of disinterest never would fly with her mother, so Sadie had had to come up with a plausible excuse. Stomach bug always did the trick. She thought back to the interview questions, the instances Baz's name was brought up, the way she felt Willa tense up. "Pretty much the same as every other interview. Skiing, family, Pops. Although, I guess it was a little different with Willa there."

At that, he whipped his head around, sending his sandy brown hair into a *swish*. "Willa was there? Why?"

"It was a joint interview. You know, the media loves seeing us together. Trying to drum up excitement for the season."

"Oh."

Did his cheeks pinken or had she imagined it? Hard to tell with the perpetual suntan. Still, Sadie's belly did a little somersault. *Oh, so you would have wanted to go if you'd known she'd be there?* She steered the conversation away from Willa.

"Mom was pissed."

"Hmm."

She took his response as the end of their exchange. Sadie watched as he continued to play, this time scouring a deserted war zone. She didn't get it—how could video games be so much more entertaining than spending time with her? What happened to the nights of endless talking, making plans for the future? When was the last time they'd taken a vacation together outside of ski events?

Sadie's marriage to Baz Tanner had caused a splash in the skiing world. Two equally talented athletes joined to create one super, impossibly beautiful duo. The fans devoured it, which Sadie would come to learn was the point.

If only they knew the whole story.

Now, when she looked at him, she saw a shell of who he used to be. Gone was the laugh that made his eyes crinkle. Sure, he was still as fit and handsome as ever, all lean muscles and a smile that would knock most women off their feet. But it didn't have the same effect on her—not anymore. His touch no longer made the hairs on the back of her neck stand up.

"I guess I'll let you finish," she said, though he didn't hear. She retreated to their bedroom, the largest of the three in the apartment, the one with the attached bathroom. She sat on the edge of the bed and grabbed the chenille throw, pulling it to her stomach in a ball. She could have asked him to turn off the game, could have initiated a conversation long overdue, but going down that road felt impossible. What was the point? Sometimes sticking with the status quo outweighed disrupting everything. Sadie lowered her chin onto the pillow. Her throat tightened and her eyes prickled. This wasn't what she'd envisioned her life to be…in more ways than one. She needed a diversion.

Sadie opened Pinterest on her phone and scrolled through the collage of images the app curated for her—perfectly designed homes, living rooms and bedrooms with magazine-worthy aesthetics. Captions like "Interior Inspiration" and "Step Inside This Modern Boho Oasis" made the wires in her brain fire alive. She clicked on pictures that caught her eye, adding several to her variety of saved folders. In another life, maybe she'd be using her eye for decorating as more than just a means of distraction on her phone. She closed her eyes and let herself go there—picturing herself at the helm of a design firm, working with influential clients, spreading her creativity throughout homes, her work landing in *Architectural Digest*.

On the bed, her phone buzzed and the daydream popped. Sadie opened the text from her mother.

Great interview today. Hope Baz is feeling better.

A zing made its way through her core. She didn't like lying. It wasn't how she was raised, a stark contrast to those strong Christian values. But she wasn't ready to admit the truth yet. More than that, she wasn't ready to believe it herself. Nonetheless, like a race buoy, it was coming whether she liked it or not. She just needed to decide whether she was going to lunge for the turn or miss it completely.

* * *

Baz stared at the screen absentmindedly. How can a sixteen-year-old kid know what love is? They were children. They were infatuated. Teenage boys were nothing more than hormones and erections. But on top of his lust, Baz did love Sadie, starting all the way back in tenth grade and for a while after that. The world fell in love with the *idea* of them. So that's what happened. Baz and Sadie became a thing. And some things are hard to break. Only, circumstances had changed; things had *happened*. And now, there they were. Twelve years is a long time to be with someone, especially when you haven't even reached your thirties.

On screen, a zombie jumped out from behind a wall and attacked Baz's player. The avatar crumbled into dust. Game over. Baz tossed the controller to the couch and leaned back into the plush cushions. He ran both hands through his hair. This was getting old. He needed a job. Tagging along to Sadie's events made him feel like nothing more than a lost puppy. If skiing was no longer his future, he'd have to come up with something else. But what?

Baz closed his eyes, trying to formulate a career. He'd taken a few college classes, but gave up when the pro circuit proved far more fun than two-hour lectures. Then it all came crashing down—literally—and the idea of doing anything else was hard to grasp. He rolled his shoulder in forward circles, feeling a slight pull with each rotation. Twenty-eight and already his body was betraying him. He tried to mentally tally his other interests like a high schooler taking a career assessment test, but came up blank. Something—someone—blocked his focus.

Willa.

It was a name he wished he could get out of his mind. A name that attached itself to his blood cells and traveled freely through his veins. Willa and oxygen, two necessities of life.

The off-season was easier to navigate because it meant distance between them—him in Jacksonville and Willa in Orlando, even if the cities were only two hours apart. But around this time every year, his skin started to itch, knowing the ski season was upon them. With the ski season came Willa. There was no avoiding her. Not when they were three of the biggest names in the sport, even after his retirement. Fans wanted pictures with them, announcers hollered their names like a single unit. Sadie Norcross, Baz Tanner, and Willa Betts.

Baz closed his eyes, picturing Willa's long dark hair, so different from his wife's. How it fell across the scar on her forehead. That one time he'd reached out and touched it. He wanted to do it again. The desire to see her was like a panging sweet tooth after dinner, one he couldn't quell.

He opened Instagram and typed in her handle, @WillaBettsSki. Nothing new since he'd looked four days ago, so he clicked on the pinned post at the top of her grid, a skiing video from last year, and watched it for the dozenth time. The way her body bowed to each turn, the celebratory fist pump at the end. Her energy came through the screen, penetrating his fingertips. He typed her name into Google to find the latest tabloid sighting, a silly piece from Page Six with the headline, WILLA BETTS STEPS OUT FOR A MID-DAY TARGET RUN.

He wondered what she was shopping for. He pictured her buying one of those matching workout sets that Sadie often wore, and then the thought sent a stab of shame down his back.

From down the hall, the sound of the shower turning on was enough to make him jolt. Baz quickly closed out of the app. His and Sadie's lives felt more like parallel streets than a double-laned highway. The spark long gone, left only with a public show. There was a time when he would have bounced off the couch and gone to join her—flinging open the curtain to hear her squeal, then stepping into the hot stream, body against body.

But today, Baz stayed put. He wasn't thinking about Sadie at all.

Chapter 6

Willa's chest burned every time she pulled into her dad's driveway. She'd been playing the what-will-I-find-today game her whole life. It used to be, *Will he be passed out at eleven in the morning?* Now it was more like, *Will his liver make it through the night?*

She supposed the two questions were linked.

Willa used her key to open the front door and stepped onto the sisal doormat just inside, removing her shoes. It was a habit instilled from when her mom was alive—Autumn was a hot mess, but she had a thing about dirt—and even though her father regularly wore his sneakers all around the house, Willa just couldn't shake the tendency.

"Dad?" she called, shifting the paper grocery bag in her arms so she could drop her purse on the floor. She heard shuffling coming from the bathroom, followed by the flush of a toilet. *Well, whaddya know,* she thought. He'd actually gotten off the couch. It wasn't uncommon for Dale to wait all day to pee, and even then it sometimes came out dark brown. One of the many side effects of end-stage liver failure. Willa listened when his doctors relayed information, but she stopped short of doing her own Google deep dives. That was for daughters who cared.

Or so she told herself.

Dale came slowly around the corner, holding onto furniture and door frames at all times. "Oh, hey Wills," he said, voice thick and hoarse. "I thought I heard someone come in." She bristled at the nickname. Only good parents should get to address their kids with such presumption. Dale didn't even know her favorite band. Did he know she'd developed an adult allergy to shellfish?

She took him in for the briefest second. At only fifty-four, he should have still been in his prime, not looking like an eighty-year-old man. Fathers of friends her age were running marathons, reaching the pinnacles of their careers. One lunatic dude, the dad of an acquaintance, just had a baby with his second wife. A few months ago, Willa took Dale shopping and the cashier had thought he was her grandfather. That was the last time Dale had left the house. Today, she was certain his skin looked even more yellow than last week, and he had to have lost another ten pounds everywhere but his distended abdomen. Skin hung from his jawline and neck, creating what Willa remembered her grandmother comparing to a turkey gobbler.

But what did she care? He'd done this to himself.

"They didn't have the tuna you like," Willa said robotically, emptying the grocery bag and putting everything into its proper place in the pantry and refrigerator. "So I got this kind instead." She held up a different brand, one she knew would taste just the same, but that her father would probably grumble about.

"Whatever," he mumbled. It would be a miracle if he even opened it.

She placed a fresh half-gallon of milk in the fridge and tossed a bag of wilted spinach into the garbage can. Dale didn't need much—he barely ate anymore—but she made sure he had the basics. Milk, bread, eggs. Clean sheets every week. Care she didn't owe him in the slightest but that she gave anyway, her sense of duty walking the fine line between love and hate. She regularly asked herself why she did it. He'd barely taken care of her as a child, yet now they found themselves in an emotionally-complicated role reversal.

"I need to sit back down," Dale said, turning back toward the living room. He couldn't stand for long periods of time. The nausea overtook him and he had to use every ounce of energy to get across the house. Apparently, his trip to the bathroom was it for the day. From the other room, she heard him grunt as he collapsed back into his recliner.

Willa finished unloading the groceries, then joined him in the living room. She looked around. It was strange to see the house from the eyes of an adult. How much bigger it seemed when she was a kid. How little had changed in almost three decades. After her mom died, her father didn't touch a thing. And so the small brick house on the outskirts of Orlando was very much stuck in the mid-nineties—floral wallpaper and all. So many memories of that time, her childhood one big bad dream. Her mind threatened to carry her back, but she dropped a mental blockade. *No. Don't go there.*

"When's your next tournament?" Dale asked through jagged breaths, still regulating after his brief walk from room to room.

"Clermont always kicks off the season the first week of May." He should know this. She'd only been skiing the Swiss Pro Slalom in Clermont, Florida, for over ten years.

"Right. Would you sit? You're making me nervous."

"I can't stay."

"Just sit."

She sat. Appeased, Dale laid his head back.

The doctors had given him eighteen months back in October, but Willa's gut said he wouldn't make it that long. Not with the decline she'd seen in recent weeks. With the season starting soon, she wouldn't be around as much to look in on him. The pro circuit took her not just across the country, but around the world. Her training was intense. She'd have to talk to him about setting up nursing care, something she knew would be met with resistance.

Willa picked at a hangnail. Being in her childhood home was bittersweet. It meant spending time with her last remaining parent, the man who had only become sober in the last two years once the doctors told him he was going to die. It figured. Get a terminal diagnosis and decide to turn your life around.

But being there also meant reliving painful memories. Forgotten birthdays, social worker visits, overflowing recycling bins filled with empty glass bottles. Too many things she'd witnessed and tucked away.

Time was short, and it was running out. How unfair that this was what was left. A terminally sick father who didn't know anything about his only child. Shouldn't he be repenting? She could have left long ago, run away from this place and never looked back. But that's not what happened. That's not the turn of events that played out. A terrible secret held her there and by that time, she was stuck. If it weren't for Roxanne, who knew where she'd be? It turned out, as Willa learned slowly, family wasn't bound by blood; it was what you made it.

Only now, Willa unwillingly craved a connection with a man whose hugs she could count on one hand. *Why?* she asked herself daily. She had Roxanne, the woman who'd brushed out her wet hair after every race, and who later accompanied her furniture shopping for her first apartment. Why did she put herself in this position with her father? The answer was too entangled to sort out. At the end of the day, she supposed a child's desire for parental love trumped everything.

"Dad, remember how you let me drive around the old factory parking lots when I was a kid?" Willa said, a surge of nostalgia and nerves mixing together and forcing words from her mouth. Dangerous words.

"Ha," he laughed, eyes still closed. "You couldn't have been more than twelve."

"Ten."

"No way," he guffawed.

"Yes, I'm positive. I was ten. I remember because I felt so cool turning double digits and you letting me whip around in the Camry."

"That busted-ass thing." Dale laughed at the memory and the absurdity. A ten-year-old behind the wheel. It wasn't just reckless, it was embarrassing. Incompetent parenting at its finest.

Willa wasn't laughing. She'd slipped into a trance-like state, her conscience taking her back to a darker time. Something threatened to come up from the depths of her belly. Something she'd wanted to say for a long time. She should say it. She should tell him. He didn't have much more time here, and did she really want him dying without knowing the truth?

Willa snapped out of it. She blinked several times, then stared long and hard at her father. Did she owe him anything? The answer came swift and sure: No. She loved him, but despised him. Wanted him to stay forever, and also die that very night.

She pushed the truth back down. Some favors simply weren't owed.

They sat there in heavy silence for a few minutes, the only sound a faint ticking from a cheap plastic clock on the wall. Willa knew her father was asleep once the snoring started. Head tipped back, mouth agape, he rested one hand on his stomach, the other limp to his side. Willa stayed another beat, then stood and walked over to him. She picked up a pillow. Held it in her hands and squeezed. How easy it would be. The coroner would assume his liver had finally given out.

She'd be free. Wouldn't she?

Her breathing accelerated, fingers tingling. A hard ball of hate blocked the back of her throat. Willa dug her nails into the fabric.

She couldn't do it. She'd never do it, even if her irrational mind entertained the thought for even the briefest moment. Instead, she used one hand to lift his head and the other to slide the pillow behind. She brushed his thinning hair with her hand, then stood back. She wouldn't kiss his cheek—that was an intimacy they never shared. And with that, she left and returned to her modest house across town, wondering if he'd be alive the next time she came.

* * *

A package waited for Willa on her doorstep. She brought it inside, placing it on the kitchen counter, and sliced open the top with scissors. From inside, she removed a notecard with the O'Neill logo.

Willa,

Merch drop! We're excited for you to try this new comp vest. Also including pieces from the new spring/summer line. Enjoy!

Your O'Neill family

Willa unfolded the tissue paper and pulled out a teal neoprene vest with a chunky zipper running down the front next to the company's signature spray decal. She slipped it on over her top and went to the full-length mirror behind the bathroom door. The vest was sharp, and even though Willa didn't *need* a new one, it was part of her contract to sport the newest gear. Brand partnerships were mutually-beneficial—O'Neill got her as one of their faces, and she got free stuff. The excess of it all was something Willa was still getting used to, coming from a childhood where she was never the first owner of the clothes she wore. For once, she didn't feel like the last one getting picked at recess. These companies *wanted* her.

Willa returned to the box on the counter and pulled out two pairs of board shorts, a pink rash guard, three graphic tees and a ball cap with a chunky logo across the front. Willa held each up, determining her favorites. The shorts, for sure. Getting free clothes and equipment from her sponsors was a perk she enjoyed, but it was the checks in the mail that really mattered. Between O'Neill, Radar Skis, and Malibu Boats, Willa made enough money from sponsorships to cover her living expenses—but just that. She wasn't rolling in extra dough, and she regularly shopped sales at the grocery store, largely because it was the only thing she knew.

Many girls on tour had part-time jobs—some, like Christina Bear, were even in college—but Willa considered herself lucky that she'd been able to stop doing freelance social media work, and focus solely on skiing in the last few years. The sponsorships were a blessing. She relied on them, which was why she promptly laid out the new merchandise on the table and snapped a picture on her phone, then uploaded it to social media. "I love being an #ONeillGirl," she wrote in the caption, tagging the brand and adding a few additional hashtags. The post immediately flooded with likes. One jumped out at her.

Baz.

Her heart did a weird flutter. She clicked on his name and his profile filled the screen. How many times a week did she visit his social profiles hoping to see something new? More often than she'd like to admit. She scolded herself. Baz was a married man. She shouldn't be thinking about him at random hours of the day. But that didn't stop him from entering Willa's dreams at night.

She closed out of the app with a long exhale. There were so many eligible guys in Orlando—the barista at her favorite coffee shop, that hot one at the gym, even Dillon, whom she used to work with and who she knew had a crush on her—but no matter what she told herself, it was always Baz who remained in her crosshairs. He knew everything about her, the goods and the bads.

Someone like that was impossible to forget.

Chapter 7

Sadie was already awake when the phone rang at seven. She'd been sitting up in bed for close to an hour, computer on her lap and a gazillion browser tabs open to various interior design schools. It was her secret pastime, a guilty pleasure she kept to herself.

The other side of their king-size bed was empty—Baz often left early for the gym. No lazy morning breakfasts for them. Saying she minded would be a lie.

The phone rang again. Who it was would determine whether she'd answer. Meg, her closest high school friend (the only one who liked her for her and not her money)—yes. Her mother—no. She couldn't deal with her mom this early in the morning. Conversations with Deb required at least a cup of coffee, or something stronger. Espresso. Amphetamine.

But to her surprise, it was neither name that flashed across the screen. When she saw his name, she instinctively closed out of the browser completely, as though she were being caught looking at something forbidden, then slid her thumb across the screen and answered.

"Morning, Pop."

"Hi, champ," Leather's booming voice came through the line like he'd been awake and already taken a few ski runs before the sun even rose. His energy was boundless. Sadie smiled and slid onto her back, stretched one arm up to press against the gray padded headboard.

"What's up?" She talked to him like she would a friend, their connection via sport a dowel rod pressed through their centers, holding them firmly together. She'd felt special when he'd take her out for early morning ski runs, just the two of them. They'd bundle in sweatshirts and he'd bring her hot chocolate to keep her hands warm. And then they'd take turns slicing the glass surface of the lake. Back and forth, driving each other. She'd tuck her icy toes under his thigh as he drove back to the dock, savoring the moments. But it could never stop at just a fun thing to do together—it was always something more, something bigger. A destiny, whether she liked it or not.

For the record, she did not.

Sadie had long felt a buffer between them, one that said his love came with conditions. It was dependent on her trajectory, her success. Her following in the Norcross way of life. She often wondered if her mother felt the same, whether Leather as a grandpa was the same as Leather as a father. He'd coached Deb to the top, got her into the water ski hall of fame. But every time Sadie got brave enough to bring up any less-than-positive opinions about skiing, an inner voice talked her down. The inner voice sounded a lot like her mother.

"Gonna be a gorgeous day, kiddo," Leather said. "We should get out there and work on your—wait, hang on. Your mom's joining in. Just a sec..."

Sadie dropped her hand over her eyes with a flop. So much for a nice morning chat. She should have known better. A conference call. This was business, after all. Their lives revolved around skiing, and skiing was a twenty-four-seven operation, even during the off-season. It's all Sadie had ever known, and for a long time, she assumed all kid skier families were the same. Didn't every girl have a gym in her basement? Didn't every kid film commercials for their church? She went along because nothing told her not to.

But then high school came, and Sadie wasn't allowed to stay out as late as her friends because it would affect her morning training. She could never attend a sleepover on a Saturday because the next day was church. Her twenties were dedicated to growing her social media presence, but she couldn't post what she wanted unless it tied directly to the sport.

Slowly, Sadie realized her life—her family—was different from everyone else. There were athletes who were competitive, and then there were the Norcrosses. There were pastors, and then there was Jed. Two different levels. For Sadie, keeping up was exhausting.

Sadie heard a click on the line and then her mother's taut voice. "Hello? Can you hear me?"

"Yep, we're here, Deb," Leather said.

"Sadie?"

Sadie took a deep breath and released it. "I'm here."

"Good."

"I booked us another promo," Leather said. Sadie rolled her eyes. By "us," he meant *her*. Wasn't this her mother's role? She clenched her jaw. Leather continued. "Got a call from Jed yesterday, and we think it's time."

"A solo spot?" Deb said.

"She's been on top for years, and with the Goode sponsorship and interest from MasterCard, it makes sense to push this now. Her face is at a new level of recognition. It could really boost our congregation after that *People* magazine piece. Open us up to a whole new generation."

Deb made a noise of agreement. "Well, it's not like she's never been in an ad before. Remember the whole group shot? She would have been what, seven or eight? But you're probably right, now makes sense."

Sadie listened to them go back and forth, speaking about her in the third person as though she wasn't part of the call, like she wasn't laying there trying to get a word in. Finally, she broke through, interrupting her mother mid-sentence.

"Would someone like to fill me in?"

"The Church," Leather said. "Jed and I have been talking about getting you more in front of the camera. We could use a new face. Mine is, well, getting older." He laughed. "And Deb, well...sorry sweetheart, but I think it's Sadie's turn."

"No skin off my back," Deb said. "I've done my fair share."

Sadie's gut clenched. Jedidiah Abraham (she was fairly certain that wasn't his real last name) led the mega-church of which her grandfather was now a top member. Leather was the Tom Cruise to Jed's David Miscavige. And while Sadie had grown up with the big worship and rules and meetings, the whole thing never sat quite right in her gut. There was always something creepy about Jed. The hypnotic smile he could turn on and off. The teachings about good and evil, behaviors that were sins, things that would surely send her to the fiery depths of hell. But Sadie justified it all because her family was in so tight. Deb had been a talking head for them for years. If Leather and Deb said it was right, it was right. Who was Sadie to stray?

Still, the battle raged in her brain. Two sides. One, follow along; the other, question everything. Once, as a teen, Sadie had been sucked into a documentary series about Amish youths breaking free from their strict cultural rules. Wearing jeans, using electricity, drinking alcohol, all things that were forbidden before. Some found freedom in their new lives, while others couldn't handle the shock. Maybe it was guilt? Or familial influence? Either way, more than one returned. Sometimes Sadie felt like that. Leaving the thing you always knew wasn't as easy as outsiders thought—even as an adult.

But no TV show could lessen the knot that formed in her stomach whenever such topics came up. They'd danced around it for months. And now, what she'd been dreading for the last few years was laid out on the table. She would be taking a bigger role in an institution that gave her more questions than confidence.

"I think it's a great idea," Deb said. "Sadie's the poster child, and what a perfect way to bring more attention to the Church, right, Sade? It makes sense."

Sadie swallowed hard, fighting a wave of nausea even though she'd yet to eat. "I don't know..."

"What's not to know?" Leather said. "The Church has always supported us, and it's our duty to give back. Your mother did, and now you can."

"Yeah, but—"

"No buts," Deb said. "It's not like we're asking you to lead Sunday service. We'll take your headshot and put it up on a few billboards. They'll run a new commercial or two. Maybe even one with Baz."

Baz. Sadie glanced over to the empty side of the bed. Her heart pinched at the thought that he'd slipped out this morning without so much as a kiss, and at the same time, she was relieved. The flip-flop of emotions made her dizzy. She never quite knew what she wanted, and that only made things harder.

"We don't even need you to do anything, really," Deb added. "Not yet at least. Right, Dad?"

"Right. Exposure is exposure. It's just positioning for now. I'll be sure to work out a fair deal." He let out a whoop. "How can you say no to more money?"

Deb joined in on the laughter, but Sadie remained silent. She ran her hand from her forehead to rest on her ribs. Let it sit there like a weight. The heaviness felt crushing.

"I'm just not sure that—"

"Enough talking," Deb said. "Your grandfather and I agree this is what's best, so that's the end of it." A beat of silence, then, softer: "You know we're always looking out for you, Sade. Trust us."

"Norcross will be a name no one will forget," Leather added. And because obedience dictated everything in her life, Sadie clamped her mouth shut and didn't say another word. She could have taken this opportunity to come clean, to remind them of the dirty secret they'd hidden for over a decade, but that would have taken more courage than she had. It would have ruined everything, and she couldn't bring herself to do it. If there really was someone up there in the sky looking down over them, goddammit, she didn't want to disappoint Him.

Sadie hung up and dropped her phone with a thud. Once again, she'd remained tight lipped, thinking it was for the best. Consequences, however, have a funny way of picking and choosing their debuts.

Chapter 8

Baz hadn't looked at her when he'd tiptoed from the bedroom in the early morning hours; his conscience wouldn't let him. Here she was, the most famous athlete in their sport, a golden princess, beautiful, what any man would want—but none of it mattered. He'd tried and tried to make his heart feel things it didn't. Attempted to stay back in that teenage land when they were high on thirst and endorphins and couldn't keep their hands off each other. He knew every curve of her body, the pattern of her hairline, how that one pesky zit still showed up on her chin at the same time every month. But that was young love, as they say. And young love isn't always lifelong love.

That is, unless you get swept into something bigger. Something you can't get out of, at least not without shattering hearts and images along the way.

He couldn't swallow that burden.

So Baz had gone along with it all. He'd stayed. He loved Sadie, loved her more than anything for a long time. In the grand scheme of relationships, he was lucky. He'd hit the jackpot. She made for a good girlfriend when they were younger, and would probably make for a good wife now—to the right person.

The guilt ate at him. Sometimes when he knew he was being distant, he imagined her crying into her pillow at night, and he wanted to smack himself. Why couldn't he show her the affection she must want? There was only one reason he could claim: It's hard to give yourself to someone when your heart's in another place entirely.

Baz turned the corner outside their apartment on foot.

"Baz! Hey, Baz!"

He looked across the street. A paparazzi aimed a camera at him. Baz waved and continued forward, heading to his favorite café, the one that served the best coffee—nothing fancy, no shapes drawn with milk. Just piping hot brew, black as raven hair.

Willa's hair.

Dammit, why couldn't he stop thinking about her? The urge to talk to Willa felt like a compulsion that grew by the year. A necessity, like breathing, more constant than the ebbs and flows of waves. What began as a childhood friendship eventually transformed into something more. But by then, he was attached to Sadie, and well...it wasn't exactly easy to get out.

His communication with Willa had slowly declined as the years went on and as the rivalry between she and Sadie steamrolled forward. Still, they exchanged birthday texts, sent the occasional funny meme, asked how training was going. It was one of those friendships that picked up where it left off. He'd check in on her dad, she'd ask how his shoulder was healing. But now, it had been months since they'd talked, for no other reason than life taking them in parallel yet separate directions. The radio silence cast a darkness over his days, like an eclipse that refuses to move from in front of the sun.

Inside the café, Baz ordered his coffee and took a seat by the window. He twirled the ties of his hoodie.

He should text her.

No, he shouldn't.

Why not? They were just friends.

Maybe it was something in the spring air—a sense of hope, throwing caution to the wind—or maybe he simply let his heart take over, but Baz pulled his phone from his pocket. He considered an appropriate lead-in, something that would ease his conscience. He typed a new text.

heard you were with sadie yesterday

There. Innocent enough, right? A warm swell bubbled inside his chest. He held his breath as he waited for her response. The message sat there, fat and hopeful. She could be busy, or still sleeping even. He willed her to see the message—he might not be able to talk later. Now, he was alone. Now, he could text without anyone looking over his shoulder.

Finally, the status changed from Delivered to Read. A breath caught in Baz's throat. He looked around, as though someone would scold him if they knew what he was doing. *She's just a friend*, he reminded himself again. A friend for nearly two decades. That meant something, didn't it? They weren't the same kids from all those years ago, but that didn't stop him from knowing her phone number by heart. Didn't stop them from catching each other's eye at tournaments and pretending it was nothing.

Baz rubbed the back of his neck. It had to be nothing, because the alternative was what? Blowing up Sadie's world and his too?

A small TV in the corner of the ceiling was tuned to a morning show. A pair of figure skaters, husband and wife, were chatting with the anchor about their new book release, chronicling their partnership on and off the ice.

Baz listened, mesmerized, and then he disappeared into another time. He was at a tournament five years ago, the Lake 38 Pro Am in Tallahassee. He remembered that event vividly not only because he'd taken first place in the men's division, but because Sadie had won the women's after a contested video footage review. The judges hadn't been sure of her score, whether or not she'd cleared the sixth ball, and the other skier fighting for first—surprisingly, it hadn't been Willa that day—had disputed. Officials watched playbacks in slow motion over and over, zooming in until the video was grainy. Leather had been furious. Ultimately, the judges gave Sadie the buoy and she took the win. She and Baz stood on their respective podiums during the award ceremonies—men's first—after which the photographers insisted on joint photos. He and Sadie had hopped back up, this time together, wrapped their arms around each other's waists and smiled, wet hair shining against the sun.

It was a good memory, one Baz recalled fondly. The two of them on top of their game. On top of the world. From the outside, one would have questioned how their lives could have gotten much better. Looking back now, he recognized it to be about the time trouble started to scratch its way to the surface. Unease had been there long before, but they'd done a good job deflecting. These most recent five years weren't so smooth in that regard.

Baz looked to his phone again. Would Willa reply? What a dumb message to send. *Heard you were with Sadie yesterday.* Stupid. Not even a hello first. He kicked himself.

But then, three little dots appeared, and a zap of electricity traveled through his body.

It was nice to see her.

Leave it to Willa to take the high road. Baz knew the interview had probably been awkward for both women. He could imagine Sadie's frostiness—the kind that came out around her competitors, influenced no doubt by Deb and whatever strife lived between her and Roxanne, Willa's coach. Willa could have replied with a dig. But here she was, refusing to say a bad word.

Baz chewed the inside of his cheek. If bringing up the interview was his "in" to the conversation, he'd have to change it quick. The last thing he wanted to do was talk about Sadie. Willa, he assumed, felt the same. Hoping to keep the exchange going, he switched gears.

how's your dad?

Not good. Don't know if he'll make it to Christmas.

A tiny twinge hit his lungs. Baz had certain feelings about Dale Betts and the fact that the man was about as useless as a rock. He'd let Willa down more times than she could count, and now she carried far too much on her shoulders. Far more than any daughter should. Men like that didn't deserve daughters like her. The last time he'd spoken to Willa, she'd indicated Dale's health was rapidly failing, but hearing that he could be gone before the end of the year made it real.

shit, i'm sorry you're dealing with that

It's a lot.

Baz's heart gave a pang. He ached for her. Couldn't imagine being in her place. Not after being raised by parents who attended every event, still kept all his childhood medals and plastic trophies in a glass case in their den.

He waited, sensing there was more Willa wanted to say. He'd been her sounding board once. Promised he'd never tell her secret, never tell a soul. It was a promise he didn't keep, and also the biggest regret of his life.

When Willa didn't elaborate, his pulse began to pound. That couldn't be the end. He shot off another quick text.

he's lucky to have you

Is he?

of course

I feel so guilty about you know what.

there's still time to come clean

I don't know if I can.

The barista called his name and Baz got up to retrieve his drink. The cup was warm against his palm, and holding it gave him the smallest dose of comfort, like being on the water under the midday sun.

How should he respond to Willa's last message? *I don't know if I can.* Context was hard to interpret through a phone, far more difficult than talking face to face. He wished he could see her in person. She only lived two hours away, but how would he arrange it? And what excuse would he give Sadie?

Baz was mid-response—some throw-away comment about the upcoming season—when another message from Willa came through.

I've gotta go. Nice chatting.

His hand dropped to the table and he stared at the text, a sinking feeling taking over. His fingers twitched, wanting to beg her not to leave. But what was there to say?

Do you love me?

Can we be together?

Are you as miserable as I am?

No, none of those things would work. None of them were fair. So instead, Baz replied with two words he hoped were true:

talk soon

* * *

When he returned to the apartment, Sadie was at the island, cutting up strawberries for her morning yogurt.

"You're up," he said, coming through the door, coffee in hand. He took a sip.

She eyed him, then the cup, then returned her gaze to the counter. "Couldn't bring me one too?"

His eyes ping-ponged from drink to his wife. "You said you weren't drinking coffee anymore. That it upset your belly."

"Oh, so you *were* listening. That's nice to know."

Baz cocked his head, defensively. "What's that supposed to mean?"

"It means we hardly ever speak anymore, so I didn't expect you'd remember something as insignificant as me no longer drinking coffee."

Baz's head went from cocked to a full loll. "Are we seriously going to do this now?"

"Why not?" She dropped the knife next to the bowl and pressed both hands firmly on the counter. "You've been distant for months. We might as well talk about what's going on."

Baz let out a sigh and came to sit at one of the tall stools. "I'm just going through a weird patch, that's all. My shoulder, my career. Things are just different now, and it's not exactly easy."

It was a half-truth. The injury that put a full stop on his skiing career had shaken Baz to his core, practically altered his brain chemistry. But that wasn't all. There was more, and he knew it.

"Are you seeing someone else?" Sadie asked.

The question hit him like a surprise bullet. "What? No, of course not." His insides burned. They stared at each other, and then Baz's defenses got the best of him. "Are you?"

Sadie laughed. "When would I have time to be seeing someone?"

"That wasn't a no."

"No, Baz. I'm not having an affair."

"Fine. I just don't think it's fair for all the blame to be on me. What about all the cold shoulders, huh? Or how you have your earbuds in all night? You're not exactly giving us a chance to connect either."

They'd reached a stalemate. Both spoke the truth and both knew it. But how could they say what needed to be said? For two people still so young and with so much unknown ahead of them, they couldn't bear to step out of the safety net they'd lived in for over half their lives. And so, as had become routine, things would get overlooked. Arguments would get temporarily patched. It was what was required.

Sadie reached a hand out to cover his. Their tan skin matched in a shade of honey. She knew these hands well. "I'm sorry," she said, coming around the edge of the counter and putting her arms around him. His forehead pressed into the hollow below her collarbone. She breathed in his mussed, morning hair.

"I'm sorry, too," Baz said.

And because neither of them was truly convinced, but both were too afraid to admit it, they let the hug do the work, as if it would magically solve all their problems. Three seconds later, when they parted, they exchanged small smiles as a Band-Aid.

"Mom and Pop called a bit ago," she said, diverting the conversation away from the danger zone. "They want me to push into the Church more. Marketing and stuff."

"Haven't you been doing that since you were born?"

"Yes, but that was small stuff, and always with my parents. Now, they think I can make a bigger impact on my own."

"Doing what?"

"Billboards, maybe a commercial. I don't know." She hugged her arms around her middle. "It's all so weird, and I honestly don't know how I feel about it."

"Why? You've been around that stuff your whole life. Leather's successor. You're pretty much the perfect fit." He said it as if his family were as devout as hers, as though they weren't the type of people who only showed up at church on Easter and Christmas Eve. At least the Tanners weren't atheists—Deb would have squashed that attraction like a mosquito on a summer night.

Sadie's eyes drifted off, like she was somewhere else entirely. "Yeah, well..." And then under her breath, so low he almost didn't hear: "Some things aren't always what they seem."

Chapter 9
THEN
1963

Leather Norcross wasn't supposed to have this life. The money, the prestige. The overall comfort. Life didn't pan out like this for babies who were left at the steps of a church in the 1940s. Abandoned by his single mother who, even at twenty, knew there was a future for this little boy beyond what she could provide. So, she wrapped and tucked the scratchy blanket into a cocoon, a tiny pink face poking out into the sticky air of a Deep South night, and walked away with nothing more than a prayer.

She could never have imagined the life she'd just given him.

Little Leather would never know his mother, only three sets of foster parents who were decent, if not at all devoted. There were small gifts at Christmas, even a single trip to the ocean shore. And yet, he slept in a bed with another boy's name carved in the wood. One foster mother refused to read bedtime stories because she said they were a waste of time.

Leather survived with his spirit intact, albeit still searching for that feeling of place. That sureness of home. Love.

Awarded emancipation early at sixteen, Leather sought employment as his only means of independence. He'd save up money and move far away from central Florida, a place that held so much disappointment. Start a new life somewhere else—the North, the West; he didn't really care. Maybe he'd buy his first pair of fur-lined boots and a heavy coat and live where snow covered the ground. A complete reversal from all he'd known, something to clear his palate.

When he came across a maintenance position at the big church a few towns over, he took it without reservation. He could empty garbage. He could mow the lawn. He'd been doing chores at the foster homes since he could walk. It wouldn't be glamorous, but any paycheck, even a small one, was a step in the right direction.

The work was mindless and the pay was measly, but at least Leather could spend hours outside breathing fresh air and soaking in golden rays. Within the first month, he'd acquired a solid farmer's tan, his forearms deep in color, the back of his neck blending into his tawny hair.

Leather liked to watch the parishioners from afar. The women in their nipped-waist floral dresses and heels. The men in checkered suits, hair combed over and greased in place. And the hats—so many hats of all kinds. He'd never seen such finery. Leather's wardrobe consisted of a couple worn shirts and pants, shoes that were wearing thin at the soles. He wondered if good wool trousers were as scratchy as the kind he owned. He'd probably never know.

Church life seemed glamorous and mysterious. He'd listen to the roaring sermon through the closed doors of the lobby, but didn't dare step foot inside the assembly room. Not his place. He hummed along to the hymns as he swept the halls, trying to make sense of the words. God's redemptive plan. Proclaiming the gospel. It intrigued him and puzzled him at the same time. How could a God be so kind and just if there were people suffering in every corner of the world? If babies could be abandoned by their mothers only to live a life of near poverty?

He pondered these questions, and others, as he worked. Mostly, Leather stayed in the shadows, giving polite smiles to members of the congregation in passing. He was neither happy nor unhappy. But about a month after he started working at the church, he met the man who would change everything.

"You've got a way with the land," the voice said, as Leather was spreading a fresh layer of mulch across a flowerbed. He turned to see a well-dressed man with a young face, a hand up to his forehead to block the sun.

"Can I help you with something, sir?"

"What's your name?"

"Bill," Leather replied, because of course he was not yet the famous Leather Norcross. He was just Bill, a boy with no family and a last name given by foster parents he no longer even spoke to.

"Hi Bill, I'm Jed. I'm the pastor here."

Leather tried not to reveal his shock. This was the booming voice he heard through the doors? The one who made women weep and men empty their pockets in donations? This man didn't look old enough to cause such an effect. Studying him now, Leather thought Jed couldn't be more than twenty-five. Jed was thirty, to be exact, but his baby face—full cheeks, high, raised eyebrows—made him appear younger. He wasn't a tall man, but any stature he lacked physically, he made up for in charisma. Even outside, without four walls to contain him, Jed owned the room. The air around him buzzed with energy. It was a presence Leather couldn't quite describe. Like stepping into the company of someone *great*.

Leather gave a nod of courtesy. "Nice to meet you."

"I've been watching you over the past weeks, and I have to say I'm impressed with your work ethic. You're not like other boys your age. You've done well here."

"Thank you, sir."

"You like it?"

"It's well enough."

Jed made a small noise, a *mmm* of understanding, like he knew something about Leather that Leather didn't yet know about himself. "What are your plans?"

Leather stuttered. "My plans?"

"For the future."

The future. Such a big idea put so bluntly. Sure, Leather had thought about it, about moving away and starting a new life. But there was nothing concrete to it, nothing he could definitively say. In many ways, it felt more like a dream than anything. Who knew if he'd ever make enough money to do anything? So instead, he improvised. "I'm not sure I have any plans."

Jed nodded slowly, a sly grin on his face. "Good, good."

And then a silence hung between them, one where Leather felt like he was being examined, analyzed. He fanned out a pile of mulch in a grand rainbow sweep.

"Listen," Jed said. "What do you think about coming to work for me?"

"Aren't I already working for you, sir?"

"Please, call me Jed."

"Jed."

"I mean work in a more professional setting. Learning the business side of things. I could really use a right-hand man, and I think you might just be that guy."

Leather gaped at him. Business? Professional? Leather was none of those things. He had dirt under his fingernails that never quite washed away no matter how hard he scrubbed. He'd barely made it to high school, and then didn't even finish.

And yet...

The magnetism Jed exuded was a force Leather couldn't resist. The warm smile, the openness. It felt like an invitation to an important party—and an opportunity he'd be a fool to pass up.

Leather looked to the ground, then back up. "Sure, I mean, I can try."

"No need to try, just *do*. You'll be great, I can already tell. Now come on, let's go inside and chat."

And so Leather stood, brushed off his hands, and followed the leader of the church through the big double doors. It was the beginning of something huge. He didn't know it at the time, but their partnership would flourish, the church would grow exponentially, and Leather would have a life his birth mother could only have dreamed of.

Jed would not only become a father-figure to Leather, but would provide him with the security he'd always craved. An early form of braces to straighten his teeth. Clothes that came from department stores instead of thrift shops. Education via sacred texts. Confidence he never knew possible.

But most importantly, weekends at the lake, where Leather discovered his athletic ability and freedom in the water. The first time he put skis on his feet, it was as though he'd been skiing for years. He was steady in the water, whereas most first-timers bobbed around, struggling for balance. The skis didn't control him, he controlled the skis. He popped right up when the boat sped forward, perfect posture, just the right amount of tension on the rope. On his second try, he exited the wake and started crossing it with ease.

One of Jed's friends whooped, "This kid's a natural!"

Another proposed, "He should try course skiing."

That very first tournament, when Leather took home first place, Jed was watching from the bank with pride in his heart and dollar signs in his eyes. There was only one thing going through the young pastor's mind.

This could be big.

Witness #2 Statement

What do I think when I hear the name "Norcross"? Well, certainly skiing comes to mind first, but a close second is all that religious bullshit. Like a cult, that church is. Yeah, I said it. They're so far right, they're basically off the spectrum. Whatever happened to being moderate? Anyway, the whole thing is a business, really. And that family is at the top. But then again, it's not like the Betts girl doesn't have her own questionable history. You've heard the rumors about her mother's death, right? I mean, come on…both those girls are fishy. Ha! Fishy, get it? Water, fish, skiers. I crack myself up.

Chapter 10

NOW

May 1
Swiss Pro Slalom
Clermont, FL

YouTube Live:

"Good morning, everyone and welcome to beautiful Lake Caroline and the Swiss Pro Slalom, kicking off the 2023 water skiing pro tour. I'm Greg Redding, and I'll be leading today's live coverage. If you're new to the sport, the way this works is that skiers earn points throughout the season at all major events, which are used to help seed the skiers, and also to determine the overall tour champion. Each skier will have two rounds with multiple course attempts at shorter rope lengths during each round. We've got an incredible line-up of talent for you today, including the incomparable Sadie Norcross, who has won this event for the past seven years in a row. The longest winning streak in Swiss Pro history! Let's hear it for Sadie!"

* * *

The crowd went wild, and Sadie's stomach did a somersault. The first race of the year always gave her butterflies, as though she hadn't been training every day. Her body was more ready than her mind. The buzz that traveled around this event got everyone amped up, including her mother, who had been fluttering around since they arrived at six that morning. Winning today would set Sadie's season up on a high note, and since she'd done it for the past seven years, it had become almost expected.

Swiss Pro, a lock.

A drone flew by overhead, and Sadie watched it soar out over the water. The lake stretched into two long lines with a narrow strip of land dotted with trees down the center like a roadway median. Along the west side, sprawling ranch homes with clay tile roofs and screened-in lanais nestled in a cluster. On the opposite side of the water, a golf course stretched across the lush terrain. The area screamed retirement goals. Much of Florida boasted Northerners who migrated to the warmer climate, many of whom had become ski fans. The older gentlemen would chat Leather's ear off about *back in our day*, and Sadie would shake her head at how people seemed to gravitate toward her grandfather.

Greg Redding continued with his pre-event rundown and announcements, but Sadie's mind had already turned inward, preparing for her first run.

"You've got this in the bag," Leather said next to her. He looked around at all the people, a smile spreading across his face. He nodded, satisfied. Yeah, this event was theirs. "Where's Baz?"

"Hmm?"

"Baz."

"Oh." Sadie glanced right, then left. "He's around here somewhere. There he is." She pointed to a group of guys chatting near a vendor table, Baz among them wearing a backward hat and bright board shorts.

"Baz!" Leather hollered, gesturing for him. Baz jogged over. "Don't be wandering off now. The lineup is starting. We don't want to miss a photo opp."

Greg read off a list of the day's competitors, ranked according to last year's points. When he got to Sadie, a roar came from the crowd.

Leather gave Baz a little nudge toward Sadie, and Baz stumbled, coming side by side with his wife. With a flick of his hand—*Go on, get out there. Greet your people*—Leather compelled them forward.

They obeyed, stepping out from the shadow of a large sycamore tree. Baz put his arm around Sadie, and they both waved again with plastic smiles and rehearsed body language.

"You didn't have to come," Sadie said through her teeth, never breaking her smile.

"Of course I did," he replied just the same.

She didn't know if he meant *of course* as in he wanted to be there, or *of course* as in he had no other choice. In truth, it was both, but Baz would only admit the former.

As soon as the noise died down and the athletes dispersed, Sadie's smile fell. She didn't notice Baz drift away, but he was no longer next to her. She looked around for a second, but then shook her head. No worry. Time to focus.

"All right, champ," Leather said, giving Sadie a pat on the back. "Let's do this."

They made their way to a grassy area where they'd set up Sadie's gear. Deb was there, shaking an instant protein smoothie. She held it out to Sadie, who took it and tossed back a gulp. Sadie pulled her shirt up over her head, then adjusted the straps of her blue bikini top. It was a new one from Nike, cut like a sports bra, but with thinner straps that criss-crossed like lattice in the back. Leather had originally protested—the female skiers had always worn one-piece suits in his and Deb's era. But for once, Deb had been on Sadie's team, telling her father that it wasn't a big deal, it was what all the girls were wearing, and anyway, her vest and bib would cover her entire stomach anyway. Once he learned the power of social media and the subtle connection between sex appeal and followers, he'd acquiesced.

Just as Sadie was about to slip out of her shorts, an official in a red t-shirt holding a clipboard stopped them. "Hold up a minute, I need to get your sample," the woman said, holding out a small plastic cup.

"Right now?" Leather said, annoyance written all over his face. "She's about to ski."

"Sorry, Leather. NADO says the tests have to be random and can be required at any time. Sadie's name was drawn."

Deb looked away, almost as if she wished she hadn't entered the conversation. She busied herself with Sadie's ski.

"It's fine," Sadie said. "I'll just do it real quick." She'd provided samples to the National Anti-Doping Organization before. It was par for the course. The worst part was having a chaperone watch you pee into a cup. A side effect of being a pro athlete: Everyone was in her business.

"I just don't see why this is necessary," Leather argued. "And shouldn't she have had a couple days notice? At least that's how it used to be."

The official laughed. "Things have changed. It's random. And now we can test samples in minutes."

"Well..." The answer failed to appease him.

"It's not a big deal," Sadie said. "There's time. I'm last to ski. Plus, it's not like I'm hiding anything."

Sadie followed the official to the bathroom where she filled the little cup with urine, handed it to the woman, and returned to the lake to wait her turn.

***

Based on last season's seeding, Willa would ski before Sadie. Twelve women in total made up this year's female competitors in the slalom category—six from the U.S., four from Canada, one from Great Britain and one from Italy. Of these athletes, the five best scores after two rounds would advance to the finals.

It was a stacked line-up, the competition growing stiffer every year.

As Willa stripped off her shorts and tied her hair back into a braid, she listened to Greg Redding at the broadcast booth a few feet away.

"These conditions are a skier's dream: perfect glass water, calm breeze, sun in the sky. I tell you what, it's going to be a feast for the eyes today, folks. All the top competitors are here ready to kick off the season. But we'd be remiss not to give a shout-out to our sponsors: ProGear Gloves, Connelly, Masterline..."

Willa let the rest drown out, as she set her mind in focus. Staring out at the lake, she envisioned herself skiing the course. Muscle memory felt the sensations of crossing the wake, rounding the buoys. She was just about to pass through the exit gate in her mind when the sound of her name coming from the announcer snapped her from her daydream.

"...the Willa and Sadie show around here. It's probably safe to say Sadie is the favorite to win—she does every time she hits this lake—but Willa is a fierce competitor and I'm sure she'd love to steal that title away."

Willa's insides fired up, as she imagined hundreds—no, thousands—of people watching the live feed. Too many times she'd come in second here in Clermont. It was almost a foregone conclusion that Sadie would win.

Almost as if everyone had just accepted the fact before any skis even touched the water.

She decided it would change today.

Willa pulled out her phone and took a panoramic photo of the lake, then uploaded it to Instagram for her 124K followers with a caption that read, *Let the season begin! #gameface #betonbetts #SwissPro*

Willa twisted her torso, stretching her back and arms. She reached to the sky and let her muscles go long. The first skiers of the day were getting ready on the dock. She'd be up soon. She pulled the red race bib over her vest and grabbed her ski. Round one. *Ready or not, here I come.*

* * *

"We're here with Deb Norcross, mom to Sadie Norcross and a ski legend in her own right. Deb, how does it feel to watch your daughter dominate the sport after all your years of skiing?"

Greg Redding held the microphone in front of Deb's face. A few feet in front of them, another man pointed a camera at her. Interviews helped kill down-time between skiers.

"Well, it sure is exciting," Deb said with a smile. "Sadie works so hard, and I couldn't be prouder. You saw her on the cover of *People* this month, right?" She pulled a copy of the magazine from her bag like a magician conjuring a rabbit from his hat.

"Quite the accomplishment," Greg said. "Those two really are incredible." Deb gave a noise of acknowledgment that some might have recognized as irritation. She'd meant to draw attention to Sadie, not to Willa *and* Sadie.

Greg continued. "It must feel like déjà vu being at all these tournaments, but then again, so much has changed."

"These girls are putting up scores like I never dreamed of. They're pushing themselves and really elevating the level of talent. I have to say, however, the buoys are a little smaller than they used to be." She winked at the camera.

"What are you expecting for today's outcome?"

Deb smiled. "A win, of course."

Chapter 11

Willa scooted off the wide platform dock and plopped into the water for her third run of round one. The first two were always a breeze, a warm-up. The third pass at 10.75 meters was when things got serious.

The boat idled forward a foot or two, no more than an arm's length from the dock, and they were off. Willa situated herself before flying through the starting gate. Then she worked her magic. Six balls later, she completed the course with a giant heave. Boom. Take that.

She caught her breath on the way back to the starting line. Next came the real test—her last run, with the rope at its shortest length: 10.25 meters, no more than half a bowling alley from the boat. It was incredibly short, making it that much more difficult to reach the buoys.

At such a distance, skiers' bodies laid near horizontal, fully outstretched with one arm to get around the buoy before zipping to the other side. They were contortionists being pulled at thirty-two miles per hour. The slightest misstep, and it would be game over. There was no room for error.

Willa took a few deep breaths to bring down her heart rate, but the adrenaline was like lighter fluid to a flame. *Let's fucking do this.*

The boat roared to life, pulling Willa up onto the top of the water for her final run. Through the gates in a flash, it sped out to the one ball. So much less time to get there. Impossibly fast. Willa managed to catch it, but not without a wobble and slack tension on the rope whipping her head back so hard that she stared at the sky. Quickly recovering, Willa bounced across the wake to the next buoy. Her ski sliced the water. Got it, but just barely. *Don't give up.* Rounded the third. Halfway there. She had to finish the course. Willa's face squeezed in concentration, and she pressed her lips together for another cross. The four ball sped toward her. She had no more than two seconds to prepare. *Lean, reach.*

But it was coming too fast.

The buoy passed by before she could get there. Willa curved out and threw her head back with a growl of disappointment. So close! She righted herself in the middle of the wake, as the boat slowed to a stop and she dropped into the water. 3@10.25 was a good run, a great effort, and it put her squarely in first place. She couldn't complain. If people were hoping for her to put pressure on Sadie, she'd succeeded.

* * *

Sadie felt it all right.

After three passes that were a piece of cake, it all came down to the last attempt at 10.25 meters. She had a perfect score going into this run...but so did Willa. If Sadie wanted to come out ahead, she'd have to score more than three balls. This was where her litheness gave her an advantage. Those endlessly long limbs—she could stretch more than anyone else on the course.

She heard her mother's voice in her ear: *This is your race.*

Sadie squinted as she focused ahead, the wind making her eyes water. She wore the champion race bib from last year—purple, the color of royalty—to distinguish her from the other competitors. The boat flew through the opening gate. Sadie held her breath. She leaned for the one ball and hooked around it with a little more jerk than usual. Her ski lurched, making her wobble.

The near-fumble rattled her, and she only had a split-second to process. *Whoa. That was weird. Okay, refocus. Finish the course.*

But crossing the wake, she lost sight of the two ball. Where was it? Had she missed it already? The course was fast, but was it that fast? And then with a millisecond to spare, Sadie spotted it. She grimaced. *Get there, get there.* She dropped an arm and extended her body so horizontal her hip skimmed the water's surface. She'd made it...right? No time to think. She was already behind in crossing to the other side. Damn! Before Sadie even got off the wake, she knew it was over. There was no way she'd make the third buoy.

Which meant...Willa was in the lead after round one.

Sadie cursed under her breath as the boat towed her back to shore. How the hell had that happened? Her body itched to rewind, to go back and try it again. But that wasn't how it worked. Everything skiers trained for could be over in a matter of seconds.

Sadie fumed. Wanting to keep her cool, she attempted to relax her face. No need for anyone to think she was anything but confident. Sadie Norcross always came out on top, and she'd do it again today. That hadn't been her best run, but it wasn't anything to worry about. There were two rounds for a reason. She'd make up the points. She'd prove her worth.

So she told herself.

Climbing from the water, she caught her grandfather's gaze. He gave her a sharp look that Sadie didn't need to interpret: *You can do better than that.*

* * *

"We're here with Willa Betts. Willa, that was textbook skiing we saw from you in round one. How are you feeling?"

Willa leaned into the microphone. "Thanks, Greg. I feel really good, really strong. The wind seems to be picking up a little more, which always complicates things, but otherwise, it's a great course."

"You've already secured your spot in the finals with those scores, but we'll have to wait to see who else makes it. I'm sure Sadie will be right there with you."

Was that a question? Willa made a noise of acknowledgment, unsure what else to say. Her pulse was still thumping fifteen minutes after completing her passes.

"Good luck in your second round," Greg said. "Thanks for talking with us."

Willa waved to the camera, remembering how, as a kid, she'd picture her parents watching from home. An illusion. Now, she knew better. That, or she no longer cared.

* * *

Round two followed the same pattern, with skiers going in order from lowest points to highest. Willa's body hummed. She would be last to ski and would get to watch Sadie.

They'd been at the lake for five hours already, and now the sun hung high in the afternoon sky. Fans had switched from coffee to ice-cold sodas. A pop-up food truck offered hot dogs with all the fixings. For the next two hours, the crowd watched all the women—Harper Cruz and the other girls—but the real hush settled over the lake when it was Sadie's turn. Knowing both she and Willa were already in the finals meant little— winning each round was more about bragging rights.

And so it was no surprise that the second round offered just as much tension as the first, and when both skiers completed near-perfect runs—4@10.25—the leaderboard remained the same. They would go into the finals with Willa holding onto a slight edge.

The atmosphere crackled with an invisible electricity. For the first time in seven years, Sadie wasn't in the lead. The lake seemed to hold its breath.

* * *

"The undefeated champion herself, Sadie Norcross." Greg stood next to Sadie, holding a microphone. "Sadie, it seemed like you were more confident in round two. Tell us what happened in the first round."

"It was really hard to see the inner balls because of the shadows on the water. I looked but just didn't see it in time." She shrugged and adjusted her suit strap.

"You're currently sitting in second place going into the finals—a bit of an unusual spot for you at this event. What are you telling yourself as you get ready for the final round?"

"I'm just trying to stay focused and not overthink. This is a great course and I know it well, and I have no reason to believe I won't bring home another win." The response came out so naturally, like someone asking for your name and birthdate. A thing you practiced since learning how to speak.

"You heard it, folks." Greg returned his gaze to the camera. "Sadie Norcross on her plans to come from behind. Up next, the final round of the women's slalom in this order: Alex Ramellow, Christina Bear, Harper Cruz, Sadie Norcross, and Willa Betts. Best of luck to you, Sadie."

She dipped her head and walked off.

* * *

Alex, Christina, and Harper all finished well—good scores, even a personal best—but nothing Sadie couldn't beat. Her first passes had been so smooth, she made it look easy. Sadie's ability to glide across the water even at the shortest rope lengths amazed everyone who watched her. Their eyes couldn't help but stay glued to the phenom. But by this time in the event, Sadie's arms throbbed. It was now pushing six p.m. The sky's blues had faded into streaks of orange, the sun getting ready to make its descent. She'd skied fifteen passes though the course that day. Her fingers had lost some of their dexterity, and she ate two bananas between rounds as a means of muscle and electrolyte recovery.

One more run. This was it, the final pass of the day. Make all six balls and she had a chance to upset Willa's lead. She needed a perfect score.

Sadie narrowed her eyes as the boat pulled her out of the water.

One ball. Sliced around, got it.

Two ball. Yes!

Pull, Sadie, pull. Three ball. Cleared by an inch.

Two more. *You've got this.*

Four ball. *Lean. Control the ski. Yes!*

So close she could taste it. The seconds were flying by. Only two more buoys to round. Sadie felt the surge of confidence. She was going to complete a perfect run. She could feel it. She'd get to keep her purple bib another year. Her grandfather's face flashed in her mind, his smile, the heavy pat on the back. He'd be so proud.

But just then, in a freak moment, Sadie's grip bobbled. The rope handle fumbled from her hands. She saw it happen in slow motion, and she stretched her fingers out to grab it. Too late. In a stunning turn of events, the rope flew through the air, and Sadie slammed into the water sideways before she could reach the fifth buoy.

Complete confusion swept over her as she breached the water's surface and let out a massive exhale. What just happened? How could she have made such a detrimental error? The rope was her lifeline to the boat, and rule number one was, no matter how hard the pull, no matter how intense the force of the turn, don't let go.

Sadie looked around as though something in the water would help make it make sense. She looked at her hands, turning them back and forth, trying to understand how they could have betrayed her. They looked no different than any other day. She punched the surface in frustration. It was a good score, but good wasn't good enough. She needed to be *great*. So much for pulling ahead. Now Willa would only need to get four balls to win.

Sadie let the boat bring her back, and as she treaded into the dock, Willa hopped into the water not five feet away. One skier done, the next about to start. They didn't look at each other—Willa going one way, Sadie going the other.

As she exited the lake, Sadie kept her eyes down, not wanting to see the looks on her team's faces. She climbed out of the water and headed toward her family.

Neither Leather nor Deb said what Sadie knew they were thinking. They didn't need to; their expressions said it all. And so, while Sadie dried off, she swallowed the disappointment. It wasn't until someone placed a light hand on her back that she spun around.

"It's okay," Baz said gently.

She didn't respond. Just wrapped the towel around her waist and walked off to watch Willa. It would take another freak slip-up for Willa not to win. Sadie felt guilty hoping for one.

****

74

Willa dunked her head and slicked back the hair that had fallen loose from her braid, then let the boat pull her forward in an idle. Sadie had crashed. She hadn't completed the course. And that meant there was a chance. Willa would only need three balls. Yes, this was 10.25 meters, the hardest rope length to ski, but she'd done it plenty of times before. Now more than ever, she needed a solid run.

The dropping sun beat down onto the water, and Willa reminded herself she'd have to really spot the buoys through the shadows. From her peripheral vision, she could see spectators clapping along the banks. She instinctively looked for Baz and then shook her head. No time to get distracted.

"Hit it!"

The boat pulled her up. Willa stared straight ahead as she flew through the starting gate and leaned out for the one ball at supersonic speed. Her ski jerked around it, nearly clipping it in half. Regaining balance, she was already bouncing across the wake on to number two. She leaned back with all her weight for extra acceleration, then pivoted edges, curving around the buoy.

Number three approached. *You can do it, you're halfway there.* She held her breath, grimaced under the intensity of the force, and circled it.

A grunt escaped her lips as she pulled back to the left. *Lean, drop an arm. Streeeeeetch.*

The rope was so short, scarcely giving her time to get across the wake. She wished she had Sadie's long limbs that seemed to extend for days. Willa was more compact, but with her muscular frame came power, and she used it to round the four ball.

Got it. Two more.

It didn't hit her that she'd already won. What she'd wanted was to finish a clean run, to get all six balls at this very difficult rope length. And so she grit her teeth and gave everything she had to the last turns. Laid her body out to reach them. Felt her ski skim past the buoys before making a quick return to the middle and out through the exit gate.

The crowd erupted. Willa let out a massive breath she'd been holding. She'd done it. Willa had upset a seven-time winner.

She raised a hand in the air, as the boat whipped her out to the side where she let go and sank gracefully into the water. A smile found her face before she went under and remained until she popped back up, exhilarated, waving to the crowd.

All the way back to land, Willa grinned, adrenaline and endorphins surging through her veins. Her heart beat threatened to explode from her chest. Roxanne met her on the dock and wrapped her in a wet hug.

"That's what I'm talking about!" she said. The two exchanged a high five, and then Roxanne grabbed Willa's arm at the wrist and yanked it skyward. The audience cheered again. Willa was on a high—the times she beat Sadie always felt good, but this one in particular carried more weight. A new champion took over—now she'd get to wear the purple bib.

Willa took in the beaming faces of fans young and old, scanning the crowd for who she thought was no one in particular, until she landed on him and realized it was exactly who she'd been looking for. Baz clapped, a genuine smile on his face, and Willa locked eyes with him for the briefest minute before an official approached with a microphone. She wished she didn't have to look away. Wished she could have done more than exchange quick glances.

"Congratulations, Willa! What a run. Six at 10.25 is quite the accomplishment. If this event is a forecast of what to expect this season, looks like you're gonna be the one to beat. How does it feel knocking Sadie from the pedestal after seven years?"

Willa wanted to be diplomatic, but the moment hummed with too much excitement. She caught Roxanne's eye, a smirk on her face. Willa leaned into the microphone, and spoke clear as day. "It feels damn good."

* * *

Photographs from the red painted podium would look different that year. Instead of the blonde princess of slalom on the throne, a new royal had come to court. Willa stood proudly on the top step, ski at her side, trophy in her hand. Sadie was a tier below. The women smiled as cameras clicked away, and then Roxanne stepped forward from the crowd. She handed Willa a bottle of champagne.

"Celebrate, girl!" she shouted. "You earned it!"

Willa set the trophy at her feet, held the bottle out and used her thumbs to pop the cork. She laughed, letting the jubilation feed her energy. *Why the hell not*, she told herself. She shook the bottle, sending a foamy spray into the first row of good-humored spectators. Sadie and Harper Cruz on either side of her recoiled as the liquid splashed in their direction.

It was a scene of celebration, with big smiles and big paychecks—four thousand dollars for Willa. Not bad for a day's work. Pulling out a win was the cherry on top of a rigorous training schedule. A reminder of why she loved the sport so much.

Even Sadie couldn't help but grin at Willa's moment of abandon. It brought her back to the days the two girls used to laugh and play. Sadie, too, knew the high of a big win, and part of her wanted to be glad for Willa—that was, until she caught her mother's eyes in the crowd. Deb Norcross, whose designer sportswear now dripped in cheap champagne, crossed her arms and grit her teeth. She spun on her heels and disappeared into the crowd of fans.

The Norcross camp had words that day, ones that if anyone had been listening close enough might have questioned. But some things fell on deaf ears. No one heard a thing. Certainly not Willa, who remained on a high as she packed her ski into her car and tossed her backpack on the front seat. A few stragglers called goodbye as they pulled from the parking lot. Willa waved in return. "See ya at the next event!"

It wasn't until Roxanne spoke that a little wind left Willa's sails.

"Who's driving, you or me?"

Such a nonchalant question, one that was asked every day in every household around the world. But for Willa, no five words carried more weight...or had the ability to make her blood run cold.

Chapter 12

"**D**addy?" Willa poked her father's cheek with her finger. "Daddy, wake up. We're gonna be late." She checked the clock above the couch where her father laid passed out in yesterday's clothes. It was five-thirty in the morning and they had an hour-plus drive to get to the event. Willa sighed. If she was responsible enough to set her alarm at twelve years old, why couldn't her parents do the same?

"Daddy, please. We have to go."

Dale grumbled and rolled over, belly flopping out above the waistband of his jeans, white t-shirt twisted around his body. Willa stood up straight and slapped her hips, frustrated. He was worthless. But... there was another parent somewhere. Maybe, just maybe it wouldn't be more of the same. She knew it was wishful thinking.

Willa hurried to her parents' bedroom, where sure enough, the only other adult in the house was equally intoxicated.

"Mama," she tried, giving her mother gentle pats on the cheeks. "Mama, we're gonna be late for my race if we don't leave right now. Mama?" Autumn's eyes fluttered open, and Willa's hope swelled. Maybe not all hope was lost for getting to the lake before her turn to ski. Her mother sat up, swayed a little, then put both hands on the bed to stabilize herself. The sapphire teardrop necklace she always wore was twisted around her neck.

"Wha—what is it? Why'd you wake me up?"

"My tournament. We have to go." She pulled on her mother's sleeve like a toddler.

Autumn rolled her head, squinting out through eyes that were slits. "Good Lord, I can't even see straight let alone drive," she slurred.

Willa's heart fell and tears threatened to follow, but she wouldn't give up. They had to get there, they just *had* to. She grabbed her mother's wrists, giving her a pull to standing. Autumn, too drunk from last night's vodka binge, obliged. She uttered a moan and put both hands out for balance.

"See," Willa said cheerily. "You're fine. You can drive. Now come on, let's go."

She'd already loaded her ski, vest, and bag into the back seat, brewed a pot of coffee, and cleaned up the dishes in the sink. All she needed was to get her mother behind the wheel. A minute later, Autumn stumbled from the room in yoga pants and a faded t-shirt. Willa knew she'd be far too hot in those pants at the tournament, what with the mid-day sun beating down on them, but there was no time to help her mother change. Yoga pants would have to do. Mama would have to find some shade. She could sleep off her hangover under a tree for all Willa cared, as long as she got her to the lake.

"Daddy, we're leaving," Willa said, as she guided her mother past the couch. "Mom's taking me, okay? We'll see you tonight."

"Mmmhhmpp," he half gurgled without budging. Willa practically tripped over the empty handle of vodka on the floor. *Great,* she thought. *Breaking my toe on a bottle of alcohol. What a way to have to forfeit.*

Forfeiting was not an option. Not when she beat her personal record last week. Not when her local paper ran a feature story on the sixth grader poised to take over the sport. She had to make every event, inebriated parents or not. Plus, her friends Sadie and Baz would be there, and she always looked forward to that.

Most of the time Roxanne was able to get her to and from events, a courtesy for which Willa was eternally grateful. It meant showing up, arriving on time, and having a support person on whom she could trust. It also meant her parents were off the hook on attending and could stay home pouring more liquor into their veins.

But today was different. Today, Roxanne couldn't pick her up. "I'll have to meet you at the lake," Roxanne had said over the phone earlier in the week. "Is that okay? Can your parents get you there?"

"Yes," Willa had lied. "No problem."

And so Willa was left with no choice. Drag her fuck-up parents out of bed, or miss the competition altogether. Staying home meant missing a podium she would surely have been on. It meant babysitting two adults. She couldn't do it again.

Willa helped her mother down the front steps to the car and into the driver's seat. She shoved the travel mug of dark roast into her hand. "Here. Drink."

"Honey, I'm telling you, I—"

"No, no. You'll be fine. Let's just sit for a minute and let that coffee work its magic. It'll wake you right up." *Sober you up* was more like it. Willa caught a peek at her mother's eyes. Red and glassy, gaze unfocused— nothing she hadn't seen before.

Willa gave Autumn approximately ten seconds and two sips. "Okay," she said, checking her watch and realizing they were cutting it close. "Feeling better?"

"Like a goat in a bowtie."

Whatever that meant. "Great. Let's go."

"Righty ho!" her mother called, as though they were on a pirate ship instead of a beat-up sedan. That coffee must have done the trick. She hit the wand on the left, triggering the windshield wipers, and she and Willa both jumped. "Whoopsie. That's not the right one. Just a minute. All right, here we go." She put the car in gear and let off the brake, but the car lurched forward instead of backward out of the driveway.

"Mama!" Willa yelled, as her mother slammed the brake, sending both of their heads whipping forward. Maybe she wasn't as sober as Willa thought.

"What in the..." Autumn mumbled, like it was the car's fault and not her own. She put it in reverse and alternated between gas and brake, bumping backward like someone just learning to drive. Willa jerked along, eyes growing bigger with each lurch. A tangle of fear formed in her gut. Before they reached the end of the driveway, before they pulled out onto the street, Willa reached a hand over to her mother's arm.

"Wait," she said, with all the disappointment in the world. There was nothing safe about her mother driving in this condition. "Maybe we shouldn't."

Her mother gaped at her. "What'dya mean? I'm fine, that coffee's—*hiccup!*—doing the trick."

Willa could see it in her mother's eyes, the tenderness that was buried deep. Autumn Betts wanted so badly to be a good mother. But that affection was masked by bloodshot veins crawling over dilated pupils, an addiction so strong it gobbled everything in its way—including her daughter.

"It's okay," Willa said. She swallowed hard, pushing down the resentment, knowing lashing out would make the situation worse. It was only one event. She'd call Roxanne and say she was sick, couldn't make it. She'd help her mom back inside, then lock herself in her room where she could squeeze her stuffed dolphin and cry properly.

Autumn put a hand on top of Willa's. "You're not—*hiccup!*—missing your race because of me." They each stared into eyes that mirrored their own. And then Autumn made a decision. She unbuckled her seatbelt. "Here, switch seats. You drive."

Willa's brows raised. "What? I can't drive. I'm only twelve." Was her mom crazy? Or just *that* drunk?

"Oh, *ppfshh*. You drive the 4-wheeler around all the time."

"Mama, a car is not a 4-wheeler."

"It's just a bunch of back roads. And at this hour"—she grabbed Willa's wrist and squinted at the numbers—"five-forty-seven, Jesus Christ five-forty-seven, no one'll be on the roads anyway." Her words slurred like the Slushie machine at the gas station.

"Mama, I—" They weren't talking about five minutes down the road. Autumn was suggesting Willa drive over an hour.

"It'll be fine." Autumn was already out of the car, bumping into the front as she rounded to Willa's side. She yanked open the passenger door and pulled Willa out. "Go on, hop in. Just for the first bit, 'til I get some more of this coffee in my system. Then I'll take back over." She slumped into the passenger seat, coffee splattering from the opening of her cup. Her blinking was long and slow, like her eyelids weighed a million pounds.

Too stunned, Willa stood there for a long minute, taking it all in, running possibilities through her mind. She knew what she should do—go back inside and let her mother sleep it off right there in the car. But then she caught a glimpse of her ski, wedged between the seats, extending from the back seat all the way to the gear shift next to her mother's thigh. She heard the crowd and felt the splashing water on her face. In her mind, she skied the course—a perfect run! The water melted away all her troubles. She climbed the podium to receive her gold medal.

Willa blinked back to reality. It was mostly back roads, she reasoned. And she was pretty good at maneuvering the 4-wheeler. Plus, Daddy had once let her drive through the old K-Mart parking lot for fun.

She glanced at her mother, all but passed out again. Then at the house and back to her ski, her head on a rotating swivel. Right, wrong, right, wrong.

In the end, the ski won.

Willa slid into the driver's seat and inched it forward a bit until her feet reached the pedals. She felt miniature behind the wheel, an infant wearing adult clothes. She took a breath, held it for a beat, then released it at the same time she shifted the car into gear. Looking intently in the rear-view mirror, she slowly reversed out of the driveway. Their street was quiet, the sky still pewter waiting for the sun to lighten it. Willa put a gentle foot to the gas, and they were off down the street. She paused at stop signs and looked both ways before crossing. She put on her blinker and made turns without hitting the curb. The whole time, her heart was in her throat. *Ten minutes*, Willa thought. *Ten minutes and Mama will wake up and be able to drive.*

But then ten minutes came and went. *Another ten*, she thought.

They were on a straightaway, down a two-lane road whose markings were old and dull. Farmland stretched as far as she could see on both sides. They were in between towns, about forty odd minutes from their destination—or maybe more, what with Willa's slower-than-normal speed.

They would have made it safely without anyone being the wiser. Autumn would have woke and been clear-headed enough to take the wheel about fifteen miles out. They would have made it in time for her run. Willa would have hit all six buoys. Would have set another personal best time, would have stood on top of the podium just as she'd envisioned—even beating Sadie.

Would have. So many would-haves.

Those things would have happened, had it not been for the white-tailed deer that bounded out from dawn's darkness, causing Willa to scream and swerve, and her mother to fly awake just in time to see a telephone pole come straight at them.

* * *

The paramedics didn't find mother and daughter trapped in the car because that would have meant big trouble for Willa. When she came to, airbag deployed in her face and glass shattered everywhere, Willa screamed again. She looked to her right. Blood dotted her mother's face like grotesque freckles. A stream leaked from the corner of her mouth.

"Mama!" she screamed, reaching a hand across and giving her mother a shake. Autumn flopped like a rag doll. The sapphire jiggled in the hollow of her neck.

Willa tried the driver's side door, and was surprised when it opened. She climbed out, stumbling to the ground and practically crawling her way around to the passenger side. Gravel and dirt pressed into her hands and knees. The passenger door was stiffer, and Willa had to use all her body weight to yank it open. When she did, her mother's torso flopped out.

Willa was crying now, frantically unbuckling her mother and pulling her from the car into the grassy ditch. She kneeled beside her, shaking violently. "Mama! Mama! Wake up!" An eeriness crept over her at the similarity—not an hour earlier, she was trying to wake her mother at home. Only that was different. Autumn had been alive then, and now Willa wasn't so sure.

In that moment, shock took over, and Willa made a quick decision. She pulled the dead weight of her mother's body to the front of the car. It couldn't look like her mother had been in the passenger seat. She had to change the scene. It had to look like her mother had been the one driving. A twelve-year-old behind the wheel? What kind of trouble would she be in? And what about her parents—would they be in trouble too? Would the police take her from them?

With trembling hands and tears streaming down her face, Willa dialed 911.

"We need help," she choked. "My mom and I were in an accident. I think she's—I think she's dead." A wail escaped her lips, and she managed to give their approximate location. Hold tight, the operator told her, help would be there soon.

Willa hung up and bent forward over her mother's face. "I'm sorry, I'm so sorry," she cried. It all felt foolish now, entirely selfish. Wanting so desperately to go to a ski competition, and now losing her mother because of it. Whatever little of a mother she had anyway. Willa's heart broke there on the side of the road. She wished more than anything she could go back and change it. She'd never get in the car, never agree to her mother's crazy idea.

When the sirens broke over the horizon, growing louder with each second, Willa's breath caught in her throat. This was a turning point—or rather, a point of no return. She'd tell a story and hope to be believed. There would be no going back. She hugged her knees into her chest and rocked back and forth. The paramedics rushed from the ambulance toward them.

"Are you okay?" the man screamed. Willa nodded rapidly, a river of blood snaking from her nose. Two men hovered over her mother, pulling and pressing, searching for any sign of life.

They found none.

The man met Willa with sad eyes. "I'm sorry, sweetheart," he said, and Willa cried even harder. How she survived with little to no injuries was a miracle, they said. By the time the police arrived to take Willa home, they'd cleaned the blood from her nose and put a few butterfly strips across a tiny gash on her forearm, another scar to add to her collection. No one asked her if she'd been driving, because why would they? She was twelve years old. She explained that a deer jumped out, and the car swerved, and that was that. It was all the explanation anyone needed. Especially when her mother's toxicology report came back showing a blood alcohol level way above the legal limit. It all made sense.

And so Willa went on living with a burden far too great for a child. She kept the secret to herself...but not for long.

Chapter 13

THEN
Summer 2006

It had been a month since the accident that claimed her mother's life at only thirty-seven, and to the world, it was a clean-cut case. Drunk woman behind the wheel, a sudden deer, a swerve and The End. The daughter survived, lucky to have been spared and given a second chance at life. A life of traumatic memories. The poor thing.

Only that wasn't how it happened. And the truth was eating Willa alive.

She arrived a month later to the Junior Semi ten pounds lighter, stress and guilt having frozen her appetite to nothing. Ten pounds was substantial for an already-fit kid. People stared, women whispered in hushed tones. Her father was little comfort, instead finding his own reprieve in a bottle, then being slapped with his second DUI in a year.

Willa had called Roxanne a few days before Juniors. "My suit's a little baggy," she'd said, to which Roxanne replied, "Well, I guess that means we better go shopping." The following afternoon, Willa left the department store with a bright, new swimsuit in one hand and an ice cream cone in the other. Perils came and went, but she'd deal with them all how she'd dealt with everything thus far in her young life: with grit and a dream. At least—amidst all the chaos—she still had skiing.

"You're sixth in rotation today," Roxanne said, as they unloaded Willa's equipment from the car.

"Sixth? Out of ten? But I always go second to last." Second to last because Sadie Norcross was always the *very* last, having ranked in the top position and getting the benefit of skiing after everyone else. Willa usually ranked just below Sadie, and therefore took the second-to-last run. It was far better to watch the competition first, to know exactly what you had to beat.

Roxanne's eyes softened. "I'm afraid you bumped down a bit from missing the last event. Two girls squeezed in between. So now you're sixth."

Willa looked away, feeling guilty for her anger. Her mother had just died, and she was more concerned with her run placement. What a bad daughter. "Okay," she said reluctantly. *Put it aside. Close the box. Place it on a shelf.* She didn't know what compartmentalizing meant, only that whatever it was—this mental ability to separate—made returning to the water possible.

Skiing was her happy place. If she got back into her routine, maybe—just maybe—she could squash some of the guilt and push away the hard ball of steel that settled in her throat whenever she thought about that terrible morning.

It hadn't worked. Nothing felt the same as before.

Willa stared at the grass, smushed a clump of blades with her foot.

"Hey, come here," Roxanne said, pulling Willa into a hug. Willa's eyes filled with tears. "It's okay if you aren't ready to ski."

Willa considered it for a quick second, but decided a forfeit would only tack onto her already heavy load. "No, I want to."

"Are you sure?"

Willa gave a quick nod, busying herself with her ski.

"Listen," Roxanne said, putting a hand on Willa's back, "don't be so hard on yourself. Just try to have some fun out there, okay? You deserve it."

A clamp took hold of Willa's gut. *You deserve it.* She didn't deserve anything.

Willa tried to smile, but it came out pathetic. Roxanne's words were a comfort, but only to a degree. And when it came to today's event, Willa had a hard time seeing anything but the negative. Her last few practice runs had been terrible. She'd missed balls completely, or didn't even try to get there. A lackluster effort, made worse by the crippling regret. Her secret was weighing her down to the point she struggled to pop up out of the water at all. Skiing felt different after the accident, like a piece of joy had been ripped away because she wasn't herself, wasn't being an honest person. Her hope that returning to the water would fix everything was proving to be an illusion, and the idea that skiing may no longer be her safe haven crushed her. She had to get her good vibes back. If skiing wouldn't do it, nothing would.

Parents and skiers sprinkled the shoreline with camping chairs set up to watch. The announcer sat under a white tent near the middle of the course. Junior events were nowhere near as exciting as the professional competitions she'd watched. But at twelve, this was her league, her age bracket, and impressing people now meant greater opportunities for the future. Skiing was her ticket somewhere—some place better, though she didn't yet know where. It had to be; she had nothing else to fall back on.

A few yards away, Willa caught sight of Sadie, stretching on the grass. Sadie looked up and waved. Willa returned the gesture. A spark of warmth lit in her chest. A familiar face.

"Careful with that girl," Roxanne said.

"Sadie? Why?" And just like that, the spark died.

"I know you girls are friends, but..."

"But what?"

"Just— just be careful, that's all. Some people aren't who they seem to be."

"She's always been nice to me."

Roxanne shot her a look that said *Trust me,* but Willa didn't understand Roxanne's comment. What was so wrong with Sadie? Out of all the girls on the ski circuit, she'd connected the most with Sadie—they were the same age, had the same retainer color, and both knew all the words to every Justin Bieber song. They'd been friends for years. There was something about Sadie that drew Willa in, something that connected them, even if Willa couldn't explain it in words.

What did Roxanne know anyway? After all, she was like forty or something. Old. Practically ancient. Roxanne didn't know anything about being twelve. Adults were basically clueless. If Willa wanted to be friends with Sadie, she'd be friends with Sadie. It wasn't like she had much of anyone else.

Willa hopped onto the dock and strolled toward Sadie. Her body ached for a friend, someone to talk to. She imagined the words spilling from her lips: *I did it. It was my fault.* How good it would feel to tell someone the truth. With each step her secret bubbled even closer to the surface.

Come clean. Come clean.

"Hey," Willa said.

Sadie pulled a wired headphone off her ear. "Hey."

"Wanna get a lemonade? It's like so hot already."

"Yeah, sure." Sadie looked over her shoulder to where her mother and grandfather were chatting. "Be right back," she called to them. Then, as she and Willa walked side by side down the dock, "Don't tell my mom. She says lemonade is pure sugar, and sugar makes you fat."

"Secret's safe with me," Willa said, and her chest prickled at the irony. So many secrets. If she kept Sadie's, maybe Sadie would keep hers. Her lips itched to tell.

They poured an overly sugared lemonade from a giant dispenser at the athlete's tent and found a shady spot near a tree to sit. Sadie showed Willa her new iPod Nano, and they sang along to Nelly Furtado's "Promiscuous" without understanding what *promiscuous* meant. When an adult walked by, they stopped singing abruptly, then laughed and laughed. It felt good to laugh. Good and bad.

"What's so funny?" The girls looked up to see Baz coming toward them.

"Hey," they said in unison.

He plopped down next to Sadie and offered them both a strawberry-flavored candy. "'Sup? Is that the new Nano?"

"Yeah." Sadie held it out. "Just got it."

"Sweet."

Willa leaned closer to see, to feel part of the conversation. She wanted a Nano—all the cool kids at school had them. And now Sadie, too. She made a mental note to add it to her birthday list, knowing damn well those lists were always pointless.

Sadie and Baz were talking about how cool Apple stores were and how Sadie's family had just got a new Mac computer that was blue and see-through. Willa had never been to an Apple store, and her family's dated computer was still dial-up. She didn't think Sadie intentionally rubbed it in, but sometimes Willa perceived herself as less-than, never quite on top of the latest trends.

She scolded herself—who cared about computers when your mom just died? But the other part of her loved the escape that came with such frivolous conversation. Kids being kids. Unless, of course, you were a twelve-year-old keeping a big secret. Her insides twisted.

While Sadie and Baz compared stories ("My neighbor has the new Halo 2"), Willa let her gaze travel out to the lake. The water, her safe place. The thing that didn't judge, who welcomed everyone regardless of what brand their swimsuit was. A boat zipped by pulling a boy at 11.25 meters. Willa watched his run. When he finished, she clapped along with the crowd.

"Oooo, someone's got a crush," Baz said, reaching across Sadie to give Willa a playful jab.

"Shut up, I do not." Her face went red.

"Why you clapping then?"

"I'm not allowed to clap?"

Sadie and Baz laughed, and Willa pushed them back, toppling them like dominoes.

"Hey!" Sadie said with a smile. "He's the one who said it, not me!"

Willa gave Baz a sassy look. "Yeah, well, I've seen you watching Amanda Ryker, so..."

Baz rolled his eyes.

"Baz and Amanda sitting in a tree," she sang.

"You better watch it!" Baz reached up and grabbed Willa's arm, pulling her down so the three of them were all mangled together on the grass, giggling away.

***

It felt good to hang out with Sadie and Baz. So good, that Willa found herself choking up. A warm, fuzzy sensation rolled down her arms to her fingertips. She didn't have many friends at school and certainly never had girls over to the house for a sleep-over. But Sadie and Baz were cool and fun, and they shared the same passion for skiing. Sadie was always lugging around a sketchbook filled with drawings, and even though half the pages were rippled from getting wet and then drying unevenly, she'd flip to a new page and say something to Willa like, "Let me draw your dream room," and then Willa would struggle to come up with anything outside her modest room at home that barely fit more than a twin bed. What the hell was a dream room?

In that way, Sadie and Baz were the perfect distraction from the dysfunction of her life. Only, that distraction came with a heavy dose of guilt. How could she be laughing and playing and singing about crushes knowing what she knew? Carrying around a secret and pretending to be none the wiser. What kind of person did such a thing?

The weight of Willa's lie sat heavy in her gut. She stared out over the water, dreading her turn to ski, predicting it would be another disappointment where she couldn't get out of her head. Like the lie was destroying her ability, taking away her talent. A thief. Lies were like that.

She needed to release it. Needed to connect with the water again.

She looked back to Sadie and Baz. These two were the closest thing she could call friends. They'd seen each other fight back tears at poor race results. Been there in some of the most character-defining moments of their young lives. If she was going to tell anyone her secret, it would be the two of them.

Willa opened her mouth to speak, the truth hanging on the tip of her tongue. *I killed my mom.*

But just then, a voice interrupted her.

"Sadie!" They all looked to the voice a little ways down the bank, coming from under a sponsor tent. Deb waved to her daughter. "Come on, you're almost up."

Willa clamped her mouth shut. She bit down on the truth, feeling it ooze blood that swam around her mouth like a disgusting sea creature.

"Ugh, I gotta go," Sadie said, standing and leaving an empty space between Willa and Baz. "See you guys later."

"Good luck," they both said at the same time. Sadie trudged away. Willa thought she could see a cross expression on Sadie's mom's face. She got the sense Mrs. Norcross didn't like her, but had no idea why. She'd probably like her even less if she knew what Willa had done. Willa was struck with the thought that she might lose her only two friends if the truth came out. Their parents—the Norcrosses, the Tanners—surely wouldn't want their kids hanging out with someone who would create such a story.

Maybe she shouldn't say anything at all.

The air hung between Willa and Baz like a missing limb. The friends were great in pairs, but best as a trio. A little bit of Willa's bravery floated away when Sadie left, and now she tried to swallow the lie back down into its place. It wouldn't go down. She'd been so close to talking, to revealing it all, she couldn't bear to hide it away again. The old Willa was scratching to get out. The Willa who skied to make everything better. She needed that again.

When she looked back to Baz, his attention was on the ground. Willa looked closer. A furry striped caterpillar inched along, the kind that curled up into a ball when touched. Once, a boy at her bus stop had found one, picked it up and tossed it back and forth between his hands like a juggler before eventually losing interest and lobbing it into the street. Willa had felt so bad for the helpless bug and had almost said so to the boy—How would you like being thrown around like that? So when she saw Baz reach toward the caterpillar, her breath hitched in her throat for a second. Only, Baz didn't pluck the insect up, didn't even poke at it. Instead, he moved debris out of its way, creating a clear path for wherever the caterpillar was heading. The gesture struck her—the kindness of it, the goodness. If he cared enough to protect the smallest living thing, it must mean he was different in some way. Trustworthy.

And that's when she looked to Baz and threw everything into the air, hoping it would land. "Can I tell you something?"

Baz was messing with the Velcro strap on his flip-flop. "Yeah, sure."

From where she sat, she could smell deodorant, and it made her think of the samples the teacher gave out in health class. Baz's smelled fresh, like an ocean breeze with a hint of mint.

"Something you can't tell anyone, like ever." Her chin was quivering now, and Baz looked up. His eyes went big.

"What's wrong?" he said.

"I did something. Something really bad." She hunched forward, tears welling in her eyes. She'd never cried in front of him before, and it felt mortifying. Would he think she was a freak? Something told her no. Something said Baz was better than that. Even if he did, it was too late to turn back. She had to keep talking.

Willa was glad they were in a somewhat private spot, away from the parents, but she still turned toward the tree so no one but Baz could see her face. For a split second, she wondered why she'd opened this box. Why now? Why not immediately after the accident? She didn't know, aside from the fact that it felt right and safe and good. Getting it out was like draining a poison that was slowly killing her.

Baz studied Willa as she tried to stop herself from sobbing. He awkwardly raked a hand through his hair. Willa knew he had older sisters, which she hoped made him familiar with girls and crying. Sure enough, he scooted closer, closing the gap. He put a hand on Willa's upper back.

"It's okay. Whatever it is, it can't be that bad. I got an F on a math test once, and my parents were pissed, but they got over it."

Willa shook her head. "It's not like that. It's really bad, and I—" She felt nervous now, wishing she wouldn't have started down this road. He'd look at her different. Maybe he'd even tell an adult. She should have told Sadie instead. Roxanne's warning rang in her ear: *Careful of that girl. Some people aren't who they appear to be.*

"You can tell me," Baz whispered. She could smell strawberry on his breath from the candy.

Their eyes met. His were as blue as a summer pool, a complete contrast to the muddy lakes they spent their time in. She could have made something up in that moment, but she didn't. Willa opened her mouth and said the words she'd been holding in for four long weeks. "I was driving."

It took him a second, like he might have misheard, but then Baz's face went slack. He stared without blinking. Then finally, no more than a breath, "Oh my god."

From a distance, it would have looked like two tweens hunched together in hushed gossip. Probably whispering about the latest fads or what they were doing over the weekend. Kids that would break apart laughing when their coaches called to say it was almost their turn to ski. Kids who had nothing more to worry about in life than finishing homework and wearing trendy jeans. Some would raise their eyebrows at them and think, *Ah, young love.* But that would have been incorrect—at least that particular summer.

All those at-a-distance observations would be wrong. Because in their tiny circle of two, Willa was detailing that fateful morning and all the chaos in her family life leading up to it. The days when her parents didn't wake up in time to see her off to school and weren't there when she got home— or had collapsed, fully clothed and stinky, in bed. How that morning all she wanted to do was make it to the event on time because skiing was the only thing that gave her a sense of control. And how when her mother suggested they switch places, she never suspected something so terrible would happen.

"Would they send a kid to jail?" Willa cried to Baz. They were forehead to forehead. "I couldn't do it. I had to lie. I was so scared. Skiing—it's all I have." Baz nodded like someone in disbelief. "You probably think I'm a terrible person. I understand if you don't want to be my friend anymore, but please, please don't tell anyone."

It was a request no child should have to make. A crime, that's what it was, and his friend was at the center of it. And now she wanted him to lie too, to keep her secret even though it was wrong. It was too much for a juvenile mind to process. All he saw was a girl who was sad and hurting. She was his friend, and he was raised with the qualities of loyalty and compassion. So, he ran a soft finger across the scar on her forehead. Maybe that was the start of it all.

"I won't say a word. You can trust me."

And she did.

For a long time, that trust held firm in more ways than one, as teens make the mistakes teens do and look for the one person in whom they can confide. For the three of them—Willa, Sadie and Baz—it was each other.

Until it wasn't.

Chapter 14

NOW

congrats on your win

> Thanks! Sorry if you got hit with champagne.

no you're not

> Yeah, you're right. I'm not.

you looked so happy up there

> Feels good to be on top for once.

Oh, so you like it on top?

> Baz!

jk

Chapter 15

"What the hell happened?" Jed folded his arms across his chest.

It was a few days after the Swiss Pro, and Leather was at his weekly meeting with Jed in the church office. The mahogany desk was so large it took up what felt like half the room. Next to it, a fern billowed from its planter, sucking in the little light that came through the cream-colored curtains.

Leather sat opposite Jed, in a chair upholstered with jewel-toned stripes. He exhaled. "Wasn't her day."

"We had a watch party in the sanctuary, and let me tell you, the outcry when Sadie missed that buoy was so loud it could have knocked the cross from the wall."

"I know it," Leather said, shaking his head. "Hard to believe her streak is over at Clermont. Seven years. That Betts girl, she's good. Think she's really been training."

"No one's as good as our Sadie. She's been chosen for this."

"Agree. But this season's gonna be tight. Sadie's not a shoo-in anymore. It's not like we can buy our way to the top."

"Says who?"

The old men met eyes and chuckled. Jed's white hair, thinning at the top and the cane he kept nearby were proof he wasn't the blossoming young pastor he once was. But the cunning influence had held strong over the years. Now at eighty-eight, Jed still had a way of soaking up every ounce of attention from anyone in his presence.

Jed leaned forward so his elbows rested on the desk. "You've got to keep her in line, Leather. Keep her focused. She seems distracted. What's that about?"

Leather shrugged. "Hard to know."

"Baz?"

"Maybe? You and I both know marriage doesn't come without bumps."

"Sure, but nothing the Lord can't fix. Maybe they need to come see me."

"I don't think this is Sadie's favorite place. She's not like Deb. Not as...pliable."

Jed's eyebrows arched. "I've noticed. And why the resistance to the new advertisement?"

"I dunno, Jed. She's not a kid anymore. She's got opinions."

"Doesn't mean she can't be...let's just say...strategically guided. You want her to fulfill her prophecy, right?"

Leather nodded. "Course I do."

"Then you make her the best. Don't forget, she's an ambassador for us now. Winning enhances our public image. We're in the business of saving souls here. Do we want to be a church full of winners? Or a church full of losers?"

"I can't control how she skis at events. We train, and then it's up to her."

A smile slowly grew on Jed's wrinkled face, like the Grinch concocting his Christmas Eve plan. "Oh, Leather, haven't I taught you anything? We control the narrative. We determine our own fates. With prestige comes great power. Remember, God wouldn't have had our paths cross if it weren't for a reason."

"What are you saying?"

"I'm saying, sometimes you have to take things into your own hands. Remember with Deb? Same thing goes this time around. We found a way to get Deb to the top. Now, we do the same for Sadie. It's what the Heavenly Father wants. I certainly didn't teach you to get walked all over. It's not how you raised Deb either. Use your name to get what you want. If that doesn't work, well, then there are...alternatives." His bushy eyebrows pulled together.

Leather nodded slowly. "I understand."

Jed extended his arms wide. "This is your home. We are your family. You succeed, we succeed, God provides for us. It's a great big circle." He narrowed his gaze, speaking right into Leather's eyes. "Sadie deserves to win and it's part of your job to make sure that happens. Yours and Deb's."

"We've got that Roxanne woman to deal with. She and Deb don't exactly have the best history. What are the odds she's coaching Sadie's biggest rival? You say it's our job to push Sadie, but it's also Roxanne's job to do the same for Willa."

"Doesn't matter." Jed shook his head like the concern was little more than trivial.

"I don't trust her. Something about her is sneaky. When I'm near her, it's like I can sense danger."

"You know what God said about snakes... 'I am sending you out like sheep among wolves. Therefore—'"

Leather joined in. "'...be as shrewd as snakes and as innocent as doves.'"

A quiet settled over the space. Leather's jaw set. "I'll talk to Deb. She'll do anything for Sadie."

"Anything?"

"Anything."

"Good." Jed reclined in his chair and cradled the back of his head. "Now, about that billboard..."

Chapter 16

THEN
1985

It's a partial tear," the doctor said. He pushed his glasses up the bridge of his nose, and pointed to the MRI image of Deb's Achilles tendon. "See this band here? It connects the muscles in the back of your calf to your heel. You're lucky it didn't rupture completely. But even so, I'd still recommend surgery."

Deb and Leather looked to each other aghast. "Surgery?" she said. "No way. I can't. I'll miss the rest of the season." She shook her head, sending her Madonna-inspired crimped hair swinging.

If inopportune had a picture in the dictionary, it would be this. Deb had gone pro two years before at nineteen. Since then, she'd been on a speeding rise to fame in the ski world, winning tournaments left and right. People already knew her name—they'd watched her grow up at Leather's events, from pigtailed toddler to talented teen—but now was her turn. Now, she was on track to clinch another season championship. Ski brands had just begun talking about the idea of sponsorships, paying the athletes who used their products—that is, the athletes who won. All the other major sports did it, they finally realized, maybe water skiing should too. It would shine a light on their sport, bring it to the forefront of U.S. athletics. Deb was poised to be the first female to secure a sponsorship, turning skiing from a hobby into a career.

This injury couldn't have come at a worse possible time.

"Non-surgical treatment isn't as effective, I'm afraid," the doctor said with lips pinched. "You risk the possibility of re-rupture."

Deb groaned and squeezed her hands into fists. "I can't believe this. All because of a stupid curb."

The real kicker was that it hadn't even been skiing that injured her. Out for a jog the night before, the sun began to set, making the sidewalk just dim enough that Deb didn't see the curb until she stumbled off of it, catching her heel and coming down hard. She'd felt a small pop, but had brushed it off. The next morning, brushing it off was no longer an option.

"Are you certain we can't just do physical therapy?" Leather asked. "Deb has a big year ahead. We really can't afford to be laid up for weeks of recovery. Isn't there some sort of steroid or pain blocker or—"

"This isn't just a muscle strain," the doctor said, tilting his head. "I'd hate to see it get worse if you don't take care of it properly."

"Dammit," Leather muttered. He ran a hand through his hair, as if it was him—not his daughter—being told he couldn't ski.

"No," Deb said again, this time more firmly. "I'm not missing months of the season for this. It's fine; I can deal with it." She slid off the exam table like a middle-aged woman instead of someone who'd just turned twenty-one. When her foot hit the floor, she attempted to cover up the pain with a brave face. "See? I'm good."

The doctor's face dripped with skepticism, but what could he do—force her? He knew enough about the family to know that what Leather wanted, Leather got. He assumed his daughter would be much of the same.

"Deb..." Leather said, a pained expression taking over his face at the sight of her.

She took a few wobbly steps. "I'm fine, Dad."

"You can't even walk straight; how are you going to ski?"

"I'll push through. It's not that bad." The podium flashed through her mind, and she pictured herself standing on the top step. Nothing—*nothing*—was going to steal that from her, not even her own body. She took another step and grimaced. Isn't this what he wanted? Wouldn't he be proud of her grit?

Leather hung his head, defeated. "I'll contact the IWWF and tell them we're pulling out of Lake 38."

"Don't!"

"Look at you!" He pointed a rigid hand down to her foot.

A new vision flashed through Deb's head. Only in this one, her rival, Roxanne Hill, stood atop the podium. Deb wasn't only on the second tier, she wasn't there at all. She hadn't made the podium. In her mind, Roxanne laughed and laughed. The sponsorship went to her instead.

Deb shook her head. She couldn't let it happen. She couldn't let her father down. The church, all the people who supported her. She was supposed to be running a kid's ski camp for the congregation that month. Jed would be pissed if he'd have to cancel it—all that money down the drain. This was so much bigger than skiing.

"I'm not forfeiting," Deb said, strong and deliberate. She crossed her arms. The doctor stood back, as though his opinion no longer mattered—this was clearly a decision between father and daughter. They were the skiing experts, not him.

The two Norcrosses faced each other.

"Are you sure?" Leather asked.

"One hundred percent."

And so Deb left the doctor's office that day with a limp and a mission. She'd take it easy for a couple of days, but no more. There was a ski season to win.

* * *

By the time the Lake 38 event arrived a few weeks later, Deb's Achilles was no worse, but no better. Rest and physical therapy might have taken her two steps forward, but the continued training brought her one step back.

She woke the morning of the tournament to a call from Jed.

"I got a message from God last night," he said in that smooth voice of his. "It said that you would prevail over pain. God is sending in His angels to carry you through the course today. He's with you, and with His strength, anything is possible."

The hairs on Deb's arms stood up. "Thank you," she whispered, a feeling of immense gratitude cloaking her body. How fortunate they were to be so close to one of God's prophets! If Jed received a message, it must be true.

"It's not up to us as humans to decide when we're hurt or injured," Jed continued. "Only God decides that." Deb's forehead scrunched as she rubbed her Achilles, trying to let that sink in, but she remained silent. "Let's pray together. Dear Lord, we ask for your almighty hand in healing your faithful follower, Deb. Christ in heaven, cover her with your gracious love. You are our rock, our savior, and your hallowed earthly suffering serves as our example for submission to you."

Deb kept her eyes firmly closed, head bowed. But then Jed's prayer took a turn. His words went from coherent to something else. Deb's lids flashed open. What came through the phone was a string of gibberish, sounds and syllables that made no sense, although Deb knew it well. He was speaking in tongues.

"Join me," Jed said, returning to English. "Let the Holy Spirit speak through you, Deb."

Deb closed her eyes again. She wanted to be on the same level as Jed and her father, two men she admired. She'd heard tongues being spoken in church, had even "practiced" in the privacy of the shower where no one could hear her. But she'd never joined in, especially not with the highest member of the church.

Jed rambled on. Against the back of her dark eyelids, she saw the words in bright, neon letters—Lala, Shaba, Baba, many rolled Rs. It sounded beautiful. It sounded like a direct connection to the Lord.

Deb began quietly plucking sounds out of thin air and stringing them together into a new, scrambled language.

"Yes, Deb. Yes!" Jed said, and her confidence grew. Her volume increased until they were praising Jesus as though they were on the pulpit together.

Finally, their voices wound down and it came to a conclusion. "That was beautiful, Deb," Jed said. "Amen. God is with you. He will not let you down. You just have to put your trust in Him and know that if He wants you to win, you will win."

A shiver traveled up her spine. She felt light, as though physical weight had been removed from her body. "Thank you, Jed."

The call ended. Deb swung her legs over the edge of the bed and stood up with resolve. Her foot felt tender, but it didn't matter. Pain was a figment of her imagination. God would see her through—Jed said so himself. She would not disappoint him. She would not disappoint herself.

***

Deb kept her promise.

The doctor would have called it impossible—or at the very least improbable—to perform at her level with a tear in such a critical body part. The foot was the fulcrum on which everything else pivoted. And yet, Deb didn't just ski that day; she dominated.

Call it stubbornness, call it sheer luck, or even God's hand. Whatever it was, winning first place proved to Deb that nothing could stand in her way. If she hadn't been so insistent with the doctor, she wouldn't be holding a three-thousand-dollar check in her hand. Wouldn't be sneaking side-eye at Roxanne next to her on the lower platform.

Pain shot up her leg in hot bursts, but it didn't matter, because seeing her father's beaming face from the crowd was enough medicine to dull any discomfort. Norcrosses were winners. They always were, and they always would be.

Her foot was never quite the same after that. Dismissing proper care did more damage than she realized. But quitting wasn't an option. There had to be a way; they just had to find it.

Find it they did.

Chapter 17

NOW

Keke's breakfast café had the best Belgian waffles, the kind that melted in your mouth and left you feeling like you needed to unbutton the waistband of your pants. Willa and Roxanne made it a special treat to go there at least one morning a month after a training session. This time, Willa ordered hers with strawberries and sliced banana on top.

"Mmmm," she moaned, as she took the first bite and chewed with her eyes closed. She did a little shimmy in her seat. "So good." Willa was a generally healthy eater, but she also burned so many calories skiing and working out that a triple stack of waffles wouldn't hurt. The same couldn't be said for all skiers, many of whom succumbed to online body image pressure. While water skiing wasn't as bad as gymnastics or cross-country running, for instance, female athletes still found themselves under heavy scrutiny to fit an image. For some, that meant salads with no dressing or plain chicken breasts every dinner. Certainly not thick, Belgian waffles.

If Roxanne disapproved, she didn't show it, and Willa was grateful she didn't have one of *those* moms.

Across from her, Roxanne gave a little chuckle. "Good?" She sliced through a spinach and cheese omelet.

"You have no idea."

On the table next to her plate, Willa's phone lit up. Willa looked down, then smiled at the text. She set down her fork to reply.

"How's your dad doing this week?" Roxanne asked.

"Same." Willa finished typing and replaced her phone. "Although I noticed the last round of groceries I brought haven't been touched."

"You don't think he's eating at all?"

"Not much. He's sleeping more and more." She speared a strawberry and popped it in her mouth. Another message appeared, and she picked up her phone.

"Have you guys talked about his...wishes?"

"Hmm?" She kept her eyes on the phone while her fingers typed.

"Your dad's wishes...for, you know...after."

A smirk pulled at Willa's mouth.

"Willa?"

"Oh, sorry." She put her phone down. "Generally, yes. He's mentioned things, but it's just so awkward. You know what it's like. Things are strained."

"Yes." Roxanne sipped her coffee. "I can't even imagine. He's so young. We're practically the same age."

"Well, that's what abusing your body does." Willa's critical defense mechanism flared. *Throw the blame. Don't get sappy.*

Her phone lit up again, and this time Roxanne couldn't help herself. "Someone's awfully popular this morning." Willa gave a sarcastic look, to which Roxanne playfully returned. "Who are you messaging so incessantly? Your waffles are going to be cold."

"Snoopy much?" Willa teased.

"Only when my breakfast date is more interested in her phone than our conversation."

"It's no one."

"No one? Hmm, you seem pretty interested for it to be no one."

Willa didn't respond. She turned her phone face down and resumed eating, chewing dramatically. *Still warm, thankyouverymuch.*

Roxanne raised her eyebrows. "I have a good idea who it is even without you telling me."

"Oh really?"

"Yes, really."

"Okay then, who?"

"Baz."

Willa nearly choked. She hadn't expected Roxanne to nail it on the head. Had she seen his name from across the table? Or was Willa really that transparent? A tingling swept up her neck.

"Good guess?" Roxanne asked.

"We're just friends." Willa felt her cheeks flush. She took another bite, trying to appear nonchalant.

"Do you always blush over your friends?"

"Stop."

"Willa..."

Her eyes went big. "What? We are. We have been forever."

"I know that. I watched you all as kids running around the junior events."

"So...?"

"So he's married."

"And I can't be friends with someone who's married?"

"Willa." Roxanne cocked her head in a motherly way. "You know what I'm saying. Of course men and women can be friends, but let's not pretend there hasn't always been a little something more between you two."

Willa clamped her jaw, feeling like a kid getting caught peeking at a classmate's test. She'd used the "we're just friends" excuse for years as justification for her intermittent communication with Baz. And it was true—they *were* friends. But if she were being honest with herself, she'd admit it went further than that. The way her stomach fluttered when his name appeared on her phone. The way she felt a pulsing in her groin when she saw him in person. *That* embarrassed and thrilled her. She'd never said it out loud to anyone, and up until now, no one had ever confronted her with the truth. Willa sucked her cheeks in.

"Baz is..." she started.

"I get it," Roxanne held up a hand like a stop sign. "He's your first love."

Willa's chest expanded. She gave a small laugh. "Yeah, and here I am, twenty-eight years old, and still not over it." A wave of relief came over her saying the words aloud. It would have been something one would confess to a best friend or a mom, and since Willa had neither really, Roxanne was the next best thing.

"There's something special about that first love," Roxanne said. "But that doesn't mean you cross the line."

"I haven't!" Willa blurted defensively. Texting was harmless. And aside from that one time after a race... oh, but that was nothing. Nothing even *happened*.

"Okay, okay. I believe you. Just be careful, that's all. You don't want to get yourself caught up in something you'll regret."

Willa pushed a waffle around on her plate. She looked down, lost in thought. Then, after a beat of silence, "What if it never goes away?"

"If what never goes away?"

"The...feelings." She peered up through her eyelashes. "What if I never love anyone else?"

Roxanne gave a soft smile. She reached out and put a hand over Willa's. "You will. Whatever's meant to happen will happen."

Willa nodded, taking Roxanne's words and tucking them into a corner of her heart. Whatever was meant to happen would happen.

Or...

Whatever she *made* happen would happen.

Chapter 18

Watching race footage made Sadie feel like an imposter. An out-of-body experience. That couldn't really be her out there slicing through the water, could it? It was like she was watching someone else, some famous slalom skier. But then it would hit her: *she* was the famous slalom skier.

"See how you cut this one a little short?" Deb said, pointing to the computer screen.

Sadie rested her chin in her hands. "Mmhmm."

"And there." Deb pressed pause so that the image stopped exactly as Sadie was rounding a buoy, laid flat, one arm reaching out holding the rope. She looked like a figure skater doing a death spiral. "Look at the angle of your ski. It's no wonder you didn't get around that one."

"Mmhmm."

Deb peeled her eyes from the screen. "Sadie, are you listening to me? You're not even paying attention. You're leaving for Europe in a matter of weeks, and now is the time to be prepared."

The European tour spanned four weeks mid-summer with tournaments in some of the most scenic countrysides. Sadie always looked forward to it, if not for the skiing, then for the incredible food and wine.

She rubbed her neck. "I've seen my replays a million times. I know what happened."

"Then you should be able to prevent it from happening again."

Sadie's lips parted, fire rising up, but she held her composure. "I'm not twelve years old anymore, Mom."

"I'm your coach."

"You might be my coach, but I don't need to be treated like a child."

Deb pursed her lips. "I'm not treating you like a child. I'm trying to make improvements so you aren't upstaged by Willa next time. The Swiss Pro should have been your event. You've never not started the season with a win."

"Is it really that big of a deal?"

Deb's eyes grew wide. "Oh, so you're fine with your seven-year winning streak being crushed?"

Sadie blew out a breath. "No, of course I don't enjoy losing, but Jesus, it was only one race."

"The first one of the season."

"And?"

Deb's shoulders hit her ears. "I'm just saying."

"Saying what?"

"I just hope it's not a foreshadow of how the entire year will go."

Sadie got up from the table, her chair making a screeching noise against the floor. "You guys have no idea."

"No idea?" Deb laughed.

"Things weren't the same when you were skiing. There was no such thing as social media. There was no live streaming of events. You didn't have an entire *church* on your shoulders."

"Oh, but I did." Deb leaned back in her chair. "Yes, technology was different then, but I was very much in your shoes. I fulfilled my role. The church is here to support you. They're our family."

"All I'm saying is it's a lot of pressure."

"Sadie, you're a very privileged person."

"And maybe I don't want to be."

Deb gaped. "Your grandfather came from nothing and worked hard to build this life for us. We owe a lot to Jed and the church. You could be a little more appreciative." Deb took a drink from the tumbler next to the computer.

Sadie dropped her head. Her mother always knew how to pull on her guilt strings. Of course Sadie appreciated the lifestyle she'd always been accustomed to, thanks in large part to her grandfather. But that didn't mean that his life should be her life. Nor that Sadie wanted all the same things he did. She thought of the schools she had bookmarked on her computer, and a tickle formed in the back of her throat, making her want to cough. "Mom, did you ever think of giving it up?"

Deb's brows creased. "Giving what up?"

"Skiing."

"What? No. I didn't even want to retire when I did, but my body didn't agree. I would have kept skiing forever."

The response only made Sadie feel worse. If she was third in line to a skiing dynasty, what did it say that she wasn't in love with it like those who came before her? How could she *not* love something she was clearly so good at?

Deb gave her daughter's hand a little tug. "Sit back down, would you?" Sadie resisted for a beat, then sat. "Listen, I know it can be demanding, but you're in the prime of your career right now. There are so many doors that could open for you, and I'm only trying to do what's best as both your mom and coach."

Sadie met her mom's eyes but didn't respond.

"Hear my words," Deb said. "You are the best female skier in the world, and nothing will change that."

A vice clamped onto Sadie's heart. She may have been the best female skier in the world, but Sadie felt small enough to hide away in a drawer somewhere. She felt like a fraud. She wanted so badly to admit the truth: that skiing *wasn't* her life, that she had *other* dreams and passions. All the hints over the years had never been enough, and she'd never been brave enough to come fully clean. Maybe now was the time. But before she could form the words, Deb stood.

"Wait here, I'll be right back."

She hurried from the kitchen toward the living room, where Sadie could hear what sounded like the shuffling of books on a shelf. Deb returned with a large photo album. She laid it on the table between them and flipped open the cover.

"Look," she said with a wistful smile on her face. "I was your age here." She pointed to a picture stuck to the album's page and held in place behind a clear protective cover. In it, a younger Deb skied a slalom course, big early-90s bangs flying in the wind, and an impossibly high-cut bathing suit showing off her long, toned legs.

"That vest," Sadie said.

Deb chuckled. "I know. We didn't have the slim neoprene you guys have now."

"Like I said, things were different."

"I can still feel the turns if I close my eyes." Deb's lids shut, and her face registered pure peace, like someone in a meditative state—relaxed forehead, slight smile, calm breaths. Sadie couldn't help but wonder at the contentment her mother seemed to experience when she talked about her skiing days. Deb said they were the best years of her life. She looked at old photos with such nostalgia, it made Sadie swallow hard. Why couldn't she love it the same way?

Sadie turned the page to find another double spread filled with ski pictures. Her mother alone. Her mother and father. The two of them on a variety of podiums, arms raised, trophies in hand.

"Dad was jacked," Sadie said with a laugh, pointing to Mark's six-pack abs.

"You and Baz are the new Deb and Mark," Deb said with what Sadie could only recognize as pride. Sadie's gut did a lurch. "Speaking of Baz...he's going with you to Spain, right?"

Baz had gone every year until last summer when his injury kept him home. It would be assumed he'd attend again. But that was when things were...different. Sadie bit the inside of her cheek. "No."

"No?"

"He's busy."

Deb gave her a look. "Busy?"

"What are you, a parrot? Yes, Baz has a life outside of my ski competitions, Mom." She thought quick. "He agreed to help run a camp two of those weekends, so he can't come." She'd made it up on the spot, but now that she said it, the idea sounded like a good one. Baz should get out of the house. He loved helping kids learn how to ski. What's more, his injury and retirement meant losing sponsorship income. They were more than comfortable financially, but sometimes Sadie wondered if a job would help Baz find a sense of purpose.

"That's disappointing," Deb said. "You know how the fans love seeing you two together."

"Well, they're going to have to use their imaginations this time around." Sadie flipped the page. Silence stretched between them, and Sadie could sense her mother staring at her.

"Is everything okay with you two?" Deb said, caution in her voice.

"We're fine." She said it too quick, and as soon as she did, her throat tightened. Heat prickled her skin. She wished she could talk to her mom about personal things, but how would Deb ever understand? Her parents were the quintessential pair. They were perfect.

Sadie's gaze floated to a picture in the bottom corner. In it, the family stood against the backdrop of a lake. Deb held a newborn Sadie.

"Look how cute you were," Deb said, trailing the photo with a finger. "I'm pretty sure you had your first swimsuit before you were even born."

Sadie studied the picture. Her mother beamed. Her father's eyes twinkled. And even a middle-aged Leather looked on with pride at the new little one who—like it or not—would carry their name into the next generation. What no one thought to ask that little girl, however, was what she wanted.

Chapter 19

WaterPro Magazine
March 10, 1994

SKI KING AND QUEEN WELCOME A PRINCESS

Deb Norcross, water skiing extraordinaire and Boss of the Buoys, announced Saturday the birth of her first child with husband Mark Avery, a daughter named Sadie Lake. The baby, weighing in at six pounds, eight ounces, may be too small for skiing, but that doesn't mean her closet isn't already full of gear.

"The sponsors couldn't help themselves," Norcross said, pulling a miniature swimsuit from the closet. "My dad's already bought her a set of toddler skis."

Excitement from family and ski world alike is no surprise, given the career that has rocketed Norcross to stardom as one of the most skilled skiers of her generation, competing for the top spot at every tournament alongside her biggest competitor, Roxanne Hill. After withdrawing midway through last year's season to finish out her pregnancy, Norcross is excited to get her feet back in the boots.

"This has been the longest break I've taken from skiing," Norcross said from her home outside Jacksonville, Florida on the Atlantic coast. "It feels weird and right all at the same time. But I'm definitely looking forward to my comeback."

The question on everyone's mind is whether that comeback will be as soon as this upcoming season, a question to which Norcross gave a categorical "Absolutely."

Born into a skiing empire led by grandfather Bill "Leather" Norcross, this new little one will undoubtedly spend her earliest days on a boat. After all, with the water sign of Pisces, it's written in the stars.

Not to be diminished by the Norcross fame, baby Sadie has ski blood running on both sides. Mark Avery currently has five American Championships and three Grand Pro titles to his name, with no plans of stopping. When asked what he thinks about his daughter taking up the sport, Avery's eyes twinkled. "Whatever makes her happy is what we want." To which Norcross smiled and added, "As long as it's a water sport."

Fans can expect to see Norcross and Avery back on the pro tour this summer, kicking off with the Swiss Pro Slalom in May. Now, race-goers can set their sights not only on the king and queen, but also the little princess somewhere in the mix, watching her mom and dad tackle the buoys.

Witness #3 Statement

Listen, I take my job very seriously. You tell me to watch the boat, I watch the boat. Security has always been my thing—my father, my grandfather, we've all been in some sort of law enforcement. So when I got stationed at the dock, I knew my role: Make sure the boat stays tied up, no one but the driver takes it out, and no funny business.

I stood there all morning from sun up. Nobody messed with nothing. I'd have seen it. Well, 'cept for that one time. But I mean, it was only five minutes! Guy's gotta take a piss at least once per shift.

Chapter 20

July 3
San Gervasio Pro Am
Italy

The European tour concluded with Willa topping the podium for half of the events. Wins for Sadie in Spain and Norway, and wins for Willa in Greece and now Italy. Once in a while, Willa felt bad she and Sadie hogged first place, preventing any of the other athletes from getting a chance.

But only rarely.

Willa took the top step on the red, green, and white San Gervasio podium, painted to represent the country's flag. The cardboard check was almost bigger than she was, but she managed to hold it with one hand, arm around her ski, and use the other to take a swig of the bottle of wine given to the first-place winner.

Willa swallowed, savoring the Tuscan red, whose grapes, the official had told her, came from a nearby vineyard. It was one of the best wines she'd ever tasted.

"Congratulations again to our top three," the announcer said into the microphone through a thick accent. "Willa Betts, Sadie Norcross, and Christine Bear. Well done, ladies!" The women, all in sneakers and dark sunglasses, hair drying in the hot Italian sun, smiled for the camera—two of them happier than the third. Some people simply couldn't find joy in anything less than the best.

* * *

At U.S. events, the skiers usually went their separate ways—some to airports to fly home, others to cars for a shorter commute. But overseas, there were no homes, only hotels, and the general consensus was that returning to a single room with not even English on the TV would be a waste. How often did young twenty-somethings find themselves in the beauty of Europe? Sadie, for one, was dying to take in the ancient architecture. Ideas she could bring home and capture in her sketchbook. The aesthetic was so different from back home, her mind burst with inspiration.

The athletes had a full evening ahead of them before most of them would fly home the following morning. And so it was Harper Cruz, the most spirited of the bunch, who suggested pizza and drinks. "When in Rome, right?" she'd said, though Rome was four hours to the northwest. The group agreed, and they took Ubers into town, ready for a respite from the weight of competition. Away from the water, many of the women could be friends.

Most of them.

The enchanting Italian village provided the perfect backdrop for a night of celebration. The bistro, with its outdoor seating and charming string lights overhead, buzzed with the sound of clinking glasses and laughter. The group, including many of the international competitors the American athletes had come to know over the years, gathered around a cluster of tables. A server brought three bottles of sparkling prosecco, and the women poured themselves a glass. Even the cautious ones—the ones who counted calories and thought alcohol was a waste of their daily allotment—sipped the bubbly liquid.

"To Italy!" someone shouted, and glasses raised into the air. Camera phones captured the perfect insta-worthy shots for social media. Willa snapped a picture of the tapas platter on the table and posted it with the caption, "A win in San Gervasio calls for celebration."

Next to her, Roxanne crossed her legs, sneaker bouncing in the air. "Huge win today, Wills. Proud of you."

"Thanks." Willa took a sip of her drink, relishing the sweet taste of victory. The only thing that could have made the day better was if Baz were there. She'd expected him to be, and her heart sank a little when the Norcross camp showed up without Baz in tow. Even if they wouldn't have been able to talk, even if she wouldn't have been able to casually brush up against him—*on accident*—she'd at least have been able to exchange a smile. Just having him near made her nerves settle, like coming home from a long trip away—even on the other side of the world. Willa wondered why he hadn't come. She eyed Sadie three tables down, as though she could find an answer. Did Sadie look more somber than usual?

* * *

Halfway through their dinner of brick oven flatbread pizzas, a quartet of musicians began playing in the square, violins and guitars strumming a magical scene. Willa let the music settle on her with a calm. The group clapped along, tapping their toes on the cobblestone ground.

Several drinks in, the mood was light. Competition had been tucked away for the evening, and women who were once adversaries let the spirit of the night draw them together in laughter and camaraderie.

Everyone, that was, except Sadie and Willa, who sat as far apart as possible. An invisible string stretched between them, one so tight you could pluck it like one of the musicians' instruments and send out a loud *ping*.

Might they have let their walls down if they weren't always in race mode? If their formidable coaches weren't sitting in adjacent chairs? Possibly. But they rarely got the chance. Coaches and athletes were like two sides of a coin. Where Sadie went, Deb went. Wherever Willa would go, Roxanne wasn't far behind. At least on the skiing circuit. For Willa, the attachment was a comfort, but for Sadie, her mother's presence felt stifling.

The evening pressed on, nearing ten. Willa was checking her phone for messages from her dad when she noticed the music getting louder. She looked up. The band, which had been centered in the square yards away, was coming closer. But not just closer to the group—coming straight toward her. The singer, plucking away on a ukulele, grinned mischievously at Willa. She looked left and right. *What is he doing?*

When he was only a foot or two away, he extended a hand to her. "Come, signora. Come dance."

Willa's face burned. The music was so loud, she couldn't even hear the words coming out of her mouth. "Oh, no. No, thank you."

"Come, come. I teach you. You love it." The rest of the band gathered around him, close enough to make Willa press back in her seat. No way would she dance in front of all these people.

The other skiers cheered, fueled by booze and the fact that it wasn't them who'd been chosen. "Dance, Willa!" they chanted.

She shook her head, embarrassed, but the band leader wouldn't give up. He reached for her hand and pulled her up, swinging her arm to the rhythm as he backpedaled from the table. She had no choice but to follow. Looking over her shoulder, she saw Roxanne howling, and Willa gave her a look that said, *You're next!*

"Like this," the singer said, showing Willa a series of steps where his feet shuffled and tapped and spun. He stood back and gestured to her. "Now you." The band members clapped along in encouragement.

Willa's body pumped heat. She glanced around, seeing not just her group watching, but diners at other tables, and even couples wandering by on foot. She would have put up more of a fight if their faces hadn't been so friendly, smiles that made her throw her arms in the air and think, *What the hell.*

Willa gave the sequence her best shot, fumbling some of the steps. Everyone cheered, and she felt her defenses softening. It was all for fun. This wasn't like their competitions on the water. Thank God the alcohol took the edge off.

"Now a little harder," the singer said, showing her another set of dance moves, this time with arm motions. Again? She thought she'd been off the hook. Being a good sport, she prepared to give it a shot.

The singer stopped her. "No, no. We do double!"

"Double?" Willa said. Did he mean for her to do it twice in a row? Another band member approached the group of skiers, arm extended, ready to pluck out another unsuspecting victim. Then she understood. It would be a dance-off. Or a dance-together. Willa watched, one thing going through her head: *Not Sadie. Not Sadie.*

He chose Sadie.

The violinist pulled Sadie from her chair, despite much resistance. Sadie tripped over herself out into the open area in front of the tables.

And then she was standing an arm's length from Willa while the band circled around them crooning, "Funiculi, Funicula."

The women's faces flushed, having been put into a situation neither would have chosen. Couldn't it have been anyone else? But there was no time to analyze—or get out of it—before the band leader demonstrated the new dance steps a second time. Sadie and Willa watched. He finished the sequence with a clap—*ta da!*—and indicated it was Willa's turn first.

Willa did her best to imitate the complicated sequence but fumbled and ended up losing her balance, nearly collapsing. The group roared in laughter, and despite herself, Willa couldn't deny the humor in the situation. She too let out a hearty laugh. "I'm a skier, not a dancer!"

The singer pointed to Sadie next. "You do better?" He demonstrated once more.

"Show 'em, Sadie!" Deb called.

Sadie looked down and repeated the steps, finishing it off with a single clap.

"Ahh!" the band cheered, and the ski group joined in. "Very nice, very nice." Everyone lifted their glasses saluting the brave dancers.

Sadie and Willa went to sit back down—the dance-off was fun while it lasted—but the band leader stopped them.

"No, no," he said. "Not done."

Again? He pulled them both back, but instead of standing them apart, he pushed them to face each other. "Hands." He extended his hands to the violinist in demonstration and the two joined. "You two. Hands."

He wanted them to hold hands?

Sadie and Willa looked at each other with flaming cheeks—maybe from embarrassment, probably from prosecco. They could have refused, laughed it off, and sat back down. *No, no. Once was enough.* The band probably would have moved onto another group.

But that's not what happened. Instead, Sadie grabbed Willa's hands.

One could have sworn the music stopped in that second, marking the moment with the briefest interlude of silence. But maybe that was just in their heads. Maybe their group hadn't gasped aloud, or Roxanne and Deb sucked in a collective breath.

It didn't matter because Willa and Sadie were face to face, hands clasped, while a lively Italian quartet directed them in a cheerful folk dance. The band hopped and played and radiated such festive joy, it was hard not to fall in line. Their vibe was contagious, and in some miraculous way, for the briefest few minutes, Sadie and Willa forgot about the onlookers, the coaches who were breathing fire behind them. Instead, they lost themselves in the fun of it all, giggling and trying to keep up with the steps. They stepped on each other's toes and once just about bumped heads, which only made the whole thing even more hilarious.

"You go that way. No, this way. Then I— yeah, now cross over. One, two. Wait, I think we—" It was hard to get the steps right when they were laughing so hard.

From the outside, no one would have suspected the history between the two—or perhaps they would. But only the good parts. They would have seen the two little girls who were friends despite their differences, or even because of them.

For those few lighthearted minutes, Sadie and Willa weren't enemies. They were two people whose stories had been written for them. And during that song, they were rewriting it. Childhood memories flooded back. Reminders of how they were more alike than different. And even though neither voiced it aloud, they both were met with surprising thoughts.

Sadie: *I could like this person.*

Willa: *I have to cut it off with Baz.*

When the song ended, Willa and Sadie fell into each other, damp with sweat and amusement. They faced their group and gave a joint bow, soaking in the liquor-infused applause.

"Didn't know you had all those moves," Harper said to Sadie, giving her a high five.

"Nice, Willa!" another called.

The skiers returned to their tables, poured a final drink and enjoyed another half hour before deciding to call it a night. As the group dialed and waited for Ubers to take them to the hotel, Roxanne and Deb held back.

"I take it Sadie got her dance skills from her dad?" Roxanne jabbed.

Deb sneered. "Very funny. Didn't you see who was the clear winner? Sadie can outshine Willa on skis *and* on the dance floor."

"Not today she didn't."

"There's plenty of season left. Don't worry, Rox. Sadie will prove to everyone who the real champion is."

"We'll see about that." And then because she couldn't help herself, or because she just wanted to get an extra little jab, she leaned in closer. "Did you hear, Deb? Baz has been reaching out to Willa lately." The surprise Deb tried to conceal told Roxanne it had worked. "That castle in the sky must have some cracks."

Deb's eyes narrowed and she glanced to where Sadie chatted with a group of girls up ahead, then back to Roxanne. Her voice was a warning. "Baz is a Norcross, and Norcrosses don't betray each other."

"Whatever you say," Roxanne said, and walked away. She caught up with Willa and linked arms with her protégé. "That was interesting."

Willa, tipsy from one too many drinks, giggled. "It was fun. Turns out I'm not a very good dancer."

"You don't get paid to dance." She gave Willa a wink.

They made their way to a waiting car. Willa's head was beginning to thump in her temples, and she craved the feel of crisp hotel sheets against her skin. A good night's sleep would be the perfect end to the day, the cherry on top of another win. But just as they were slipping into the back seat, a phone call gave the mood a sober turn. Willa squinted at her phone. She normally didn't answer unfamiliar numbers, but something made her finger slide the green icon.

"Is this Willa Betts?" the man's voice said. "This is Dr. Bashira, calling from Orlando Health Hospital. It's your father."

Chapter 21

Willa's plane landed, and she took an Uber directly to the hospital, using the time to read through messages from the fellow skiers she'd left behind.

Thinking of you!

Praying for your dad!

Even Sadie had texted. *Hope your dad is okay...Sorry you had to leave early.* The message surprised Willa. Maybe their impromptu dance had fused some sort of broken thread between them. She had an involuntary vision of what it would look like not to be so pitted against each other, but then the driver announced their arrival, and the spell burst.

The woman behind the reception desk looked up Dale's room number and directed Willa to the elevators where she zoomed up to the fourth floor. Outside room 413, Willa stopped, let her lungs fill with air. Her stomach throbbed behind the waistband of her pants, a deep cramping she credited to stress. She was nearing the end of this long journey, and while she felt guilty admitting it, part of her was relieved. The constant flip-flop of emotions left her with whiplash.

Love him, hate him.

Save him, let him go.

Willa pushed open the door. The stark hospital room smelled of ammonia and stale air. Her father laid on the bed, somehow looking even more frail than the last time she saw him before she'd left for Europe nearly a month ago. July had robbed her father of more than just time. It took weight from his frame, color from his skin, and zest from his eyes.

Willa approached the bed with tentative steps. "Hi, Dad."

Dale turned his head. "You're here," he managed, voice raspy and slow.

"I'm here."

"But I thought you were in—"

"I flew home when the doctor called."

He gave the smallest nod, closed his eyes like it pained him to keep them open for another second. Impulse would have told her to resent this reaction—she'd just flown across the Atlantic to be with him!—but she couldn't bring herself to go there. It took too much effort. Instead, in this moment that felt like one of his last, she saw him for who he was—a man with faults.

Willa tried to swallow, but her mouth was a desert. She looked around the room for a pitcher of water.

"I think...this is...the end for me," Dale sputtered.

Willa faltered. How did she respond to such a statement? Disagreeing would be both silly and pointless—they both knew what he said was true. She didn't have the ability to sugarcoat it any other way.

Instead, she avoided a direct answer. "Are you in pain?"

He shook his head. "Barely feel...a thing."

Willa glanced at the IV attached to his arm, a clear liquid dripping from a bag on a pole. Morphine, she imagined. "That's good."

Her body temperature rose, and she pulled on her collar to let out some hot air. What was she doing there? When she'd got the call, she'd felt such an immediate need to be by his side, and now was left feeling more confused than anything. Could this really be the end? Should she say goodbye?

The chorus of beeps from machines cut through the silence in the room in an exaggerated volume that Willa wondered was just in her own head. She looked to the white board where it listed a nurse's name—Michelle—next to a smiley face. Such an odd symbol to have in a terminal patient's room. She considered how nurses could care for people at the end stage of life. See patients die and families cry. The sadness would be too much to bear.

When Willa looked back to her father, he was asleep. She watched his chest rise and fall with labored breaths and wondered how much longer he had. An hour? A day? A week? A chair took up space in the corner, a place for grief-stricken families to watch and wait. Would she have to sit there until it was over? It looked like a prison.

Her mind drifted to the tour. The next race wasn't for three weeks, but that didn't mean she could blow off training. She had a life outside of this man.

A dark thought poked its way into her mind: *Please don't let this drag on.* She wished he'd just die. It would be better for him. Better for her. Right?

A wave of nausea slapped her in the face. *Selfish girl.*

She was heartless. Or human.

She couldn't tell anymore.

* * *

Some time later, Willa jumped when she felt a hand on her head. She blinked rapidly, unsure where she was, jetlag hitting her hard. Everything came to. She was still in the chair next to the hospital bed, but must have fallen asleep? Her head laid forward on the mattress, bumping into Dale's bony hip.

The hand moved again, soft, traveling from the crown of her head to the nape of her neck. A pang hit her heart when she realized what it was: Her father was stroking her hair. Something caught in Willa's throat. She remained still.

"I used to play...with your mother's...hair like this," Dale said. That made her sit up. Their connection broke. He coughed. "I'm sorry...for not being a...better father."

"Oh, I, uh—"

"I made...a lot of mistakes...I wish I...could take back."

Willa's arm hairs stood on end. An apology. After all these years. She didn't know how to respond. Was this what she'd been waiting for? She searched for an internal signal, something that would make her feel warm and fuzzy. A final gift.

Nothing came. As the seconds passed, it felt like too little, too late. Accepting it would mean accepting a childhood no kid should have to endure. She couldn't forget the neglect—what Roxanne called trauma.

A saying came to mind: You don't have to forget to forgive. But could she?

Willa's lips parted, words on the tip of her tongue. Just as she was about to speak, Dale continued. "We loved you even if we didn't show it very well. Your mother and I, we had our demons."

"Demons," Willa whispered. The word made her think of evil, of secrets. Of people doing bad things. She'd done a bad thing too. Was that her demon? Maybe she didn't deserve forgiveness either.

A sudden urge to confess hit her square in the chest. This might be the last time she spoke to her father, and the guilt tore her in half. What did she owe him? The truth? Or was it better to let him go without the burden of knowing how his wife had really died? The internal battle raged. She remembered what Baz had said.

There's still time to come clean.

"Dad, I want to tell you something," she choked. Regret overtook her, as if she were that twelve-year-old child again. It didn't matter that her parents' transgressions far outweighed her own. In the moment, Willa feared his disappointment. She took a breath and channeled the reminders she'd told herself when dark thoughts clouded her brain. What she'd done had been a chance event. Pure bad luck. A mishap. Their actions were deliberate choices. It was the only way to ease her conscience.

"That day, the day of the accident," she began, slowly. "I—"

But then the door swung open, cutting her off. Willa swiveled to see who had entered. Her breath hitched, as though she'd conjured him. "Baz."

He wore a concerned expression. "I thought you might need some support." He took tentative steps toward her and she stood to meet him. Her body vibrated. When they were feet apart, she let it take over. Her arms reached out and he took her in his.

"Does Sadie know you're here?" Willa asked.

"Not exactly."

"Baz." It was a scolding, but only half-hearted. In truth, his presence struck her with glee, followed by quick self-reproach. Sadie was on the other side of the world. She had no idea her husband now stood in a small hospital room, holding another woman. Willa's ribs constricted. She flashed back to only hours before. The group at the Italian bistro. Sadie. They'd danced together, had shared what Willa could only refer to as a *moment.* Willa had told herself right then that the daydreams about Baz had to end. It wasn't fair to any of them. And now, here Baz came crashing through it all. Staring into his eyes, breathing the same air, the idea went out the window.

Willa rolled her ankles. "I don't want to cause a problem."

"It's fine," he said. "This is more important. She doesn't need to know."

Willa bit her lip to keep the emotion in check. Her heart felt like a speeding train with no brakes. Until that moment, she hadn't realized how much she needed the support. "Thank you for coming." She pulled over another chair next to hers and they sat, hands folded carefully in their laps.

"Dad," Willa said. "This is Baz Tanner, Sadie's husband. Remember?" Even though her parents hadn't attended her races, she'd mentioned the same names of competitors and friends enough times. That, and the media coverage meant Sadie's and Baz's names were hard to forget.

"Hi, Mr. Betts. I'm Willa's friend," Baz said. "I hope you don't mind me being here."

Dale shook his head and closed his eyes, almost as though glad for someone else to fill the space and keep his daughter company. Willa and Baz exchanged nervous glances, which quickly turned to conversation about the European circuit. She recounted the races, the level of competition. He asked about her flight home, how she was feeling. Before long, Dale's breathing slowed, and Willa knew he was asleep again.

Willa rubbed her eyes. "I'm desperate for coffee."

"There's a little café downstairs."

"Oh, bingo."

"I'll walk with you."

They left the room quietly and headed toward the elevators at the end of the hall. Their sneakers squeaked against the linoleum.

"You didn't want to go with Sadie this year?" Willa said. "Italy is pretty romantic."

"I'm not sure she wanted me to tag along."

"Trouble in paradise?"

Baz rolled his eyes. "No such thing as paradise."

"I thought 'Norcross' was synonymous with 'perfect.'" Willa smirked, giving his arm a little shove, and then felt immediate shame for flirting when her father was dying in another room. A sick feeling washed over her, but she pushed it away. Baz's presence helped alleviate some of the mess. She couldn't remember the last time they'd been alone together. Years probably. He might not even be that same person. But even so, it didn't matter. Their shared childhood and sporadic texts kept them tethered.

As they made their way to the small café in the lobby, Willa found herself yearning to grab his hand. Instead, she shoved hers into her pockets, not trusting what she might do.

Chapter 22

The coffee was shit, but caffeine was caffeine, and Willa got a little zap when it hit her bloodstream. What time was it anyway? She tapped her phone screen. Eleven-oh-five. But in Italy time it would be...forget it, her brain hurt too much to think.

Willa and Baz sat on a small leather couch outside the café in the lobby. The space was a ghost town at this hour, quiet and dimly lit with only the occasional noise coming from the welcome desk. A decorative glass water wall emitted a quiet rain patter, like a white noise machine set to low.

Willa pressed herself against the armrest, despite the overpowering urge to scoot closer to Baz. Her conscience waved a finger. She crossed her legs and tucked one hand into her armpit, the other soaking in the warmth of the coffee cup.

Again, they exchanged quick glances, as though afraid to make extended eye contact. They let out tiny, electric breaths, until Baz rubbed his neck and gave her a sheepish grin. "You know what randomly popped into my head the other day?"

"Hmm."

"That time in Tuscaloosa."

"What time in Tuscaloosa?" she said, coyly bringing her cup to her lips to cover a smirk. She knew exactly what time he was talking about. Her cheeks burned, mouth twisted mischievously.

"You know."

"I don't." She wanted him to say it out loud. They were both grinning, playing a dangerous game. Any qualms she'd had earlier were long gone. Sadie who?

He lowered his voice. "I didn't think skinny dipping at midnight would be so easy to forget."

Willa raised her eyebrows. "Oh *that*. Funny, I haven't thought about that night for a long time."

Only multiple times a week.

She spun her phone in her lap, looking down to hide the full smile spreading across her face.

"You're a bad liar."

"Better than a good one, right?"

The memory came fast. It had been a moment of pure spontaneity. That summer—what, seven years ago now?—after the Malibu Open when a group of them who'd just turned twenty-one had gone out for drinks. One too many rounds of shots had led to karaoke, which led to truth or dare, which led to someone throwing out a dare to skinny dip in the lake. They'd all laughed and egged each other on, until the game fizzled when a junior skier—who'd used a fake ID to get in—puked in the bathroom. Outside, the group called Ubers to head back to their hotels or head home, and that's when Baz had told Sadie he was going to walk instead, hoping to sober up a bit.

He'd kissed her goodnight, shut the Uber door, and turned to head toward the sidewalk. The air would sober him up a bit, and he'd get almost seven hours of sleep before he'd have to be back on the water to train.

But that's not what happened. Because as Sadie's car pulled away, leaving Baz behind, another car circled back.

"Forgot my jacket," Willa said, jumping from the backseat, her long dark hair a waterfall over her shoulders. Baz had frozen mid-step, a deer in headlights—quite literally. He'd watched as Willa bounded into the restaurant and returned, jacket in hand. She flashed a megawatt smile, and his knees wobbled.

Something about that moment, them being there alone in the dark cover of midnight, pressed down on the invisible accelerator whether they knew it or not.

"You know," Baz said, approaching her car just as she was about to hop back inside, "I'm not one to bow out on a dare."

She'd stood there, skinny jeans hugging her toned legs, and for a second Baz thought maybe he'd crossed the line. His girlfriend had just left, and here he was batting eyes at someone else. But it wasn't just anyone. It was Willa.

A glint appeared in Willa's eye. "Me either."

And that's how they ended up at the lake, stripping off their clothes, and jumping into the lukewarm water lit by the moon. It wasn't romantic, and they didn't even touch, even if they'd wanted to. They simply laughed and laughed until their cheeks hurt. It had been one of the last times Willa had felt so free.

Back in the hospital lobby, Baz cleared his throat, jolting Willa from the memory. Her fingers fumbled, and her phone dropped onto the floor. Dazed, she leaned down to reach for it, but so did Baz, and their foreheads nearly bumped.

"Oh."

"Sorry."

"I got it."

Willa grabbed the phone, but neither of them moved to right themselves. Instead, they met eyes and something primal passed between them. The world made sense, without any words being spoken. Willa's body came alive with need. And then their lips were together, soft and gentle, and yet so very hungry. To give credit for the kiss would be unfair, as they'd met in the middle. A mutual deed.

Baz placed a hand on her cheek. Willa could taste mint on his tongue, and it surprised her. She'd thought he'd taste like strawberries and cream. The candies from their youth. His lips felt like pillows against hers, and she sank into them.

It was a moment a long time in the making, and yet Willa had convinced herself it would never happen. How could it? Baz was married. She wasn't a homewrecker. Still, the rightness of it outweighed the wrong, and she let her body rejoice.

That is, until the creak of a door thrust them apart.

They both bolted upright, and Willa experienced a few dizzying seconds as blood returned to her head. Her hands went a million directions, eventually landing on her hair and tucking it behind her ears. A man in scrubs crossed the lobby toward the café counter.

Willa cleared her throat. She stole a glance at Baz, whose face was flushed. The room felt buzzed, like a live wire. She squeezed her toes inside her sneakers. Had she really just kissed Baz? What did this *mean*? Her stomach clenched in a cramp. She felt sick. Maybe coffee was a bad idea.

Willa stood, turning her back to the man at the counter. "I should probably get back."

Baz stood too. "I don't have to go. I mean, unless you'd rather I—"

"No, it's fine."

"Are you sure?"

"The company is nice."

Baz nodded with a look Willa interpreted as relief. He didn't want to leave. He wanted to be with her.

When they returned to Dale's room, a nurse was fiddling with wires attached to Dale's chest. "Just checking his vitals," she said. Then, seeing the coffee cups, "Sorry it's not Starbucks." She pressed two fingers against Dale's wrist to take his pulse, then opened his chart and jotted down notes. She snapped her pen closed and tucked it into her breast pocket. "He seems comfortable. Give me a buzz if you need anything, all right? There are blankets in that top cupboard."

"Thanks," Willa said.

The door clicked shut, and silence fell over the room. Willa swore if she strained hard enough she could hear an electric current pulsing between her and Baz. She glanced at the clock. Eleven fifty. Her eyelids weighed a million pounds, and yet she felt energized enough to run a marathon.

"Are you going to stay here all night?" Baz said. "We can go somewhere. I mean, if you're hungry or something? Or, you know. Even if you're not." He bumbled his words, and Willa tried to detect his motive. She wished desperately they hadn't been interrupted downstairs. That their lips were still pressed together. His fingers in her hair. Baz's gaze didn't waver. Something in his expression told her he wanted the same.

But then what? Was she really going to do this? She brought a hand to her churning belly.

"Sure," she said, imagining scenarios for when they left the safety of the hospital. A hotel room, clothes strewn all over the floor. Her heart raced, and something clenched in her abdomen. Lust? No, she realized, a full bladder. "But give me a second, I'll be right back."

Willa shuffled down the hall, the whole time thinking about what she was about to do. An angel and devil wrestled on her shoulder. She'd gone from shock at his sudden appearance to kissing him in the downstairs café.

What the hell are you doing, Willa? It was wrong, and yet somehow completely logical. Willa and Baz. Baz and Willa. It was like a force she couldn't withhold any longer. All the clichés sprang to her mind, but one felt the most true: Meant to be.

Willa was so lost in thought that she paid attention to little else as she entered the bathroom. That is, until, she pulled down her pants and underwear. The air sucked from her lungs. A million disappointments in the span of a second. "Of course," she breathed, staring at the red stain. Perfect timing. Any visions she had for the evening flew out the window. She wouldn't be sleeping with Baz. Not tonight.

Maybe it was punishment—a sign that girls who fool around when their parent was dying didn't get the things they want. Or maybe it was a giant red flag trying to get her to see straight.

Either way, Willa left the bathroom with heavy feet. She cursed biology and fate and womanhood. As she returned to her father's room, she was taken back to years before, remembering how Mother Nature had a way of showing up at the most inopportune times.

Chapter 23

THEN
Summer 2008

Her belly had been giving her trouble for days, but Sadie chalked it up to nerves, what with the North Shore Race that weekend. She was prone to anxiety leading up to an event, and it wasn't unusual to have loose bowels the morning of. Plenty of athletes could be found making an emergency dash to the toilet. Only this time, when Sadie hit the porta potty for the third time, it wasn't diarrhea she encountered, but a brownish-red smear in her suit.

"What the..." she said, and then after it became clear, "Great." Nothing like getting her period for the very first time at one of the biggest competitions of the year. Couldn't this have happened last week instead? She thought back to last year when Kaley Oldman got her period in the middle of English class. When her standing up to answer a question on the board had caused a wave of whispers mixed with laughter to stir through the room. Kaley had been wearing light khaki pants and the blood looked like a dark blotch, almost like she'd sat in chocolate, even though everyone knew the truth. Sadie had felt second-hand embarrassment for

Kaley in that moment, and she had prayed—*prayed*—that her period would make a less humiliating appearance.

A ski race wasn't exactly what she had in mind.

Sadie wiped the rust-colored streak from the crotch of her suit, but not all came off. She hadn't brought an extra. Maybe her mom would have one stashed in the car? She layered a wad of toilet paper into her suit and pulled it up. A temporary fix. Her belly really ached now, worse than minutes ago, as if knowing the reason made the cramps even stronger.

She stood for a minute, slightly dumbfounded. Now what? It wasn't like she could ski with a toilet paper diaper. Emotion bubbled up and water filled her eyes. She took a breath there in that stinky porta potty, then pushed open the door, practically smacking the face of someone outside.

"Sorry!" Sadie said, automatically.

Willa took a step back. "I thought maybe you fell in."

"Ha," Sadie tried to laugh. She wiped her eyes, but not fast enough for Willa not to notice.

"Are you okay?"

"Yeah, it's just— My stomach's a mess." She flapped her hand dismissively. "Girl stuff." She added this at the end both as a declaration of pride—*I finally got my period!*—and as bait to see Willa's response. Had Willa already gotten her period? Or was she an even later bloomer than Sadie?

That moment between the girls, no more than seconds really, echoed the hallmark of their existence. Who would come out on top? Who would be the more advanced? And who would be the one trailing behind? Ski races and periods, one and the same.

"Oh damn, that sucks," Willa said. "Do you have something?"

Have something? Sadie nodded before she could even gather what the "something" options were, and the girls traded places—Willa going in to let out her nervous shits, and Sadie off to find the only option for help: her mother.

* * *

"You're kidding," Deb said, as she filled her cup from a coffee carafe set amongst bananas and donuts under the concession tent. "Oh, Sadie."

"It's not like I asked for it."

"Do you have another suit?"

"No, I was hoping you might."

Deb shook her head. "Welcome to womanhood. I just wish it wouldn't have been today." She dug through her purse, pulling out a tampon and extending it to Sadie. "Here."

Sadie snatched it and tucked it under her shirt. How embarrassing in front of all these people! Her mom practically waved it like a flag. *Christ.*

"Do I have to?" Sadie asked.

Deb's over-plucked eyebrows squished together. "What do you mean? You can't wear a pad in the water—it'll soak up the whole lake. And I don't think you want blood running down your legs into your boot, do you? It's fine—just stick it in and you're good to go."

Mortification didn't even come close to describing it. Stick it in? What? How? Also...ouch! But Deb was already pulling last competition's scores up on her phone to analyze results. "Harper Cruz is here today. Gotta watch out—she's really been having a good season."

"My lower back is throbbing."

"Sadie, it's less than one minute of your life."

These things—intimacies, feelings—made Deb's chest tighten. It was why she'd bought Sadie a puberty book three years ago and left it on her pillow without a word of discussion. Vulnerability threw her off balance, like a sailor hitting land after a year at sea. Better to close off those emotions, even when it came to her daughter.

And yet, Sadie's wide eyes made Deb soften. Maybe she wasn't the warmest mother, but she wasn't completely heartless. She leaned in so they were on the same eye level. "Listen," she said, "periods are awful, and yes, cramps hurt. But the O'Neill people are here, and your grandpa's working really hard to secure a sponsorship. It might not be a boat, but a vest or swimwear brand is a good place to start. You can't not ski today, period or no period. Okay? Millions of women wear tampons. You can too."

Sadie trudged away toward the porta potty, holding the tampon under her shirt like a stolen treasure, wishing this very first violating experience could have happened in the comfort of her bathroom instead of a stand-up shit stall. Her belly cramped again. She felt like throwing up. People meandered by, unsuspecting, and yet Sadie felt like everyone could see the stain hidden under her shorts. She shuffled as fast as she could, clenching muscles in her pelvic floor she'd never engaged before. Baz was somewhere around here, and she did not want him catching her with a *tampon*. She'd rather *die*.

Somehow the arrival of her period brought with it an indisputable shift. A fork in the road. They weren't kids anymore. It felt like another lifetime when they were busy catching frogs along the sides of the water. Now, her body had thrust her into a new chapter. Would he look at her differently?

Ahead, Willa exited the porta potty. "You good?" she asked with a knowing look.

Sadie liked this girl code talk. *Be cool.* "Yeah, I uh— I got something." She tapped her shirt, hiding the secret object.

"Good. Sorry that happened. Totally sucks on tournament day."

So Willa *had* started her period already. Sadie felt a warmth toward the girl she'd once played Barbies with in between ski runs. With dozens of skiers in her age bracket, she'd grown to recognize many of the same faces over the years. Everyone was cordial, would clap for each other, but at the end of the day they were all participating as individuals. Without the team mentality, it was hard to form true friendships. The ingrained understanding was clear: *this girl is my competition.*

They lingered there for a minute, both wanting something from each other, the same thing—sisterhood—but not knowing how to navigate it. There'd always been that appeal, that natural connection that seemed to come so freely. But then parents and coaches and managers got in the way. Their friendship was no longer the same as when they were ten or twelve.

Sadie gave a nervous laugh, and when she did she felt a gush of warmth between her legs. She froze, mouth open. And somehow Willa knew.

"Do you...need help?"

"Help? Oh, you mean with..." Sadie patted her shirt again. "No, I'm good. Can't be that hard, right?" More nervous laughter. And then she silently cursed for giving herself away. Willa probably thought she was so immature. A child. Sadie wished she'd have asked her mom the questions she had after reading the puberty book. Wished she'd demanded to be more prepared. Maybe then she wouldn't have shaved her legs dry and ended up with angry razor burn she had to hide behind pants for a week. But their relationship was never one to be so casual. Now, Sadie wondered if Willa had to learn everything on her own too.

She must not have been convincing, but instead of snickering, Willa took a gracious turn.

"Well, I just mean it's awkward at first. Here—" Willa pulled Sadie by the elbow back toward the porta potty, not giving her a chance to protest. She opened the door, gave Sadie an encouraging little shove, and then stood guard outside. She'd wait as long as Sadie needed.

"So, like, see if you can put a foot up on the toilet seat," Willa said, leaning her shoulder against the blue plastic and talking through the door in a low voice only Sadie could hear. "It makes it easier to get the right angle. Put it in up to where your fingers are holding it, then push the bottom to insert the tampon."

"This is disgusting."

"Don't think about it."

"Is it supposed to hurt?"

"Hurt? No. But it's sort of uncomfortable until you get used to it. If it's up there right, you shouldn't feel it."

A hand on her shoulder made Willa jump. "Wanna bite my wiener?" Baz said, shoving a mustard-slathered hotdog in Willa's face.

She recoiled. "Ew, Baz. You're so disgusting."

He howled, pleased with his crude humor.

Boys, Willa thought.

"What are you doing? Why are you hanging out against the shit closet?" He shoved half the hotdog in his mouth, chomping away.

"Nothing. Don't worry about it."

"Got the runs?"

"Baz, just get out of here, okay?" Willa didn't know if she was more flustered that he associated her with pooping, or that he was actually right—minutes ago she had been emptying her bowels. Such an undignified thought. What she did know was that she didn't need him hanging around when she was trying to help Sadie insert her first tampon.

"Sheesh," Baz said, and trudged off. *Girls.*

Willa returned her face to the door. "Sorry about that," she said. "Baz. He didn't know you were in here though, don't worry. Did you...get it in?"

"Yeah, I think. I pushed the bottom part."

"Now just pull the rest out. That's all garbage. I can get you some Tylenol—Roxanne keeps a bottle in her car."

From inside the stall, Willa heard rustling of toilet paper, a couple pumps of hand sanitizer, and then the latch sliding open. She stepped back from the door. Sadie emerged, flushed, and the two exchanged awkward eye contact.

"Thanks," Sadie said, hand to her belly.

"Don't worry about it. Just make sure the string's tucked in."

"Good call."

The girls smiled and something passed between them then. Was it trust? Some sort of pact? Neither could have put it into words had there been a gun to their heads. It was an understanding, an acceptance of this friendship that might not ever get to blossom into its full potential, and that outsiders might discourage, but one they'd nurture in their own way. Screw adults, screw parents.

If only it were that easy.

Willa wrapped an arm around Sadie's shoulder, leading the two of them back toward the lake where their respective crews waited. Deb saw the girls coming from a distance, a sense of unease settling in her gut. She involuntarily looked to Roxanne a few yards away, who also watched the smiling girls approach. Sadie and Willa would both ski in a matter of an hour, undoubtedly taking the top two spots. But only one would get first, a fact they each knew but neither would say aloud.

Chapter 24

NOW

With her father asleep for the night, the nursing staff convinced Willa to go home. He was critical but stable, they said—a distressing combination, for he could take a downward turn at any moment—and it didn't make sense for Willa to sleep in a chair all night.

Relieved, she agreed.

Willa and Baz took the elevator to the ground floor. They stood side by side against the back wall, their inside hands inches apart. Neither grabbed for the other, and yet it was like their fingers resisted a force outside their control pulling them together. When the door opened, Willa gulped air that hadn't been Baz-infused.

He extended an arm, ladies first. Willa stepped through into the lobby. Carnal energy coursed between them, even after Willa's bathroom letdown.

"Do you want to—" Baz started.

"I'm exhausted," she cut him off. "Thanks for the offer, but I think I'll just head home and get some sleep." She didn't admit the truth, that less than an hour earlier, she'd been daydreaming of spending the night together. If her period wouldn't have made a surprise visit, she might have actually gone through with it. The thought scared her. What kind of person was she?

"Can I walk you to your car at least?"

She smiled. It wasn't what either of them wanted, but it would have to do—for now. Forever?

They headed into the parking lot, which was dark save for a few scattered overhead lights. The summer Florida air held all its moisture, as though trying to win a humidity competition. Willa's feet dragged, her body reminding her of how long she'd been awake.

At her car, Willa reached for the door handle, slow and exaggerated, dragging out the moment and not wanting it to end. "Thanks again for coming. It means a lot."

"I can come back in the morning. If you want, I mean."

Willa tilted her head. "Sadie will be home by then, won't she?" The rest of the ski group was scheduled to fly home the morning after she'd left Italy. Which was...what? How many hours from now? She couldn't think.

Baz dropped his head, and a stretch of silence fell on them. A thin horned moon hung like a basket in the sky. "Listen, Willa, I—" He reached for her hands and leaned in like he wanted to kiss her again.

"Baz, we shouldn't."

"But I know you feel the same."

"And what if I do? You're married."

"Sadie and I haven't been happy for a long time." He tucked a piece of hair behind her ear. "Things could have been so different."

Their eyes told so many stories, memories of youth and first loves and heartbreak. It was too much to sustain. Everything told her to get in that car and drive away. Leave him standing there, like the night outside the bar. But then, she'd come back. They'd snuck to the lake and splashed around naked. It was inappropriate then, and it was inappropriate now.

The voice in her head screamed in warning, but Willa tuned it out. She let Baz pull her close, and just as their lips were about to meet for a second time that night, a bright flash made them freeze. It was followed by another quick succession of white flashes.

Willa and Baz broke apart, heads spinning, searching for the source.

"What the...?" Baz said.

Willa squinted into the dark, and once her eyes adjusted from the blinding light, she saw them—two men with cameras leaning from windows of a car on the other side of the parking lot. She spun her back to them. "Paparazzi. Fuck."

Baz did the same. "Paparazzi? How did they know you were here?"

"It must have leaked that I left before everyone else." She frantically opened the car door and flung her purse inside. "I have to go. Shit! What did they see?" Even as she said it, she knew. Her face had been an inch from Baz's, lips parted, eyes closed. It didn't take a genius to look at those pictures and see two people about to kiss. A lump formed in Willa's throat. She yanked the door closed.

"I'll text you," Baz called through the glass. He spun on his heel and hurried away, head down.

Willa sped away without responding, but the word was heavy on her tongue. *Don't.*

She felt like she was falling from the highest peak to the depths of something jagged, her actions digging her own grave. It was one thing for Baz to live in her own mind, but it was another for the world to catch them in a moment so intimate.

As she peeled from the parking lot, Willa saw spots. She swore under her breath. *Dammit Willa, what are you thinking?*

Chapter 25

The pictures hit the media as Sadie was boarding her flight in Naples. A TMZ notification lit up her phone, followed by a tag on Instagram. She swiped it open.

SEBASTIAN "BAZ" TANNER CAUGHT IN LATE NIGHT ROMANTIC MOMENT WITH WIFE'S RIVAL

Sadie's stomach hit the floor. Her peripheral vision went white.

"Ohmygod," she breathed at the same time she stepped over the threshold into the plane.

Behind her, Harper Cruz peered over Sadie's shoulder. "What?"

Sadie pressed the phone to her chest, a gut reaction in an effort to keep her personal business private. But that was pointless. If TMZ had the scoop, that meant the whole internet was probably already talking about it. And her mother—oh, Lord, what would her mother say? Sadie was grateful Deb's old school approach to phones and planes meant she didn't just turn hers to airplane mode; she turned it all the way off the minute she lined up to board.

Sadie peeked at the screen again. Heat pounded in her face. It was the ultimate betrayal. And to think she'd felt bad for Willa having to leave early. That *bitch!* Had her father even been sick? Was it all a ruse to fly home early and be with Baz?

Harper breathed in Sadie's ear. Sadie handed her the phone. "Look."

Harper gaped. "Are you kidding me? How could he..."

But Sadie had already tuned out. Her brain traveled in reverse over the past weeks, months looking for red flags. Sure, their marriage had been strained, but she never—never—would have expected this. The image was grainy but clear enough to make out Willa and Baz without question. Their bodies were pressed together, faces inches apart. His hand cupped the back of her head. Sadie knew the feel of that hand.

She snatched the phone back. "I need to make a call."

"Wait, are you calling Baz?"

Sadie nodded.

"Give him hell, Sade."

She found her seat and shoved her carry-on in the overhead bin, then tucked into the impossibly small bathroom at the rear of the plane. It smelled of disinfectant. The fan kicked on when she slid the lock.

Sadie dialed with shaking fingers. It was 6 a.m. in Italy, which meant it was midnight back home. Baz should be sleeping. But *where* was he sleeping? Sadie got a foul taste in her mouth.

"Hello?" He answered on the third ring.

"You bastard," she hissed, a surprising burst of water springing to her eyes. They never name-called, but in this moment, it was the only thing that felt right. "How could you?"

"It's not what you think, Sadie."

"Oh really? I think the pictures make it look pretty damn clear. Did you sleep with her? Are you with her right now?"

"What? No."

"Well, it's a logical question."

"I'm not— Nothing happened."

Sadie sputtered. "Right. I'm supposed to believe that?"

"Her dad is dying. I went to the hospital as support."

"And then made out in the parking lot."

"No, the paps—"

"Oh, so the paparazzi caught you and that's the only reason you stopped yourselves. How thoughtful."

Sadie caught a glimpse of herself in the tiny mirror. No makeup, hair pulled into a top knot. She had been ready to catch a few hours of sleep as the plane crossed back over the Atlantic. Forget that—she'd never be able to fall asleep now.

A knock on the door, followed by a woman's voice. "Excuse me? You'll need to take your seat now."

Sadie swiveled the phone away from her mouth. "Just a minute."

"Listen," Baz said. "Aren't you supposed to be taking off? Let's talk about this when you get home, okay? There's no point arguing when you're an ocean away."

"What is there to say, Baz? You're clearly having an affair. And now you want me to just come home and *talk* about it? This is great. Just great. It's on TMZ for fuck's sake."

"I'm not having an affair."

"What the hell do you call it?" she screamed.

The fight attendant knocked again, louder this time. "Ma'am, I need you to return to your seat. We're about to push back from the gate."

"I'll be right there."

"No, *now.*"

Sadie sighed.

Baz was still talking on the other end of the line. "...figure this out when you're home."

She had nothing else to say, and so she tapped the red button to end the call, then left the bathroom, passing the very annoyed flight attendant on her way back to her seat. She caught a glimpse of her mother a couple rows ahead, pulling a sleep mask down over her eyes.

"What did he say?" Harper whispered, as Sadie sat.

"Denied it."

"Oh please."

"I know. Photos don't lie."

"I'm so sorry, Sadie."

Sadie frowned. As the plane taxied toward the runway, she laid her head against the window and stared out at the sun stretching above the horizon, ready to start another day. A host of emotions swirled in her gut, but the one that rose to the top surprised her most. It wasn't sadness. It wasn't anger. It was embarrassment that the world now knew there were cracks in the Norcross name.

Chapter 26

There were paparazzi waiting when Sadie landed. Their cameras rang out in a stream of clicks, lights popping like fireworks on the Fourth of July.

By then, Deb had seen the news. As passengers had stood from their seats upon landing, anxious to stretch their legs and breathe fresh air after an eight-hour flight, Deb's head had whipped around searching for her daughter with a look that told Sadie all she needed to know—Deb had turned on her phone.

Sadie kept her head down, as she and her mother walked straight past baggage claim to the car. They'd come back for luggage later. Right then, the only thing that mattered was getting away from the airport and out of camera range.

They practically dove into the car, and with the slam of the doors, Deb finally spoke. "Oh, Sadie."

Was that pity? Or disappointment?

"Not now, Mom. Just go."

Deb stepped on the gas, speeding away from the airport, leaving a dozen hungry photographers in the dust.

"I knew I never liked that girl," Deb said, white-knuckled grip clenching the steering wheel. "Look at her role models. Absent parents. And Roxanne for a coach. Good Lord, it's no wonder she has no morals."

Sadie thumbed through social media, reading headline after worse headline. *Bad Baz,* one wrote. *Love triangle on the water,* another said. They called her a scorned wife, a victim. The flawless couple's fall from grace.

Sadie closed out of the apps and turned her phone over. "I can't believe this is happening."

"We have some serious damage control to do. I've already texted your grandfather. He's thinking we'll—"

"Can I get a second to breathe first?"

Deb gave her daughter a quick glance, then returned her eyes to the road. "Sadie, this isn't some little thing we can brush under the rug. Your husband is *cheating on you.*"

"Thank you for stating the obvious."

"Well, it's not a good look."

Emotion welled in Sadie's chest, making her breathing increase. "Is that all you care about? The look? Our image?" It was hypocritical, Sadie knew, because she'd thought the exact same thing and hated herself for it.

"I never said that."

"You didn't have to."

"Sadie."

"Can you honestly say you didn't see this coming, Mom? We've been pretending for a while."

"Don't say that, Sadie. You've had a perfectly happy marriage. You're both God-fearing, good people. That's the Norcross way. We'll have to spin this in our favor, of course. Let Baz take the biggest fall. He blindsided you. You're devastated."

"Of course I'm devastated," Sadie said, mouth agape. But was she? Yes...and no. Perhaps not in the way people would think.

"Your grandfather wants us to meet him at the church. We can craft a statement there."

"Mom, I'm tired. I didn't sleep at all on the plane. Can't it wait?"

"No. We need to get out in front of it." Then under her breath, "I can't believe he would do this to us."

* * *

"Hey champ," Leather said, opening the door for them. It was a Monday morning and the church was empty, with the exception of Leather and Jed. "Looks like we've got a bit of a pickle to sort out, don't we?" His belted shorts reached nearly to his knees, striped polo shirt tucked in, completing his version of casual. Sometimes when she looked at him, Sadie was reminded he wasn't the young, agile man in the framed photos on her parents' walls.

Leather placed a hand on her shoulder, guiding her in with a grave expression. Sadie crossed the threshold feeling like she were harboring a mortal sin rather than the one grieved. *You haven't done anything wrong*, she reminded herself. And still, misplaced guilt weighed her down. Twisted emotions desperate to burst out. Since she'd seen the first TMZ notification, no one had hugged her. No one had said, *Sadie are you okay?*

They sat in Jed's office on brown leather chairs opposite his desk. Leather extended a sheet of paper to Sadie. "This is what we came up with," he said.

Came up with?

Sadie read the headline: JOINT STATEMENT FROM SADIE NORCROSS AND BAZ TANNER

"A statement?" she said. "But I didn't write this. I haven't even talked to Baz since I landed."

"No matter," Jed said, and Sadie felt resentment that this man was privy to her business. "Read."

Sadie read, her stomach squeezing tighter with each sentence.

Like many couples, our relationship has its ups and downs, but at all times, we remain a solid, committed unit. With the love of God and our families, we're persevering through this current storm with grace. Our marriage remains our top priority, which is why we're seeking counseling from our wise pastor, who leads with God's gentle hand. We have spent the past fourteen years loving each other and have no plans for that to end. While we understand the public interest in our relationship, we ask for our fans and the media to respect our privacy.

Sadie looked to Leather. "But none of this is true."

"What's not true about it?" Deb said. She stood leaning against a bookcase, arms crossed.

"We say what we need to say," Leather added.

Sadie's face scrunched. "Persevering with grace? God's gentle hand? Marriage counseling? I don't even know if I want to stay married at this point."

"Sadie!" Deb said, aghast.

"What's so wrong with divorce? People do it all the time."

"Not in this family," Leather said. Widowed in the ballpark of thirty years, he'd never even considered remarrying. Willa had never met her grandmother, but she'd heard enough stories to know she and Leather were each other's soul mates. He talked about her with such reverence, so convinced of their eventual rejoining in the afterlife, it made Willa's skin tingle.

"So I'm just supposed to accept my husband being in love with someone else?"

"You don't know that," Deb said.

Sadie's eyes lowered. "It's always been Willa."

Jed, who'd remained cool and calm the entire time, crossed a bony ankle over his knee. "There are ways around these things. But divorce? No. Not an option."

Sadie felt heat rising to her face. She balled her hands into fists in her lap. "Since when does the church have a say over decisions I make in my personal life?" she said to all three of them collectively.

Jed was the one to respond. "Since the church started funding your lifestyle. How do you think that nice, new apartment gets paid for? We all know your race winnings couldn't cover a fraction. And those sponsorships? They just came about on their own?" He gave a haughty chuckle, and Sadie's face burned, truths she already knew being shoved down her throat. "Listen, Sadie, we're connected whether you like it or not. We scratch each other's backs, you get what I'm saying? And so, yes, the church does have a say in what happens with you and Baz. This is a business. You are a business. A very lucrative one."

Sadie felt as though she'd just been hit with a stun gun. The air sucked from her lungs. She looked to her mother and grandfather, neither of whom said a word. Deb's eyes were downcast as she fiddled with her purse strap. Leather met Sadie's gaze, but his eyes lacked the warmth she craved. It was as if she could see dollar signs in his pupils. She was a commodity, even to them.

A surge of emotion welled in her. "Really? You guys aren't even going to say anything? Mom?"

Deb looked up, her face stoic. "It is what it is, Sade."

"So my feelings don't matter?"

"That's not what we're saying," Leather said. "We just want the best chance for this situation to work out. Jed here is offering to meet with you and Baz. He knows how to work wonders with couples."

"I'm not interested in marriage counseling." She glanced at Jed. "No offense."

Jed shrugged. "None taken. But it sounds good in a statement regardless. We just don't want to see your career affected by all this."

"Maybe I don't even like my career."

"Sadie!" Deb blurted for the second time. "Don't say that."

"What? It's not like anyone's ever asked me." Water pooled in her eyes.

"Of course you like skiing; you're the best in the world."

There it was, the link that didn't quite connect. How could they not see that being good at something did not automatically translate to loving it?

Leather smacked his thighs. "We'll put out the statement later today. You and Baz can both post it on your insta-thingys, or whatever you call them. And then it will be important for people to get a glimpse of you two together. Maybe go out for dinner or something. Hold hands."

Her head spun. She'd no more than touched down on American soil, and her day was already laid out for her. She hit the ground thinking the last thing she wanted was to come face to face with her husband, but now the idea of him felt like a welcome relief from the people in this room. She needed to get home.

"Are we done here?" Sadie said, her patience having reached its limit.

The other adults exchanged looks and nods. "Keep up the appearance until the dust settles, okay?" Leather said. "Don't worry, champ. You're not the first scorned wife, and you won't be the last. Baz is a good guy who just made a mistake. Life goes on. You've got a race in a month. Don't let this throw you."

If he meant it as a means of comfort, the comment missed the mark.

Scorned wife. The same thing the internet was saying. It hit different coming from a man she admired.

Sadie clenched her teeth, grabbed her purse, and stood, only then realizing she hadn't driven herself and had no way to get home. She waited by the door like a pouting toddler not getting her way.

Deb came up behind her. "Why don't you come over for a bit? Dad will want to watch replays from Europe."

Ski tapes and criticism. It was the last thing Sadie felt like doing. Her mother was delusional. Sadie groaned. She wasn't going anywhere but home. Safety. Or at least what used to be safety. Despite wanting to crawl into bed and stay for a week, there was a discussion to be had. Like it or not, she needed to talk to Baz about what exactly he'd done.

* * *

Returning home from traveling was a feeling like no other—the smell and sights of comfort mixed with the sensation of lightness. Only this time, Sadie felt none of those things. Familiarity suddenly became foreign, as she stepped through the door into a reality very different from the one she thought she had.

Baz sat at the table, an empty cereal bowl in front of him, phone face up on the table. Sadie took a quick glance at the vintage clock hanging to his left. Ten o'clock. With the time difference, it felt more like dinnertime to her, and her bones ached for rest.

Baz turned to face her when she entered the room. "Hey."

She dropped her keys onto the counter.

"How was your flight? I hoped you would have texted me when you landed."

"I guess I didn't know whether you were *preoccupied*."

Baz tilted his head. "Don't be like that. Sit. Can we talk?"

"Pops wants us to put out a statement."

"Saying what?"

"That we're committed to our marriage, and God will get us through this, and please respect our privacy, blah blah blah."

Baz was quiet for a second. "Are we committed to our marriage?"

Sadie met his eyes and held them there for longer than felt comfortable, seeking something to give her answers. She'd fallen in love with those eyes as a teenager, maybe even before. They'd been the last thing she'd seen before falling asleep for so many years. And now she didn't recognize them at all. Her voice came out as a whisper. "I guess I should be asking you that question."

Baz sighed. "Will you please sit?"

Sadie took a chair opposite him, folded her arms on the table. "How did we get here?" She felt the first prickle of tears threatening, and she blinked hard to keep them at bay. She didn't want to cry. She wanted to be angry, wanted to hate him. But instead, the sadness that had been absent on the plane had worked its way to the surface.

"I never meant to hurt you," Baz said. "I'm sorry."

"Do you love her?"

He opened his mouth but nothing came out, and that stung more than anything. His hesitation said it all.

"You love her," Sadie said.

Baz ran a hand through his hair. "I don't know what I feel. Willa has been part of my life for so long, as long as you have. You know we've always been friends."

"But she's not your wife. I am."

"And I love you."

"Do you?"

"Of course I do."

"Then how could you..."

"You're right. It shouldn't have happened. Maybe I shouldn't have gone to the hospital at all. I was just doing what I thought was right to support a friend. And then all sorts of weird feelings came up, and let's be honest, it's not like you and I have been in the best place lately."

"Do you regret marrying me?" Sadie said in the softest voice.

"Never." Her shoulders relaxed with the confirmation it hadn't all been a lie. But then Baz continued. "It's just... we were so young. And your family... you know how entangled it all got."

She nodded, eyes low. "So where do we go from here? How can I ever trust you again?"

For a long minute neither said a word. Sadie picked at the edge of the table, causing a chip in her nail. Baz stared out the window across the room. Outside, the sky was bright. Too happy for what was happening inside.

"They're not going to let us split up," Sadie finally said.

Baz didn't need her to explain 'they.' "Is that what you want? To split up?"

"It doesn't matter what I want. My family is all about image, and part of that is you and me as a couple—forever."

Baz swallowed hard, unsure how to respond. How did one wrap their head around the idea of being a puppet in a bigger storyline? "That's unfair."

"Doesn't matter." The defeat in her voice crushed him.

They stared in opposite directions. Sadie's nails made a little plucking sound on the table.

"So..." Baz said.

Sadie pushed back from the table. "So, I guess we go about things as usual. But let me make one thing clear. I'm pissed at you. You hurt me. And I won't ever be able to forget it."

When she left the room, Baz watched her go, somehow feeling an even bigger weight on his shoulders than before. He hadn't thought it possible.

Chapter 27

I probably shouldn't even be texting you, but I'm sorry about last night.

it's not your fault.
i shouldn't have asked to walk you to your car

I shouldn't have agreed.

a lot of shouldn'ts

How pissed is Sadie?

she's hurt

I saw your statement.

yeah

I hope you're doing what makes you happy.

you'll always be my friend, Willa

Right. Friend.

Willa...

if i could change things i would.

Why can't you?

Chapter 28

Willa wiped a stray tear from the corner of her eye and shook out the rest of the emotion through her fingertips. She unrolled her yoga mat in her living room—paps would surely catch her going to the studio. It had been three days since the kiss at the hospital. Three days since everything blew up in their faces and people starting calling her a homewrecker.

She'd been buried in her bed when Roxanne showed up that next morning.

"You can't hide forever," she'd said, *I told you so* dripping from her voice. At least she didn't say it out loud. Willa was already kicking herself enough.

"Are you here to scold me?"

"No. You're not a child, and I'm not your mo—" She stopped herself. "Yes, it was a lapse in judgment. No, you're not a bad person."

Willa had wanted to believe her.

In the end, Roxanne had left it with a single piece of advice: Be careful.

Willa let out a long exhale. She stretched her arms skyward, then folded forward, feeling the stretch in her hamstrings. It would be a fast flow session. She needed to burn some energy, and only had an hour before picking up her father from the hospital. Like a stubborn mule, he'd held on the past few days, neither worsening nor recovering. A stalemate with death. The doctors agreed he'd entered the final stage, but how long he could go remained a mystery. Staying, they both knew, was draining the little savings Dale had managed to collect in recent years.

"I want to go home," he'd told Willa yesterday. His final wish.

And so, with the approval of his medical team, Dale would be spending his last days in the comfort of home under the care of hospice and a steady stream of meds. Willa would be in charge of decisions. She'd still stop in daily despite the around-the-clock care. It wasn't exactly what she'd planned for this summer, the incessant thoughts of wanting her father to just die already, piggybacked with a whopping amount of guilt for even considering such a thing. She sometimes daydreamed about the relief lifting from her, like a physical being, and how good it would feel. She was a monster.

Nonetheless, in between training runs at the lake with Roxanne, Willa would spoon-feed her father chicken broth—on the days he'd eat at all— and watch an unhealthy amount of daytime TV. Hospice nurses would keep him comfortable until his body decided it had had enough. And then, Willa thought as she pressed back into downward dog, she'd be an orphan.

The realization landed as confusing as a jigsaw puzzle with no edges.

No, she reminded herself. She had Roxanne. Roxanne was her family. Willa tried to let that be enough, but it never quite hit the same spot.

She led her body through another flow sequence, each time her face coming close to the mat, another few tears collected in a puddle. She'd never felt more alone.

Chapter 29

Sadie's feet pounded the pavement to the music pumping through her earbuds. She loved running through Jacksonville University's campus, not only for the pretty scenery but because she could picture herself there. She imagined what it would have been like to live in a dorm, walk across the quad to classes, go to the football games. Maybe she would have joined a club or sorority like Phi Beta Kappa. She could have been the type to run for student government. Or perhaps taken a work-study job in the mailroom.

All of that was a daydream. College, her parents had told her, wasn't necessary—not when you were a rising star making good money already. Skiing, they said, was all she needed. And Sadie had listened. Once, when she'd taken a career match test in high school, her results had come back with jobs in interior design, architecture, and project consultancy. She'd had to sit on her hands to keep from clapping right there in class. *See*, she wanted to say to her parents, *this is what I'm good at.* But when she'd cautiously shown her mother the career list at home, Deb had barely looked. "That's a cute hobby," she'd said, "but obviously skiing will be your career."

Now, as Sadie ran along a brick path, weaving in and out of co-eds who were almost a decade younger than her, she wondered if she'd missed her chance. She thought of the information she regularly browsed online about admission packets and degree requirements. The websites made it sound so easy. Click here. Apply now. How could she go back now when her life was already set in motion?

Sadie passed a young couple wearing backpacks and holding hands. She caught a toe on an uneven brick. Baz's face flashed through her mind. Maybe that could have been them. Or, what gave her even more of a jolt, maybe that could have been some other boy completely. How different her life could have been. Would she have stayed with Baz if they'd both gone off to college? Who would she have met instead? It wasn't even a fantasy, really. Fantasies implied some sort of desire. All Sadie felt was uncertainty.

The song changed, and Sadie sped up. She turned out of campus and continued along University Boulevard, matching breath to pace. Sweat drenched her sports bra. Nothing beat a good workout. This was her longer loop. She'd finish up by running across Mathews Bridge, which was always a pretty view of the river, and then head home.

It was a route Sadie ran often, and one she knew well, which was why her heart lurched when she came upon something new. Something unexpected. She saw it just before taking a right onto the bridge's walkway. There, near the intersection, high up for all to see. Her face, plastered across the billboard her grandfather and Jed had been talking about.

Sadie came to an abrupt stop, so fast that her knees almost buckled, and she wavered in place, unsteady and breathing hard, as she took in the scene. It was one of her many professional headshots—one where her hair was done and she wore a nice top that felt far too formal. A wide smile, but not one that brought out the crinkles around her eyes. Next to her photo, a big, bold headline read, "Rise Up!" followed by a quote:

"I Discovered the Power of Ministry, and You Can Too." —*Sadie Norcross, 5-time World Waterskiing Champion*

In smaller font across the bottom was their church name and phone number, proclaiming to all who read it to *Call Today!*

Sadie brought a hand to her forehead to block the sun, and read it again. Her stomach squeezed. It was all so bogus. She wasn't even a regular church-goer for goodness sake! The only times she set foot in the sprawling building were when someone needed something of her. It wasn't a place she went voluntarily. Wasn't a sanctuary.

Sadie stared at the giant picture like she was staring at a stranger. Who was this person? The image she portrayed, what people thought they knew, what she kept quiet. None of it matched. Where was the line between truth and fiction? Her skin crawled at the realization—she didn't even know who she actually was.

Across the street, a man eyed Sadie then followed her gaze up to the billboard. He did another couple of double-takes, as though making the connection—*Wait a minute, is that you?*—and just as he lifted a finger to point in her direction, Sadie sprinted off. The billboard, the ads, the fake testimonials, they all came with a truckload of embarrassment. The urge to speak up. But whenever she tried to challenge anything, she was met with nothing but criticism.

Be grateful.

Don't ask questions.

Trust us.

She'd been raised as a people pleaser, going along with whatever her family said. And look what that had gotten her: an unfulfilled marriage and an involuntary job as spokesperson for a religion in which she didn't even believe. Being a pawn with no voice made steam blow from her ears. She didn't know how much longer she could keep it up.

Sadie grunted, forcing herself to run even faster. She pumped her arms and lowered her chin. So much was out of her say. And so she'd push her limits here on the blacktop road for one reason only: because it was something she could control.

Chapter 30

International Waterski and Wakeboard Federation (IWWF) Instagram

Voting is officially open for IWWF Awards! Who tops your list? This is your chance to crown your favorite. Visit the IWWF website or click the link in our bio to cast your vote for Best Female Athlete and Best Male Athlete, and to see the full list of categories! Results will be announced at the annual IWWF awards ceremony on October 25. Tune into our YouTube channel for a live stream of the event, starting at 7 p.m. Until then, VOTE!

#TeamWilla #TeamSadie #SadieVsWilla

Chapter 31

August

The doctors couldn't explain how Dale Betts held on so long, but come August—a whole month since Willa rushed home from Italy to his side—his heart still beat in that dilapidated chest. He slept almost around the clock, opening his eyes less and less frequently as each day passed. Eating had all but ceased, and hospice told Willa it was only a matter of time. It could be hours, or it could be days. She didn't venture far, and soon, a quick trip to the grocery store or a morning ski run were her only outings.

It was a Tuesday afternoon, as Willa sponge bathed his face and arms, when Dale grabbed her hand mid-wipe. She looked up, surprised to see his eyes open and seemingly alert.

"Dad?"

"I'm ready," he whispered. His gaze traveled to the ceiling, and his forehead smoothed of all wrinkles, a peacefulness settling over his bony frame.

Willa was struck with a sudden burst of panic. *Wait*, she thought. She still hadn't confessed her secret. All these weeks, she'd come close a few times, but either chickened out or convinced herself it was inhumane to burden a dying man with such a blow. Besides, he kept hanging in there, day after day. But this time felt different. The look on his face, the way his eyes stared up like he saw things she couldn't.

"Dad," she said with an edge of frenzy, dropping the washcloth into the tub of water at his bedside. "Not yet. There's something I have to—"

"I know," he said, returning to face her, his voice no more than a raspy whisper. He squeezed her hand. "I know. It's okay."

Willa winced at his admission.

Dale lifted his hand in a final act of stamina and touched Willa's cheek. "Forgive yourself." And then his breath hitched. He sucked in a last gulp of air and it wheezed out through his parted lips, at the same time his eyes closed for the final time.

"Dad," Willa said, voice trembling. "Dad." She gave his arm a little shake, but it just wiggled with no response. She held a finger under his nose. No air. His chest failed to rise.

Willa stepped back from the bed with feeble steps. She studied her father, what remained of him, lying there, and she imagined his insides hardening, his skin turning cold. All the years of her childhood came rushing back into focus as if they were yesterday. She was a kid again, staring at a grown man unconscious on a bed. Only this time, he wasn't just in a drunken stupor; he was gone. Then came the image of her mother, dead on the side of the road. So much blood, such a horrific scene. Here, Dale seemed peaceful. He hadn't struggled to take his last breath; it had just happened like any other. In, out, and that was it.

Willa reached behind her for the arm of a chair and slid down into it, never taking her eyes off her father. She scanned herself for a reaction—her dad was dead, both her parents were, and she was only twenty-eight years old.

Willa struggled to pinpoint the emotions that swirled inside her, but one came out the clearest: relief.

***

With her father's body on its way to the funeral home, Willa sat on his couch with heavy limbs and a heavy heart. The house already felt different, in a way she couldn't yet articulate. She pulled her phone from her pocket and dialed Roxanne.

"Dad died," she said upon her coach's answering.

"Oh Willa, I'm so sorry."

"It was a long time coming. Just feels...I don't know...weird. Weird and...final."

Roxanne's voice gave a sense of calm. "He was lucky to have you, especially at the end."

"Mmm." Willa drifted, lost in thought. "I'm making arrangements tomorrow. I think I'll take the morning off from training."

"Of course. Do you want me to meet you? The house or the funeral home? Whatever you need."

"I'll be fine."

"Are you sure? I don't think it's good for you to be alone."

"I promise. I think I just need to work it all out in my head, you know?"

"Okay, well, call me if you need me. Hugs, honey."

Within minutes of disconnecting, a few condolence texts appeared on Willa's phone—fellow skiers, her sponsor, even the local broadcaster who'd announced all her childhood races. Turned out, the skiing world was a small one, and news—both good and bad—traveled fast.

Willa typed *thank you*, then copied and pasted it to each reply. She appreciated the messages, but the one she wanted the most hadn't come— at least not yet. Into the evening, she waited, wondering if Baz would text or maybe even call. He had to, right? He'd been there at the hospital; he knew the complicated nature of her and Dale's relationship.

But when the sun went down and he still hadn't reached out, Willa resigned herself to the fact that there would be no message. Her heart shriveled. Maybe the public statement had been true. Maybe Sadie and Baz were working it out. And if so, where did that leave her and the indisputable energy that had coursed between them?

Willa drowned her sorrows that night with a pint of ice cream and a sappy movie. She resisted the urge to stalk his social media, telling herself it was over—whatever it was, whether it had even started, it was over. Somewhere in a whole other city, Baz was probably going about his life with Willa the last thing on his mind.

* * *

Baz heard from Sadie, who heard from Deb, who heard from another coach, who'd been told by Roxanne that Willa's dad had died. The ski world was indeed small.

His heart hurt for Willa, picturing her going through her father's things, making all the arrangements on her own. Once when they were kids, he'd asked her if she wished she had siblings. Her parents never came to events, and Baz thought that was strange. Willa always had a pensiveness about her. Maybe it was because she wished her home life were different; maybe having brothers or sisters would have helped. Her answer had surprised him. *No, I'm glad I don't have siblings.*

He wouldn't understand it fully until they were older. She didn't want another kid to deal with the dysfunction.

Baz wrung his hands in his lap. Instinct told him to pick up the phone and call. It would be the bare minimum when what he really wanted to do was hop in the car and drive to Orlando. But that would be impossible. Not even a phone call was feasible sitting in a room with his wife's family.

"Such a shame," Deb said, shaking her head. "No one should have to lose a parent so young. You girls aren't even thirty yet."

"He didn't exactly live the healthiest lifestyle," Sadie said.

"Certainly not."

By that point, Willa's upbringing and Dale's drinking problem were a poorly kept secret. There'd been whispers when they were younger—poor kid, such a sad situation—but like Pandora's box, the subject was one no one wanted to get too close to let alone touch.

Baz listened, caring less about Dale than Willa. She was probably wrestling with the grief. Holding everything in, trying to be strong. If he were there, he'd tell her it's okay to be vulnerable. He imagined wiping tears from her cheekbones, letting her rest her head on his shoulder while she cried.

His mind teetered on running away into fantasy land. *Forget it*, he scolded himself. He had to stop thinking about Willa. "Do you think we should go to the funeral?" he asked, and immediately regretted the question. Everyone whipped their heads to look at him, as though he had three eyes. He bumbled his words. "I mean, she is a friend, right? A fellow athlete..."

"Are you crazy?" Leather said. "How do you think that would look?"

"I just mean—"

"You just mean nothing. It's a hard no. Not with everything that happened last month. Can you imagine the headlines? Adulterer attends funeral for mistress's father."

Mistress. That's not what this was. Baz's temperature rose. "Sadie and I could go together to show our support."

Sadie coughed a laugh. "I'm not going anywhere near Willa."

It was a reach, he knew. Baz grumbled. If it weren't for that stupid paparazzi picture, things wouldn't have gotten this bad. He looked to

Sadie, who curled into the corner of the couch, legs pulled up into herself. Closed off, cold.

So much had changed between the three of them, and a piece of him naively longed for the way things used to be. It was silly—kids didn't stay kids. Still, nostalgia transported him back to the bank of the river on that warm day when they were ten years old. The way their hands had stacked on top of each other's. A pact. Friends forever, they'd declared. Weren't friends supposed to be there for each other in times of grief? Didn't a pledge mean something?

Baz reached over to grab Sadie's hand. "But what about our—"

"Don't say it, Baz. We're not kids anymore. And besides, I think you broke that promise."

He withdrew to his side of the couch, burned.

The family continued whatever conversation they'd been having—something about a possible brand partnership—but Baz checked out, his mind stuck in the past when times were easier and he wasn't being pulled apart by the opposing forces of love and loyalty. It would nag at him for hours.

That evening, Sadie went to bed first. She hadn't kicked him out after the scandal broke, not even to the couch. It was almost as if she didn't care enough. They still shared a bed—even though opposite sides of a California king felt like different continents.

Baz watched her disappear down the hall in her sweats and slippers. He hated to admit he'd been waiting for this moment. When the bedroom door clicked shut, he pulled out his phone and texted Willa.

i'm so sorry about your dad. hope you're hanging in there.

He waited for the three dots to appear. A second later they did, and his heart leaped to his throat.

Thanks. It's been a weird two days.

A zing hit him. Two days. Willa was clearly acknowledging his silence. He wanted to hold her. *You're all I've been thinking about.*

Baz glanced down the hall again, making sure it was empty.

are you having any services?

Just something small at the graveside.

No specifics, no date or time. Did she not want him there? He was spiraling trying to interpret her tone when another message came through.

Friday, 10:00

His shoulders should have relaxed—she wasn't ghosting him—but the reality of the situation prevented the agony from fading.

wish I could be there.

You could if you wanted.

it's complicated. i'm trying my best here.

A full three minutes passed, and Baz worried she wouldn't respond at all. That would crush him. When her reply finally did appear, it hit with the same effect.

Understood.

184

* * *

Willa didn't understand at all. She couldn't comprehend why Sadie and Baz were treading water in a marriage that was destined to sink. Didn't see how he could stuff away his feelings like they weren't bursting from him in the same way hers were. There were fireworks, for Christ's sake. Nothing made more sense in the world.

Sure, the Norcrosses were some sort of prodigal family, but did that really justify a miserable existence? When she stepped back and thought about it from a thousand-foot view, it made her head spin. Maybe none of it was real. Maybe she'd been living in a fantasy world. People were scared, and people stayed. Money talked. Love was for fools.

All Willa knew for sure was that as she watched her father's casket be lowered into the ground on a misty Friday morning, surrounded by a handful of people whose names she couldn't recall, she felt the same surge of jealousy that had plagued her for over a decade.

Baz hadn't come. Once again, he chose Sadie over her.

Chapter 32

THEN
Summer 2010
Swiss Pro Slalom
Clermont, FL

Willa shivered, from nerves or the cool morning, she couldn't be sure. Wasn't Florida supposed to be warm? The afternoon would heat up, but that did little for her six a.m. wake-up call—the best ski conditions happened before the dew dried from the grass. She yawned. Even after all these years, she still hadn't turned into a morning person.

But this morning wasn't a normal one. It was the first competition of her professional career. And while nothing would be all that different— same course, same expectations—going pro added a whole new level of pressure for a sixteen-year-old.

Willa rubbed her upper arms to get the blood flowing. A light fog hung on the water, and the sky painted itself a hazy gray-blue. The banks were mostly empty, but they'd soon be filled with spectators: former athletes, water sport fans, kids with big dreams of following in her footsteps.

Her phone rang. Dale's number flashed on the screen.

"Hello?" Willa answered, never knowing if it would be some sort of emergency.

"What the fuck, Willa?" His voice boomed, and Willa held the phone away from her ear. "You don't just dump someone's liquor! I need that!"

"You're going to kill yourself."

"You don't know shit. And now I'm sitting here with nothing to stop the shakes, all because you thought you'd try to prove a point."

"Good!"

"It's not fucking funny. How dare you—"

Willa hung up and shoved her phone into the pocket of her boardshorts. Dumping the booze had been a last-second decision before she left her dad's house the night before to return to Roxanne's. Why she still even continued to visit was beyond her—her dad was nearly always drunk or on his way there. When he'd dozed off in his recliner, she'd snuck into the kitchen, snatched the bottles, tucking two under her armpit to carry them all, and poured them into the toilet, finishing with a satisfied flush.

Vindication was futile—he'd simply go buy more—but the thrill she got from watching the toxic liquid swirl down the drain was like finally talking back after years of having your lips glued shut.

Now, Dale was pissed, and Willa couldn't care less. She gazed out over the water, mentally running through her passes and turns, putting her father far from her mind. She closed her eyes and felt the pull of the boat, the leans, the slices, the—

"There you are." Roxanne plopped down beside Willa on the edge of the dock. "Whatcha thinking about?"

"Nothing."

"Not nothing." Willa rolled her eyes. Roxanne knew her well. "Stuff at home?"

"Just Dad being Dad. He's mad that I—"

Approaching chatter cut her off mid-sentence. She and Roxanne pivoted.

"I can't believe we got Nature Made. I mean, they're the number one vitamin brand in the country." Deb Norcross came down the embankment, clipboard in hand, husband at her side, followed by Leather and Sadie bringing up the rear. She turned and pointed to Sadie. "Now you just need to start taking the women's multi, or at least pretend to."

Deb's voice lowered when she realized they weren't the first ones on the water. A sudden coolness transformed her. Her lips pinched. Willa swore she could see Deb's nose tilt up in the air.

"Roxanne," Deb said, as her group passed.

"Deb."

The greeting couldn't have been more clipped, and a second later it was over. Deb, Mark, and Leather kept walking, but Sadie held back. "Hey," she said to Willa.

"I'm going to go get some coffee," Roxanne said. "Here, I got you all checked in." She handed Willa a bib to go over her vest and strolled away. Sadie took Roxanne's place, sitting next to Willa, shoulder to shoulder. Their feet dangled in the cool water. Purple polish shined on Sadie's toenails.

"What's the deal with them?" Willa said once Roxanne was out of earshot.

"Right? If daggers could kill."

"Adults are fucking weird."

Sadie nodded in agreement. And they left it at that, because why would they have dug any deeper? Sixteen-year-olds don't tend to think of anyone but themselves, so there'd be no reason for them to wonder about the chilliness between Roxanne and Deb. After all, the girls hadn't even been born when that rivalry took hold. Twenty years might as well have been a lifetime ago for a teenager.

The girls sipped their morning drinks—tea for Willa, Red Bull for Sadie (Deb was working on securing a sponsorship)—and talked about anything but the competition. Having both recently gotten their drivers' licenses, the conversation naturally turned to that: afterschool activities, weekend parties with friends, finally a sense of independence. When the conversation circled around to skiing—because how could it not?—it wasn't the conditions or leaderboard they focused on, but mostly how Baz had shown up that morning four inches taller, with *muscles*, and no more braces.

"I seriously did a double take," Willa said.

"I know! I was like, 'Hey Baz,' and he was all 'Hey Sadie,' but like, his *voice*—I was like, 'Who is this *man?*'"

"Right? He's like—"

"Hot, right?"

"Yes! Like, what the hell—it's *Baz!*" They burst into muffled laughter.

Sadie's hair flung forward into her eyes and she whipped her head back like a model at a photoshoot. Of the two, she possessed the most conventional beauty. Perfectly symmetrical features. No scar on her forehead. Ballerina body. Beneath that trim build was a master ready to fly across the wake with centripetal force up to 4Gs.

Whereas Sadie was long and lean, Willa had blossomed into a more womanly figure. Fuller thighs, larger breasts. Willa's healthy curves and the power coming from her muscular frame meant it was impossible to take your eyes off her on the course.

Between Sadie's grace and Willa's might, the duo were superstars before they could even legally vote.

And yes, they'd been noticing boys for a while, at school, at races. But never Baz. Not their Baz. He was the kid who gave them annoying nicknames like "Willa Butts" and "Braidy" (in reference to Sadie's long, blonde braids). He played and teased in equal measure. He was the third piece of the Three Musketeers.

But puberty hit later for boys, and while Willa and Sadie had had boobs and periods and prescription acne creams for years now, it wasn't until that summer that Baz came into his own.

They might have suspected, but never would have known for sure, that their world was going to change from that moment, the moment they acknowledged Baz's hotness. And maybe it was their joint agreement, the fact that they both knew they were thinking the same thing, that made the girls clam up, never to utter it aloud again.

* * *

Based on points, Sadie skied last that day. She was hoping for 3@10.75. She wished she could go shorter than that, but she would miss balls. "You'll be at 10.25 before you know it," Leather liked to tell her.

At the starting gate, Sadie went through her routine: Dunk, soap, gloves, rope. The movements were so habitual, she moved from one to the next without a single thought. The announcer called her name. A roar of applause. This was it, her professional debut. Along the bank, sponsor tents symbolized her future—as her mother liked to remind her. A good showing today could mean the difference between a top-tier sponsor like Goode or Malibu, or a shitty one like some no-name athletic brand.

Sadie scanned the line of banners, her eyes dancing around the people scattered about. They landed on Willa, next to the MasterCraft tent, standing not next to her coach, but Baz. New and improved Baz. A little pang shot through Sadie's chest. She recognized it right away: Envy. Even from the dock, she could see Willa blushing. Of course he'd go for Willa and her C-cup boobs. Sadie was all straight up and down. Fucking genetics.

Willa waved and gave two thumbs up. "You got this!" she yelled.

And then Sadie was off, cruising through the gate and pulling out toward the one ball right in front of Willa and Baz with an extra *umpf.* Sixteen-year-old girls might not be aware of everything in the world, but they're aware when a handsome boy is watching. *I'll make him like me more.* Sadie was determined to put on a show.

She didn't disappoint.

* * *

"Damn," Baz said, as Sadie flew past. It was no more than a whisper, but loud enough for Willa to hear. "She's on fire today."

No, no. Don't watch her. Look at me! She swayed awkwardly. "I guess pro is a whole new game. Time to kick things in gear." Willa's eyes bounced between wanting to watch Sadie and not wanting to look away from the divine specimen paying her attention. Her mind spun. *This is so bizarre—Baz!* Heat pumped from her chest, as hormones she didn't know existed raged on.

Sadie, of course, finished a perfect run, and as the driver idled back toward the dock, posed herself on the engine hatch. She shook out her hair and locked eyes with Baz. She looked like a supermodel. Sun glinted off the droplets on her tanned legs. Willa's gut twisted.

It was her turn, which meant she'd have to leave Baz's side, opening her place for someone else to fill—someone she knew would be Sadie. As she got in the water, she prayed he'd watch her as closely as he did Sadie. She also prayed he'd reserve the sexual tension for when she returned.

* * *

191

By the final round of the day, the girls were neck and neck. Willa went first, hoping to make up the slim margin Sadie had on her. She took a massive inhale then blew it out hard. She wanted to win, but she wanted to impress Baz more.

"Focus," Roxanne said, as Willa scooted off the dock into the water. "Don't think of anything—or anyone—on the sidelines." Willa gave her head a sharp turn, meeting Roxanne's grin. Apparently her flirting wasn't so discreet. "This is your race to lose."

The boat took up the slack. *This is my race*, Willa repeated. With a quick "Hit it!" and press of the throttle, she glided to the top of the water.

Willa pulled back on the rope, sending herself outside the wake with all her might. A quick edge change, and back the other direction. She grimaced, eyebrows knitted, mouth tight, as the force pulled her left and right around the buoys. There was barely time to think—just let the motion take her, as it had done hundreds of times before.

In thirty seconds that felt like the snap of her fingers, she made all six balls without penalty. The crowd roared, a standing ovation chanting "Bet on Betts," and when Willa sank into the water after her run, she gave an enthusiastic wave, then smacked the water in excitement. *Hell yeah!* Had Baz seen it? Was he watching? She climbed from the water with a bit more saunter than ever before, picturing herself in slow motion, like one of those James Bond girls.

Roxanne greeted her with a wet hug, swiftly bringing her back to reality. "Amazing, Wills!"

And she was sixteen again.

* * *

"Nice run," Baz said, as Willa dried off with an old Speedo towel she just couldn't part with. The edges frayed and it was paper thin, but even water skiers have superstitions.

"Thanks." She squeezed out her ponytail and slipped on her board shorts, purposely leaving her shirt off. *Let him look.*

Butterflies danced in Willa's stomach. Baz had watched her. Not just watched her, but seen a perfect run. It was like having a good hair day on the first day of school—a huge win. Suddenly, Willa was hit with an influx of thoughts. She wondered if Baz was single. If he'd find her as attractive as she found him. Was she skinny enough? Was her skin clear enough? She wondered a lot of things about him, including how soft his hand would feel in hers, but like any normal lovestruck teenager, she kept her lips sealed and hands to herself. Instead, she fiddled with her gear, stuffing things into bags. *Say something, stupid!*

She opened her mouth. "I heard there's a—"

"Sadie's up!" Baz said at the same time, cutting her off and making her face flame. "Oh, sorry, what were you saying?" But he wasn't looking at Willa; he was staring at the dock where the pretty blonde was getting ready.

"Nothing. Just that I heard there's a new ice cream place nearby."

"Oh, cool. That's, uh...that's cool. Sorry, I just don't want to miss her run."

"No, of course. Me either." Willa turned to face the water and bit the inside of her cheek. *Idiot!*

By the time Sadie got in and the boat lined up, Willa was cursing under her breath. *Make her fall, make her fall.* Everyone thought Sadie was so perfect, but Willa herself had just completed a perfect run—that had to count for something, right? She envisioned Sadie catching an edge and biting it face first into the water. Not a ski to the head—she wouldn't wish that on anyone—but just a little blow to her pride...in front of Baz. Surely he'd want to hang out with the winner. And the winner would be her.

Willa peeked at Baz out of the corner of her eye as though afraid he could hear her inner thoughts. She didn't like feeling this way, this jealousy that showed up uninvited. Sadie was a friend. But a new factor had entered the equation—a friend turning into a crush—and with it opened a new chamber of Willa's heart. She wanted Baz, but something told her there was going to be another person in the way. In that moment, standing side by side with Baz, feeling all sorts of new emotions that made her question herself, Willa discovered something profound: there was a fine line between friends and enemies.

"Here she goes," Baz said, transfixed.

Willa held her breath. Sadie flew through the gate and rounded the first two balls with ease. Three. Four. Five.

No, no, no. Not today, Willa begged to the universe. *Let me take this win.*

And then, just as Sadie extended out to the six ball, her edge caught the water, and she yanked on the rope to stay upright. In less than a second, the buoy passed—Sadie had missed it.

The audience gave a collective *ohhh*, and Willa gasped. Had she made it happen? A quick stab of guilt pierced her lungs.

"Aw, man," Baz said, to which Willa echoed the same: *Yeah, darn. Bummer*. They watched as Sadie climbed into the boat. The crowd clapped, and she gave a gracious wave, then a shrug. Oh well, next time! The crowd clapped louder. Everyone loved a humble loser.

For once, it wasn't a perfect score. Sadie lost points with that last buoy, which meant the results were effectively sealed. Willa had won her first pro event. She peeked at Baz again. Would he congratulate her? Sweep her up in a hug?

"Well, I guess that's it," she said.

"Top dog today, huh?" He put up a hand for a high five.

"Looks like it." No hug?

"That's awesome, congrats."

Willa blushed. She hoped he would ask her to stick around to watch his runs.

"I better go get ready," Baz said. "See ya next month at Malibu."

Wait, what was happening? That was it? He was leaving? Willa fumbled with her hands. "Yeah, sure. See ya." She watched him go, disappointed. Her ears went impossibly hot. She suddenly felt foolish for expecting anything more—how dumb to envision him falling in love with her just because she won a single event.

Willa wavered in place, clumsy, unsure what to do with her hands, and ultimately tucked them into her armpits. Despite feeling let down by Baz's reaction, she held onto one small thing. She—not Sadie—was the last one to talk with him before he went to suit up. As though the final word was a contest she'd won. She'd be the one he'd think about as he traveled home later. This, she thought, had to be leverage.

As she packed up the last of her things, a familiar voice came up behind her, an excited whisper.

"Oh my god, Willa. Willa! Guess what just happened? You'll never guess." Sadie, still breathing heavy from her run, squatted next to Willa on the grass. Her suit dripped a stream of lake water onto Willa's dry bag. Willa blinked. She started to ask, but her subconscious already knew what was coming. After all, it wasn't as though Sadie would be flying high after her ski performance. No, this was the type of excitement Willa recognized from girl talk against lockers at school. Something not related to the tournament at all. It could only mean one thing.

"You're not going to believe this," Sadie continued. "I mean, it's so weird, but like, so freaking awesome."

Willa stared, unable to form words.

"Baz just asked me out."

"Asked you out?" Her throat went tight.

"Yes! He wants me to stay to watch his runs, and then said there's like some new ice cream place around the corner or something. Can you freaking believe this? Like, who would have thought? I guess I've always had a little crush on him. I guess he feels the same!"

Willa swallowed. It tasted sour. "That's—that's incredible, Sade." Her insides burned like a fire pit. Not orange, but blue—the hottest.

* * *

When they stood atop the podium that day, it was Willa on the top spot with the first-place trophy in hand, Sadie to her right with the silver. And while the sponsors took note, and made deals and eventual offers, and while everyone smiled and said how cool it must be to be up there next to your friend, one girl was soaring and the other simmering. It wouldn't always be like this—along the way, they'd switch places many times—but another benchmark in their complicated relationship had begun.

They knew it, their coaches knew it. Only the world didn't.

196

Witness #4 Statement

I was standing along the course, parallel to the starting line. There was a real buzz that day, with the rivalry and all. People kept betting on which of them would win. I had my favorite... now I'm not so sure.

For goodness sake, I had my kids there to watch, and then this happens? How am I supposed to explain it to them?

[Witness pauses to collect herself.]

I'm sorry, I just can't believe she's *dead*.

Chapter 33

NOW
September 24
Mastercraft Pro
Polk City, FL

After the European tour, followed by her father's passing, Willa was happy to stay put in Florida for a while. The temperature rose into the triple digits through the end of the summer, making it miserable to be outside. She planned her trainings for even earlier in the mornings, then spent the rest of the day inside. O'Neill sent another package with gear to take her through the fall months. From the selection, she wore a crisp, white t-shirt to the next tournament.

The Mastercraft Pro, only about a half hour outside of Orlando, felt like her hometown race. Compared to other events where she had to drive for hours or even fly, it was nice to travel without needing a GPS. There in Polk City, it was the one stop of the year where she could count on more fans with "Willa" signs than "Sadie" signs. And sure enough, as Willa pulled into the parking lot the morning of the race, spectators were already lining the arm of the lake that stuck out like a pot handle.

"Willa! Willa!" a few voices cried as she got out of her car. Two young girls ran toward her, posters in hand. They bounced on their toes. "Can we get your autograph?"

Willa smiled, taking the Sharpie and signing her name. "Are you skiers?" she asked them.

The girls nodded with enthusiasm. "We want to be just like you and Sadie."

The marker jolted like it had hit a speed bump, leaving a little glitch in her otherwise smooth signature. Willa pressed on a smile. "Keep training and pretty soon you'll be at the top of the podium. But don't forget to have fun, too." She patted each of their heads.

"We will. Thanks!" they said before scampering away.

The mention of Sadie's name made Willa's ribs clench. Today would be the first time they'd seen each other in person since the hospital photos leaked. In the two months since then—one month since Willa had buried her father—much of the media frenzy had died down thanks to the never-ending stream of salacious news. A reality-TV couple breakup, a singer's whiskey-fueled rant caught on tape. There was always something. Thankfully, she and Baz were no longer that something. But Willa had a feeling today could very well dredge back up her business. Tour photographers weren't the same as paparazzi, but photos were photos, and they'd end up on social media one way or another. With the increased interest in their personas, Willa had a feeling the tabloids would pay for just about anything—they had a special way of making news out of nothing.

Which was exactly what would happen today—nothing. She'd keep her distance. She'd learned her lesson.

Only it wasn't that easy. The mind is a strong thing, and Willa found her resolve fracturing. She wondered if Baz had come. She nonchalantly scanned the warm-up area for him. Just a glance wasn't wrong, was it? She peered up and down the lake. Even in a sea of faces, she'd pick his out with ease. She jumped when a hand squeezed her shoulder.

"Looking for someone?" Roxanne said with a grin.

"Jesus," Willa exhaled. "You scared me." *How the hell does she always know?*

"You're going to be able to stay focused today, right?"

"Why wouldn't I?"

Roxanne gave her a look that didn't need explaining. "This is your turf. Don't let them distract you. Or should I say, don't let *him* distract you."

"I've got this," Willa said, pulling her ski from the car. "Have you already checked me in?"

"Not yet. I was just over at the dock. I'll walk with you." Roxanne put an arm around Willa's waist as the two headed toward the athlete's tent. The gesture made Willa's insides warm. Roxanne might not be her mother, but their relationship ran just as deep. There were few things left on the table when it came to coaches and their athletes—both the good and the bad. In many cases, they'd do anything for each other.

* * *

The Mastercraft Pro was bittersweet for Sadie. On one hand, it was her sponsor's big event, but on the other, Willa got home-court advantage. As Mastercraft's top athlete, Sadie knew she had to put on the charm at this tournament—she'd be photographed with not only her boat, but enough marketing material to make her jaw hurt. She'd do her best not to be swallowed by Willa's fans. Mastercraft could plaster her face on a giant flag, and the crowd would still lean in Willa's favor. Their hometown hero. Rags to riches stories were hard to top.

And yet...none of that would matter when she hit the water. It would all come down to pure skill. Only one person could come out on top.

Losing here—especially after Baz's cheating scandal—would only add insult to injury. As Leather reminded her, the Norcrosses didn't do insult well.

Sadie returned to wiping down her ski, a pre-race ritual that served as a sort of meditation. She used a quick-dry shammy towel, just like her mother had taught her. It left the ski shiny and smooth, as though it were headed to a trophy shelf instead of a dirty lake. Pointless, really, only seconds before getting in the water, but as her mother said, when you look good, you ski good.

Sadie's name boomed from the loudspeaker and the crowd cheered. She looked over her shoulder and spotted Baz standing on the bank with her parents. He gave her a thumbs up, and she nodded in acknowledgment, burying any thoughts that didn't serve the mission at hand. Now wasn't the time to fall down a rabbit hole of relationship woes. *Forget what happened. Pretend all is fine.*

Feet in the bindings, she extended a hand for the safety spotter to hand her the rope. And that's when her heart skipped a beat. Her eyes fixed on a spot a few feet down the line from the handle, right where it changed colors. The braided rope appeared to be frayed—something wildly unusual for monofilament nylon of this caliber. Race ropes were virtually indestructible.

"Hold on," Sadie said to the driver. She pulled the section of rope closer for inspection. "What the...?" She fingered the smooth braid, which now had spiky little ends poking out. "This rope is damaged. It looks like it will snap on the first turn. I can't ski with this."

The driver narrowed his eyes, then waved over an official. "We've got an equipment malfunction."

Something suddenly felt off, like a sixth sense setting in. Sadie's fingers tingled, pulse higher than normal.

Race officials, seemingly unconcerned, quickly swapped the rope for another one, but that wasn't enough for Leather.

"What the hell's going on?" he said, trudging onto the dock.

"The rope's all frayed," Sadie said, looking to him for reassurance.

Leather eyed the rope. He went to speak, but the official interrupted him. "We switched it." Then, "Better go, clock's ticking."

Rules were rules. Once the skier was on the course, they only got a 1-minute delay for any issues that arose. Sadie's gaze remained focused on her grandfather, who was nose to nose with the official.

"These ropes don't just fray," Leather was saying. "They're brand new."

Sadie's mind raced. In all her years of professional racing, she'd never seen a rope do that. They used the strongest tow ropes made. Underwent pounds and pounds of pressure from the pulling of skiers across the wake. So if the rope didn't fray on its own, that must mean...

"Sadie? You good?" the driver said.

Sadie did a quick glance at the race clock, which was counting down her minute delay. Nineteen seconds left. If she didn't get in the water now, her run would be disqualified.

The eeriness nipped at her. She should insist on further investigation.

"Sadie?"

Ten seconds.

What would be worse—a crash or a disqualification? One was a maybe, but the other would be a certainty if she didn't go. She slammed her feet into the bindings, grabbed the handle of the new rope, and slipped off the platform into the water. The boat pulled away from the dock. A wave of clapping circled through the crowd. She let the sound soothe her nerves. As she waited for the boat to straighten, a tidal wave of thoughts infested her brain. *Focus!* she demanded of herself.

And then the boat was off, pulling her up and out of the water. Sadie had only seconds to gain her balance before she leaned to the right and prepared to round the first ball. She pulled on the rope with all her might and barely managed to circle it. Not good. Back across the wake to catch the second. She clipped it, nearly crashing but managing to hold on. Anyone watching would know this was not a typical ski run from Sadie Norcross. By the time she reached the fourth ball, they were simply coming too fast. She missed the fifth and sixth. The rope debacle had thrown her completely off.

The boat slowed. Sadie let go of the handle and sank into the water, muttering a string of curse words. It was by far her worst performance in years, and what's more, it opened the door for Willa to sneak into the lead.

When she stepped onto dry land minutes later, Leather was waiting.

"Don't," she said, hand up, before he could get a word out. She stomped past him, eyes focused ahead on one thing. That rope had been manipulated. There was no question in her mind. And she knew exactly who was behind it.

* * *

Willa was giving her hamstrings a final stretch when a fiery voice attacked from behind.

"I know it was you."

Willa turned to find Sadie, red-faced and dripping wet. She hadn't even slid her sandals on before trudging over.

"What are you talking about?"

"Don't play dumb, Willa. You saw what just happened. I know you fucked with the rope."

"Why the hell would I fuck with the rope?"

"You wanted me to fall so you would win." Sadie gave an exasperated laugh. "Jesus. I mean, I get that we're competitors and all, but I can't believe you would stoop so low as to put a skier in danger."

Willa stepped forward. "Sadie, I didn't touch the rope. Why would I? We all use the same one."

"Well, clearly not after I would have fallen on it. You would have got a new one after that. And anyway, that's not the point. Maybe they would have let me redo the run, and so the rope wouldn't have even mattered. The point is you were trying to mess with me. Get in my head."

"You're crazy. I wasn't anywhere near the boat. It was probably a bad rope, that's all. Geez, Sadie. Chill the fuck out."

"Chill the fuck out? Really? Pretty choice words coming from someone who was sneaking around with my husband."

There it was. A bolt hit Willa's chest and she had to pause to make sure her heart was back in rhythm. She'd hoped Sadie wouldn't bring it up, not here, not for everyone to see. "Can we not do this right now?" she said. "If you want to talk, I'm happy to. But can it wait until after the event?"

"Oh, so sorry. Wouldn't want to interrupt your race. Heaven forbid you get rattled right before your run. That would just be mean."

"Sadie."

"You've always had a thing for Baz. I know it and you know it. But guess what? He picked me. He's my husband. So you better back off. Got it?"

"Baz is my friend. You can't dictate who I am friends with."

"Oh yeah?" Sadie stepped closer and lowered her voice. "Well, if you want your little secret to stay hidden, I suggest you take my demand seriously."

Willa's eyes grew. Heat coursed through her body to the point she felt like she might be sick. "I...I don't know what you're talking about."

Sadie sneered. "You know exactly what I'm talking about. Don't act so shocked. Husbands and wives tell each other everything."

It was a dig, a reminder that Baz belonged to her. Willa felt lightheaded. Her heartbeat pounded in her temples. Baz had promised never to tell. And he'd broken that promise. It felt like a stab—not in the back, but directly in the chest.

"Keep fucking with me and I'll make sure everyone knows how your mother died," Sadie said.

"You wouldn't."

"Maybe, maybe not. But I don't think you want to test me. You'd be in pretty hot water if the truth came out."

"It was sixteen years ago. I don't think—"

"Doesn't matter. Imagine what the media would say."

Suddenly, Willa's defense skyrocketed. She gritted her teeth. "I'm not the only one with a secret, don't forget."

Sadie's face slackened at that, and despite her best effort to keep the upper hand, Willa could see her retort had hit the mark. At the end of the day, both women had skeletons in their closets, things very few people knew.

They stood face to face in a stare-off until a new voice sliced through the tension. "Sadie, come on. Let it go." It was her mother. "Shake it off. You've got three more runs."

"Did you see the rope?" Sadie asked.

"Yes. Clearly someone's doing." Deb looked to Willa. "We're not idiots."

"I didn't touch the rope," Willa said.

"Could have had help."

"Careful, Deb." Roxanne was there now too, quietly coming up alongside Willa, the four women forming a messy, estrogen-fueled catfight. Willa versus Sadie. Roxanne versus Deb. "Last I knew, it was the Norcrosses who were the shady ones."

Willa and Sadie looked at each other, aware of the rivalry between their elders—but only to an extent. Never in a million years could they have guessed the true reason behind such a clash. Only three people knew *that* truth, and two of them were standing right there, mouths zipped firmly shut.

Chapter 34

THEN
Summer 1990
Miami Pro

It had been a long season, a constant battle between first and second for Deb Norcross and Roxanne Hill. Both were tired, but too stubborn to give up. They'd keep going so long as the other did, determined to be the last woman standing in this sport. The one with the most championships under her belt, the one the people would be talking about for decades to come. Finally, the last event of the season arrived, and it all came down to this.

They'd been at it for years, neck and neck, but somehow Deb always inched by with just enough points to take first. The amount of stamina it took, the amount of determination to try again when you always came up just a little short required superhuman mental vigor. For Roxanne, second place was getting old. Nothing she did, no amount of extra training, early-morning runs, or strength building could cinch that top spot. It wasn't fair. Shouldn't everyone have a moment of glory? It was like watching Jack

Nicklaus continually get the green jacket at the Masters. At some point, fans were like, *Okay, we get it, but can't someone else win?*

Roxanne's parents liked to say, "You're never a loser until you quit." And she was no quitter.

But still...

Maybe it was the universe telling her second place was good enough. Take the winnings and be happy. But it wasn't just the constant runner-up finish that rubbed her wrong—it was the fact that the same person always beat her. The same person, with her perfect blonde hair and crystal blue eyes, who waved from atop the podium like she owned it. It was always *her*—Deb Norcross. Sometimes Roxanne swore there was something bigger at play, something she just couldn't put her finger on. How could the same person always end up on top, year after year? It didn't seem right. Didn't seem natural. What was she missing?

* * *

Away from the crowd, Deb laid on a yoga mat while her father, the legendary Leather Norcross, stretched her leg into the air.

"Ouch," Deb said.

"This is it. Few more runs and then it's post-season. Think you got it in you today?"

A rhetorical question. She winced as he pushed back another inch, straining her hamstring to its limit. "Of course I do."

"Atta girl."

A group of spectators passed by with whispers of, *That's him!* Leather was used to it—after all those years of skiing, the fame had become part of normal life. Whereas most men his age had retired from the sport, Leather pushed his body to the limit, still competing at the age of fifty-five. Sure, his ankles cracked when he got out of bed, and more than once he woke up with a stiff neck for no good reason, but he'd never let it show. To outsiders, he was an untouchable beast. They didn't say he put the Master in MasterCraft for nothing.

"Hiya, folks," he said with a bright smile and a tip of his head. "Beautiful day for some skiing." He lowered Deb's leg and massaged her quad with the heel of his hand.

"Passing the buck to your girl, I see," said one of the older men. Then to Deb, "Big shoes to fill, huh?"

Deb smiled from her upside-down perspective. They were big shoes, all right. Leather had more awards than anyone in the history of the sport. Deb was better than most—she'd been skiing since age four—but the competition was stiff. The sport had evolved to new levels, courses getting tougher. For a long time, she easily placed first. And then more and more talent showed up, putting additional pressure on her to win. Every Sunday, Jed led the congregation in a joint prayer for Deb's triumph. She trained harder, terrified of letting her parents and the Church down. It was enough for a while.

Until Roxanne found her groove and her talent skyrocketed.

Spooked, the Norcrosses had gone back to the drawing board. And that's when they came up with their secret weapon. A skeleton kept between Leather and Deb, just the two of them. At first, it made her sick to her stomach if she thought about it long enough, but soon it became second nature. If it helped her win, it was worth it. Plus, her father wouldn't lead her astray, would he?

The spectators walked along, leaving Leather and Deb alone once more. Under a tent a couple dozen yards away, skiers gathered, picking bananas and granola bars from the food table, standing to the side and stretching their limbs. No one thought twice of the well-known father/daughter duo off in the grass. Everyone had their own pre-run rituals. Some stretched, some jogged, some did jumping jacks. Skiing came with a sense of solitude—it was just you in your head. If anything, others were jealous of the closeness Leather and Deb shared around a common love.

So, everyone minded their business, focusing instead on the task at hand: get around as many buoys as you can without falling. The clock ticked down until start time. Chatter scurried across the glass-smooth lake. Kids ran by, chasing each other with plastic water guns. Events came with lots of commotion, lots of diversion. Which is why no one ever noticed when Leather slipped a small syringe from his nylon waist pack and covertly jabbed it into the side of Deb's hip. Not just that competition, but every competition. For the last five years.

A covert prick, quick rub of the skin, then back in the waist pack went the empty needle. That's all it took for Deb to have a little more energy, a little more stamina and strength. Just enough to repeatedly knock out the competition.

No one would notice.

Unless you were the one always getting second place and beginning to wonder why. Why could Deb always reach that last ball at 10.25 meters, but she couldn't? How did Deb manage to fly across the wake like lightning at a mere hundred and ten pounds?

Someone was suspicious. And that someone was Roxanne Hill.

That day, while Leather stretched Deb like he always did, and while he greeted fans with his signature charm, and while he discreetly pulled something sharp from his bag, hidden behind his large hand, and while he stuck it into Deb's skin all while carrying on a seemingly normal conversation, Roxanne watched from behind a tree. She saw the whole thing and it finally made sense.

And that's when she knew what she had to do.

***

Finding a minute alone with Deb was next to impossible with a father like Leather Norcross. The two were inseparable, from boat to land and back again. Roxanne swore if an event existed for father/daughter pairs, they'd be the first ones to do it.

Making her new revelation go public wasn't the plan. Roxanne didn't need a scene. Just a quiet moment to throw down the ultimatum. Her belly fluttered with eager anticipation. This could change everything. She looked around. The bathroom—that's where she'd wait. Surely, Leather wouldn't escort Deb there.

Roxanne paced the gravel sidewalk next to the outhouse. Arms crossed, darting eyes, lungs in her throat. Had anyone else seen what she saw? She thought hard, replaying the scene in her mind. It was almost too wild to believe. Maybe her mind was playing tricks on her. Maybe she'd imagined the whole thing, a hallucination of wishful thinking. Deb couldn't really be doping, could she?

But then her chest expanded, as certainty swelled. She knew what she'd seen. Leather had stuck a needle directly into his daughter's skin. Deb hadn't flinched, hadn't recoiled. She knew what he was doing. She was in on it.

Roxanne's muscles quivered. How dare they! Her thoughts swirled. Did officials already know? Impossible. Deb would have been banned. The IWWF wouldn't have let it go on this long—and Roxanne knew, without proof, that it *had* been going on for this long. All those wins. There was simply no other explanation.

The time ticked down. Roxanne fiddled with her ponytail. She couldn't stand there forever. She had to get herself ready before it was her turn to ski. Couldn't sacrifice her own warm-up just to wait for someone who might never come.

But then Deb did come, and Roxanne's pulse spiked.

"You in line?" Deb gestured to the door.

Roxanne clenched her jaw. Her hands turned clammy. "No, no. Go ahead."

Deb passed with a nod, but Roxanne was one step behind, following her competitor into the single bathroom. She locked the door behind her, the click making Deb spin in place.

"What are you doing?" Deb said, a mix of confusion and fear on her face. Mistaking the bathroom for multiple stalls was one thing, but locking the door? The oddness of it made her reach for the sink edge.

Roxanne's heart knocked away at an alarming clip. It was now or never. "I know what you and your dad have been doing," she whispered. Her eyes held firm, peeling back Deb's outer layer.

"What are you talking about?"

"Don't play dumb."

Deb laughed nervously. "Seriously, Roxanne. I don't have time for this. Can you just get out? I'm trying to pee here."

"The drugs." Roxanne's voice rose, no longer a whisper. "Whatever they are. I saw him inject you. And something tells me it's not anything you want the officials to know about."

"You're crazy." Deb took another step back. She shook her head, trying and failing to dismiss the absurdity. Roxanne saw through it.

"I'm not. I know what I saw. You're cheating, and you have been for years, haven't you?" Bitterness flew through the roof. Athletics were supposed to be about good, fair competition, not cheating your way to the top. Roxanne had always played fair, and this awakening came with a heaping of rage. The color drained from Deb's face, like a mouse caught in a lion's sights. She went to speak, to defend herself, but Roxanne wasn't having it. "How could you? After everything this sport has given you?"

Deb's mouth opened and closed. "It's not what you think."

"You're a fraud. All those wins—they should have gone to—"

"What? To you? So this is all just you whining about second place? Who's to say you would have come in first anyway even without the—"

"So you're admitting it?"

"I'm not admitting anything."

Roxanne exhaled through her teeth. Of course she would have won if Deb didn't exist, or if Deb wasn't doping. But now wasn't the time for pride. "This is bigger than you versus me. This is about the sport, and all the other athletes involved. No one's had a fair chance. And you've known it all along. I'd rather be honest than impressive."

Deb stared, face white.

"Think about all the other girls," Roxanne continued. "Or are you really that self-centered?"

Something came over Deb at that. Her lips pulled down, shoulders rounded forward. "You don't get it. My dad, he's—"

"Oh, so you're going to blame it all on him? How mature."

A beat of silence hung between them, there in that cement brick bathroom at the Greater Miami Ski Club. The biggest tournament of the season, the culmination of their efforts for the year, waited moments away. They were due to hit the water in minutes. And yet, all of it rested on that instant and what Roxanne would say next.

Only one thing seemed fair.

"Pull out," Roxanne said.

Deb's eyes filled with tears. "What?"

"Pull out of the competition. I don't care what you say or the reason you give, but you leave this bathroom and you go to the officials and tell them you're out. You don't talk to your dad first, and you don't tell them about this conversation. My name doesn't leave your lips."

"And what if I refuse?"

Roxanne stepped forward, closing the gap between them. Breath mixed with breath. "Then I tell them you've been doping, and your career is done." She thought she heard a little cry escape Deb's lips, but she couldn't be sure. What she did know for a fact was that Deb's eyes went from icy blue to fire red, and at once their unspoken clash was drawn in the sand for real.

"What about next year? And the year after that?" Deb said, voice shaky.

"Something happens to you starting next year. You miss balls you don't normally miss. You can't quite run 10.25 like you used to. You'll still be good; you'll still win some comps—but not all of them, because I'll win the rest." Roxanne lowered her head, staring deep into Deb's eyes. "You understand what I'm saying?"

Deb's face turned to stone. "I understand. You think you've won, but you haven't. I'm not doing it; I'm not throwing away my career."

"Don't be stupid."

"You don't scare me."

Roxanne hadn't prepared for this, hadn't expected Deb to put up such a fight once the truth was thrown in her face. She needed something more, an extra layer to drive the nail home. Evidently, it wasn't enough for Deb to lose everything. But what if Roxanne pulled the rug out from the top?

"You do realize your father will be arrested, right? Banned from the sport. It won't just be your name that's tarnished; it will be his, your mother's too. Isn't he tied in with that church leader? I wonder how long it would take for the house of God to fall..."

If Deb Norcross could have breathed fire, she would have. Instead, she gritted her teeth, balled her fists, and left the conversation with a warning:

"You'll pay for this."

Chapter 35
NOW

"**L**ast I knew, it was the Norcrosses who were the shady ones," Roxanne said.

Deb's jaw hardened. "You'll say anything to throw me under the bus."

"It doesn't take much. People wouldn't even have to look that hard; they just can't see past the blinding *perfection*."

Deb blew out a laugh. "Whatever you say, Roxanne. I'll let my world records speak for themselves."

"You wouldn't even have them if people knew the truth."

"The truth? The truth is you're jealous. Always have been. First of me, and now of Sadie."

"This has nothing to do with jealousy. It's about fact. And the fact is, I could destroy you."

Deb's face went white. She stretched her neck forward, hissing her words through her teeth. "You'd regret it. That's a promise."

Roxanne stepped forward, body trembling, but determined not to back down. "Really? It sounds like a threat."

The women's eyes zeroed in on each other, as though they were the only two on the planet. Their voices lowered to a menacing whisper.

"Trust me, you don't want to mess with me and my family," Deb sneered.

Roxanne's lips curled in a snarl. "The world has no idea who the Norcrosses really are."

The truth of it landed hard. Deb pinched her lips. Sadie and Willa looked to their respective leaders. *What the hell is going on?*

Color returning to her face, Deb straightened up and gave her chin a little upward flick. "You're living in la-la land, Roxanne. I won't stand around listening to my name dragged through the mud by some bitter ex-athlete. Come on, Sadie, we have a tournament to win."

She led Sadie away by the elbow, and the twosomes separated like fighters to their respective corners of the ring, as though space between them would douse the bad blood. When she was a few feet away, Deb called back over her shoulder, "Here's a suggestion, Rox—why don't you go shopping? Jealousy doesn't look good on you."

Roxanne seethed. She wanted to lunge after Deb, jump on her back, and claw at that pretty face. The audacity of that woman! Lying through her teeth. Roxanne's torso leaned forward, like a torpedo about to be sling-shotted forward. Her breaths piled on each other at a rapid pace.

"Whoa. Easy, killer," Willa said, putting a hand on Roxanne's arm. "What was that all about? What did you mean by *if people knew the truth?*"

"I've kept it in for almost thirty years." She kicked the ground.

"Tell me."

The fury drained from Roxanne's body in heaps of pent-up energy. She'd said what she wanted to say. Telling Willa would only stir up more distraction from their mission. Roxanne shook her head. "Let's go. You're up. It's time to kick Sadie's ass."

***

Willa did not kick Sadie's ass, but she came close.

After four runs, the skiers were tied. The confrontation between the two had shaken more than just Sadie. Both girls were off their typical rhythm, missing balls they never missed. One run bumped Sadie in front, and the next Willa caught up. Then vice versa. A see-saw of first and second place until finally they balanced the same. The crowd went wild. A tie meant a run-off—another opportunity to see the two best in the sport go head to head. Even after a long day in the sun, no one could dismiss the excitement of a showdown.

The announcer's voice came over the loudspeaker.

"Ladies and gentlemen, here are the rules for the run-off. The tie-breaking run will begin with the scheduled speed and rope length of the last complete pass and conclude with the first miss. If another tie results, the tie will be run-off in the same manner with another new drawing for order. This process will be repeated until a winner is determined. Who's ready to crown a champion?"

The crowd roared. On the dock, Sadie and Willa stood side by side. Their smiles read as confident, but any skier knew that a run-off came with even more pressure than a normal race. This was it—do or die, sink or swim. A mistake would cost someone the race.

The two refused to look at one another. Water glistened off their tanned, toned skin. Their race bibs stuck to their abdomens above their bikini bottoms. Other racers—those who'd already finished—stood by, anxiously waiting, as though they were watching gods instead of mortals.

The announcer, along with a race official, joined Sadie and Willa on the dock.

"And now for the coin flip to see who goes first," the announcer said. "Sadie, as the first skier of the day, you call the flip." The official flicked the coin into the air.

Sadie watched it fly in slow motion, and wondered which was better—setting the bar as the first skier, or going second and knowing what she needed to do to win?

There was no time to waste. The coin began its descent. "Heads," Sadie said.

The official caught the coin and smacked it onto the front of his hand. Everyone leaned in. He lifted the cover to reveal the flip. "Tails," he said.

Sadie's heart dropped.

The announcer held the microphone out to Willa. "What'll it be?"

***

Willa wasted no time. "I'll go first," she said with confidence. Waiting and watching would only make her nerves worse. She was ready.

"You heard it, folks," the announcer said. "Up first we have Willa Betts!"

The crowd cheered. *Bet on Betts! Bet on Betts!*

Willa peered around the throng of people and found Roxanne's face. Her coach gave a nod, a quick point, and mouthed, *You got this.*

Ski on, rope in hand, Willa plunged into the water, taking in a mouthful and spitting it out. She rolled her shoulders and gave her neck a swift crack. *Forget about what happened earlier. Forget about Sadie. Do not think of Baz. Do. Not. Think. Of. Baz.* Her heart hurt each time she pictured him telling her secret to Sadie. She willed herself to put it out of her mind, if only for the next thirty seconds.

The boat pulled the slack from the rope, getting in position. And then, with a quick signal, it accelerated to speed, pulling Willa up onto the water.

Through the starting gate, she flew, then out to the side, slicing the water with the edge of her ski and rounding the one ball. Back across the wake, right, left, right, left. *Baz, Baz, Baz.*

Breeeeeeathe. The sixth buoy came into view. She was almost done. One more cut and it would be a perfect run.

Willa flew across the wake, absorbing the bumps with her knees. She dropped a hand, leaned. *Bazzzzzzzz.* And that's when it happened—again. Her edge caught, and before she could catch the last buoy, she faceplanted, the water hitting her like a thousand knives.

She could hear the crowd's collective cry even underwater. When she blasted up through the surface, she inhaled a deep breath, then brought two hands to her head. *No!* She'd been so close. Disappointment flooded her. She leaned her head back, wishing she could sink below the water again and stay there.

The boat brought her back to land and clapping fans. Willa gave a wave of appreciation. Faces smiled at her, but she felt like she'd let them down. She'd let herself down. All she had to do was complete the course—like she'd done endless times before—and she failed. Now, the only thing to do was wait to see if Sadie would mess up too. It was her only chance.

* * *

When Sadie saw Willa crash, she couldn't help the giddiness that tickled her ribs. *Karma*, she thought. But then an altogether new sensation appeared. She'd seen Willa's face when she got back to the dock and knew the feeling all too well. The sense of failure, the desperate wish to go back and relive that split second and make it have a different result. To correct whatever mistake brought her there. Willa wore a smile, but it wasn't real— any athlete could see. Sadie could tell from yards away.

Sadie shook the feelings away—now wasn't the time to feel bad for Willa Betts. Now was the time to crush the course. She imagined her grandfather lifting her up in celebration after her win. It would all be worth it.

In the water, Sadie breathed out long exhales through her mouth. Sixteen seconds and the run would be over. She saw herself on the top of the podium. Manifestation, she'd learned, was a powerful tool.

"Hit it," she hollered to the driver, who put the boat in gear and sped forward. Sadie cruised around the first ball, then the second, then the third. Halfway. She could do this. She held her breath as she shot across the wake, leaning hard, pulling with all her weight. Four ball. Five ball. One more and it would be a perfect run.

Sadie let her body do what it had been trained to do. Her muscles knew the tempo. She heard her mother's voice. *Trust it. Don't overthink.*

And then she was reaching for the last buoy. She cut into the water, leaning into her edge. Dropped an arm so low it could have skimmed the water's surface. Yes! Sadie cleared it, coming back into the middle of the wake and crossing the exit gate with an arm pumping triumphantly in the air.

She'd done it. Another trophy her family could be proud of.

A thunder of applause came from the crowd. Sadie dropped into the water, giving it a celebratory smack with her hand. Back on the dock, she waved to the crowd, then high-fived Leather, who came up to give her a wet hug.

"Way to go, champ!" he said, then took a victorious spin himself, both hands up and waving to the excited crowd. Sadie bent and put her hands on her knees, heart rate not yet subsiding.

Within an hour, the podium area was set up, three tiers in front of a backdrop sprinkled with sponsor logos. Some of the audience had filtered out, but the most loyal fans stuck around to see the awards. Skiers mingled in the grassy area, dry and changed into t-shirts and ripped jean shorts.

Some were pleased, others dissatisfied. All were hungry for the next chance.

The announcer got back on the microphone. "What an event! A big thank you to our gold sponsors, Mastercraft and Action Water Sports for another incredible day of skiing. Did everyone enjoy themselves?" A chorus of clapping echoed around. "And now, it's time for the awards ceremony. Coming in third place, we have Harper Cruz!" Harper took the lowest platform on the podium, and an official handed her a red and blue plaque. "In second place, after a hard-fought battle, and winning an $8,500 prize...Willa Betts!"

Willa forced a smile. She carried her ski to the podium and stood it next to her on the second-place platform. She accepted the check handed to her by the official. The money was nice and certainly helpful, but bragging rights beat a cash prize any day. It was a hard pill to swallow, the fact that one measly ball could mean the difference between 8K and over double for first place. Still, she told herself to take in the moment. Making the podium was a win, and she shouldn't take it for granted. Smiling faces met her from the crowd, and she did her best to return them as authentically as possible. These were her people; they loved her, and they were proud of her.

But then she locked eyes with Baz, and all that goodwill floated away. A sword of betrayal stabbed her back, twisting dangerously close to major organs. It felt impossible to breathe. Her Baz. Well, not in that way, but a friend nonetheless. She heard Sadie's voice from earlier: *Husbands and wives tell each other everything.* She'd trusted him with her darkest secret, and he hadn't kept it. Seeing him now was like seeing a stranger.

When he smiled at her and she didn't return it, his brows knit together. Willa looked away before tears could form. She gripped her ski with white fingers.

"And now," the announcer said, "today's winner, taking home a cash prize of $18,000...Sadie Norcross!"

Cheers all around. Sadie climbed to the top step, ski in hand. She raised her other arm and waved. All three women held their plaques and smiled for the official race photo that would be posted to the IWWF website, along with numerous social media accounts. Willa stared past the camera and focused on Roxanne, whose eyes narrowed and mouth pulled in a tight line. Roxanne's gaze didn't match Willa's—she looked the slightest bit higher. No question, she was glaring at Sadie.

The clicking of cameras faded. The show was over; time to move onto the next. As they stepped down from the podium, Sadie and Willa's skis bumped.

"Sorry," they both said at the same time.

Their eyes held each other's for the briefest second before darting away. Gone were the days of congratulatory hugs, of post-race chit chat, or even group gatherings. Too much had happened. Too much that pulled them apart instead of together. What neither of them could see was the potential that existed if they combined their star power instead of fighting for the biggest shine. Together, they could have rocketed the sport through the stratosphere in a positive way. But not with the outside influence that kept them pitted against each other. People loved a feud far more than friendship.

Chapter 36

Sadie was on such a high after winning that she almost forgot about Baz's little indiscretion. She posted the podium photo to her 275K social media followers with the caption, "Big win today! Thank you to my #Mastercraft family." Comments rolled in.

Long live Norcross!

You're my favorite skier to follow.

Congrats, GOAT

She and Baz made it home late that night after the two-and-a-half-hour drive along Florida's east coast interstate. Sadie had fallen asleep in the car listening to her favorite interior designer-turned-lifestyle-mogul's podcast through her earbuds, and woke with her head on Baz's shoulder. She blinked for a second, forgetting where she was, and then quickly realized the intimate position she held—the crown of her head nestled into his neck. She could smell his cologne—the one she'd bought him several Christmases ago. It was far too cozy an arrangement given what had happened. But instead of jerking away, she stayed put, smelling the scent on his shirt and letting it bring her back to a different time. They'd been together since sixteen, grown up together, faced the lowest of lows and the highest of highs. She didn't know another person as well as him—or at least, she used to think.

In that moment, as the Jacksonville city lights brightened the darkness of the car, Sadie wondered if she could let go of what had happened. Baz had made a mistake, nearly crossed the line. But could she really blame him? It wasn't like their relationship had been on the most solid ground. If she were being honest, she'd admit she was partly to blame for that. Relationships were a two-way street, and hers had been blocked off with heavy concrete barriers for a while.

Were his actions really as bad as everyone made them out to be? If so, why hadn't she felt more? She recalled hearing a famous actress talk about the memoir she wrote after the darkest, most bleak days post-divorce. The woman had gone on and on about being so low she could barely crawl through the days. How her husband's infidelity was a deal breaker, full stop.

Sadie wondered if she should feel the same. Maybe she should stop comparing herself and Baz to everyone else. Some couples called it quits, but others worked through things. No one had room to judge. Perhaps she could put everything behind them. Force herself to find the love again. Her family seemed to make it sound possible.

A new intention solidified. She'd try. For herself, for him, for her family.

"Let's pick up a bottle of champagne," she said, sitting back up and feeling a sudden burst of spontaneity. She smiled and reached for his hand, which he took with a look of surprise. It had been so long since they touched voluntarily, without the pressure of onlookers and an image to uphold. It felt good.

"It's ten o'clock," Baz said. They'd been up since five a.m., and even though he hadn't been the one skiing, the day felt more like a week. Also, since when did Sadie want to drink champagne?

"So?" she said, almost giggly. "It was a big win, and I feel like celebrating. We haven't had fun in so long." She gave his hand a squeeze, and her eyes looked too bright, so hopeful, he couldn't say no.

And that's how they found themselves buying two bottles of cheap Korbel bubbly at the grocery store, along with a block of sharp cheddar cheese and a bag of green grapes. At their apartment, Baz popped the cork, and Sadie yelped when it hit the ceiling. He poured them both a glass. She raised hers. The mood was weirdly intoxicating. A flash of abandon.

"What are we toasting to?" he said.

"To my win, of course." Then, looking into his eyes, "And to us."

She wanted so much to believe it. That a single flute of gold liquid could patch up any holes. *You love him, you love him. He loves you.*

Delusion.

They clinked glasses, and instead of sipping, both gulped down the champagne in its entirety to ease the strain. Then they laughed at the lack of tact. *Who cares?* Baz gave each a refill. For two people who had known each other since the days of Legos and Barbies, the nerves were strong. One would have thought they were on a first date, using alcohol as a crutch.

And it worked. By the time they popped the second bottle, Sadie and Baz fell into a pool of calm. Sadie pulled the elastic from her hair, letting her ponytail fall into a curtain of blonde that touched her shoulder blades. She laid back against the couch cushions, stretching her arms above her head, in turn revealing a sliver of tan midsection where her belly button rested on top of defined abs. She caught Baz looking. When was the last time he took in her body? His noticing made her tingle. *See?* she thought. *We can get this back.*

Finishing the second bottle meant they were both properly tipsy. They had scooted closer to each other on the couch, and it didn't take long for one thing to lead to another. His mouth was on hers. Her tongue wrestling with his. So familiar. Almost *too* familiar? *This is good*, Sadie told herself. *You guys need this*. They fumbled for a minute. Why wasn't he taking off her shirt? She didn't wait. She took it off for him. Baz followed her lead, slipping down his shorts. And soon, though they did it all themselves, they were naked. He carried her to their bedroom. Skin to skin, they found the rhythm they'd known for years.

Sadie tried to let go of all else, clear her head, be present in the moment. She closed her eyes tight, hoping imagination would take over. *Think back. Remember how it used to be.* She wanted her heart to gush with passion, and yet she couldn't look at her husband as he moved on top of her. She kept her eyes shut, wondering, but too scared to see if Baz's were shut too. She imagined him admiring her and felt a wash of guilt that she couldn't force herself to do the same.

* * *

All Baz saw was the dark insides of his eyelids. His body knew what to do, but his mind couldn't get on board. If he opened his eyes, the bubble would burst. This wasn't how it was supposed to be. They shouldn't have to rely on two bottles of champagne to perform what used to come so naturally. Sadie was probably gazing lovingly at him, and he couldn't even bring himself to open his eyes and return the sentiment.

Still, sex was sex, and it reached its predictable conclusion regardless of what was happening upstairs in his head. Baz rolled off Sadie, breathing deep. The room was dark, lit only by a sliver of moon coming through a break in the curtains.

Neither of them bothered to clean up, and as the seconds ticked by, the possibility got less and less likely, until both fell asleep exactly where they laid and without as much as a word to mark the end of the evening together.

Alcohol ushered them into the land of the unconscious, and they both slept like logs until morning, when Baz woke up with a pain deep behind his eyes. Recalling the events of the night prior—ah yes, too much champagne—he blinked awake expecting to find Sadie by his side, equally hungover. Instead, the sheets were pulled up and he was alone. A mix of emotions hurled his way. Shame? Relief?

He reached for his phone on the nightstand. A string of text messages filled his lock screen—all from the same sender. Reading the first one, his gut twisted.

I can't believe you told Sadie.
How could you?
I thought I could trust you.

He struggled to breathe. Somehow Willa had discovered that Sadie knew about the accident. But how? The messages were sent individually, short and snappy like bullets, rather than one long painful scolding. Each one dug the knife deeper. He was in big trouble.

Baz checked the timestamp. Willa had sent them in the early morning hours after he and Sadie had already passed out. He couldn't help but wonder what she'd been doing at one o'clock in the morning when she typed out these hurt-filled texts. He pictured her red-nosed and weepy. Guilt coursed through him at lightning speed. He'd broken his promise.

It had been years since Willa's secret accidentally slipped from his lips one random night. Completely innocent, without an ounce of malice. Just one of those verbal mishaps he immediately kicked himself for. But for all of Sadie's surprise at the time, she'd given her word that she'd keep it between them. Baz had believed her. Just like Willa had believed him. Turned out none of them were as loyal as they seemed.

Now, Baz found himself in damage control mode. He sat up in bed, wincing with a sharp pain in his head, and waited for his vision to stop spinning. With timid fingers, he typed out a response to Willa.

i'm so sorry. i never meant to tell her, it just happened and I regretted it immediately

He still didn't know how Willa found out, but asking would make him sound even more lame. Three dots appeared, and he held his breath, waiting for her reply.

How long has she known?

He felt his neck growing hot. He was already in deep, and now this wouldn't make it any better. But there was no sense in lying at this point.

a while

How long is a while?

ten years?

Ten years! And you didn't even tell me? WTF Baz!

i didn't think she'd say anything. i'm sorry! i messed up

Well it would have been nice to be

**a little more prepared when she
threw it in my face yesterday.**

fuck I'm sorry

There was a long pause, and for a few minutes, Baz thought she'd ghosted him. His stomach churned and he wanted to chug a glass of water but was too scared it might come back up. Finally, Willa responded.

I feel so betrayed.

That hit him like a dagger. Baz ran a hand through his hair. It was greasy and needed washed. He looked around the room as though for an answer to his problems. All he wanted was to make amends. He had to figure out a way to smooth this over, but that was hard to do over text. If they could only talk and hear each other's voices, he'd be able to express his remorse. She could chew him up and down; he'd take it. Anything for her to forgive him.

His fingers typed in triple speed.

can I call y—

But before Baz could hit send—and good thing—he heard their apartment door open and close. A familiar foot pattern, keys dropped to the counter. Sadie was home. *Damn.*

He deleted the message, but that couldn't be it. He couldn't *not* say something. Baz thought fast and sent a quick alternative, one he hoped she'd accept.

please forgive me. i promise i'll make it up to you.

229

As soon as the message sped off into the ether, he realized the irony. It was a slap in Willa's face. Promises made to fix a broken promise somehow fell flat.

Chapter 37

Going through a dead person's belongings was like walking into an alternate universe, one with spine-tingling music and where you aren't quite sure what is reality and what isn't. How could a human being be there one day and gone the next?

The upholstery on Dale's recliner faded to threads on the seat and arms, an imprint from the body that sat there all those long weeks and months. His presence still lingered in the house, and Willa found herself inspecting mundane items, amazed that such objects remained without her father in connection to them. His slippers sat by the end of the couch. His toothbrush probably still smelled of his breath. The TV remote probably carried a hundred of his fingerprints.

But he was gone. Along with her mother. And that made Willa parentless at twenty-eight.

"How many T-shirts does a man need?" Roxanne said, pulling open a dresser drawer. She thumbed through a stack of at least twenty.

Willa managed a small smile. She was grateful to have support and help in this strange process. It felt very much like erasing a person's existence. If she got rid of all his things, would that mean he hadn't been real? She'd been too young to remember any of this when her mother had died. She'd never witnessed Dale go through her mother's belongings, but somehow—

was it slowly? Or all at once?—their home had changed. Clothes, cosmetics, even some decor—gone. Who'd done it all? Her father and aunt? Did they have a service come in and sweep the home of all things Autumn? How did these things work?

Willa pointed to the drawer. "Make a pile of anything worth donating," she instructed Roxanne. Willa was busy tackling the closet, where stacks of papers and albums and Lord knew what else filled three deep shelves. She pulled out a box of paint color strips from the home improvement store and sifted through the rainbow of hues. "Why do people keep all this stuff?"

"Maybe they were into painting?" Roxanne offered.

"Yeah right."

Painting, like a slew of other things, fell into the category of good-ideas-lost-to-booze. Priorities weren't exactly in line when Willa was a kid, and she recalled times when her mom would tell her they could spend the day rearranging her bedroom furniture, or her dad saying he'd help her build a fort, only for them to find a bottle and get sloshed before they could even get started.

Willa pulled a 1984 yearbook from the shelf and flipped through it, looking for one of her parents. Near the front, she found him: Dale Betts, junior. His dark hair sat full on the top of his head, tapering at the sides, and trailing down to the back of his neck. She stared at this younger, mullet-haired, clear eyed version of her father, wondering if the boy in the picture would ever have guessed his life would end so prematurely. People were living to one hundred more and more, and here he was dead at fifty-seven. Had alcohol already trapped him in its grip when this picture was taken? Or was there a chance for this boy—an alternative life where he would have walked a different path? Willa shook her head. Choices.

"Here's one from a Billy Joel concert," Roxanne said, holding up a faded blue tee. "You should keep this one."

"Billy Joel?"

Roxanne cough-laughed. "Yes. Piano Man, Movin' Out, Only the Good Die— Nevermind. Just keep it. Billy Joel is classic." She tossed it to Willa, who caught it and instinctively brought it to her nose. The smell disgusted and, oddly enough, comforted her.

Willa returned to the crowded shelf and dug out a small box wedged toward the back. She opened the lid. Autumn's necklace—the one with a sapphire teardrop on a silver chain. Willa's throat prickled. She touched the gemstone, remembering how it laid perfectly in the hollow of her mother's neck. How the blue stone had been covered in blood on the day of the accident. How did it get here? And why would her father have kept it?

It had been so long since she'd touched anything belonging to her mom. Everything left behind after her death had been utilitarian items— dishes and furniture and linens, things Dale would need too. But this, this was different. It was hers alone. A precious treasure Autumn wore daily, including her last minutes on this Earth. It being tucked away in the closet only meant one thing: her dad had saved it for her.

Willa removed the necklace from the box, and despite the memories that came with it, unhinged the clasp and put it around her neck. It fell to the exact spot it had on her mother. A ray of heat shot through Willa's chest, as though connecting her heart to the stone. A strange, confusing sensation. She tucked the necklace under the collar of her shirt without a word.

Determined to get the cleanout over and done with, she moved on. She pulled out an oversized album with the word "Scrapbook" in goldleaf on the front. Must be one of her parents' mementos, she thought. More old high school things. But when she opened it, Willa was surprised to find the pages empty. A handful of loose newspaper clippings shoved inside the front cover fell into her lap. Willa shuffled through them. A shiver zapped her. The scrapbook wasn't her parents'. The clippings were all from Willa's ski events.

Local ski star takes top spot at Junior U.S. Open

Bet on Betts: Twelve-year-old skiing phenom headed for Nationals

Norcross, Betts go one-two at junior skiing event

Willa's brow furrowed. Her parents had never been to a single race. Not one. And yet, here were dozens of write-ups someone had clipped and saved.

Willa checked the scrapbook again, and that's when she noticed the opening page, on which she recognized her mother's neat handwriting.

WILLA'S SKIING MEMORIES

Her mom had saved everything from those early days. The clippings might not have made it onto individual pages with cute scrapbooking details and coordinating gel pen inscriptions, but maybe that would have been too much to ask. Despite everything, here they were. Proof of...something? The mere presence of the clippings stirred something in Willa—an emotion she hadn't felt for a long time.

She missed her mother.

Roxanne came up beside Willa. "Are those...?"

"They're all mine." Misty eyes took Willa by surprise.

Roxanne's mouth formed into a soft smile and she put a hand on Willa's back. "Are you going to keep them?"

It felt weird to throw them away, like tossing your history in the trash. These were Willa's personal accomplishments, and the fact that her mom had the sentiment to cut them out meant Willa couldn't just dump them. Instead, she tucked them back inside the scrapbook and placed it on the floor next to the Billy Joel t-shirt. The two things and the gemstone around her neck represented her "save" pile. Almost everything else would go.

Willa sniffed. A hard lump had formed at the base of her throat.

"It's okay to grieve them," Roxanne said.

"I have."

"Have you?"

Willa looked up. "Trust me, it's not hard to get over parents who were never there for you."

It was her armor talking. Because for all of Willa's outward stoicism, there was a part of her that would always be a little girl hoping her dad would take her to the father/daughter dance, or her mom would be waiting for her on the dock after a race, just like Sadie's mom.

Roxanne acquiesced, and Willa resumed her purge of the closet. In the end, the house and the majority of the items in it would be sold. Willa could have upgraded her apartment or taken a vacation with the money, but after settling a few of Dale's small debts and paying off the funeral expenses, she put what remained in the bank for another day. Something about using her dead parents' meager estate to celebrate just didn't sit right. And besides, the end of the ski season was quickly approaching. Cash prizes only went so far with fewer than ten events in the season—and that was if she placed in the top. She thanked God for the sponsorships that kept everything afloat.

Dale's death functioned as somewhat of a clean slate for Willa. With October right around the corner, she had two more major events—both of which she planned to win. She and Sadie had been neck and neck all season, but the last two races came with major accolades. Willa wanted them. And she could feel it in her bones that she was going to make it happen, no matter what it took.

Chapter 38

October

Sadie normally did her HIIT workout with ten-pound weights, but today those damn things felt like boulders, so she switched them out for five-pounders instead. She followed along with the instructor at the front of the room, the whole time wishing she would have done a YouTube workout in her living room instead. People kept looking at her differently. Judging. She could sense it. Reverberations from the scandal back in July. She'd thought most of it had settled down, but once in a while a paparazzi still caught her unaware—like an hour ago on her way into the gym. Bastards had nothing better to do.

In the wall-to-wall mirrors, women in spandex leggings and matching sports bras lifted weights above their heads, then brought them down and across to touch their opposite foot. Back up, and down. Over and over—how many reps were in this set? Her thighs burned.

Sadie breathed harder than normal. She felt off, and knew it had to be because she wasn't sleeping well. Too much going on in her head, everything with Baz. Ever since their spontaneous rendezvous last month, a ball of dread had settled in her gut. She'd woken that next morning and spent a solid fifteen minutes watching Baz sleep. The whole time, her brain had whirled, trying to come to terms with what she knew deep down was the truth: Their marriage was in trouble, and not even a sexual rekindling could save them.

That morning, she'd slipped out of the house for a training session before he woke up and they'd have to address the awkwardness. She'd cried on the way to the lake. Cried because of what would surely be inevitable, but also cried out of fear. She couldn't keep going on like this. It wasn't fair, and it wasn't healthy. Would her family ever let her live life on her own terms? Would she ever be free to make her own decisions?

In the time since "the parking lot incident," as she'd come to think of it, she and Baz never addressed the elephant in the room. Instead, they kept up the facade in public and retreated to separate ends of the apartment at home. It wasn't that they hated each other. Only that their love had run its course, and after so many years there was no more to give—not in that way at least. She'd tried to hate him but couldn't. They were two people with shared history who weren't destined for a shared future.

Back in the gym, the woman to Sadie's right got a little carried away with her lateral raises. Her dumbbell grazed Sadie's arm, jolting her from her daydream.

"Oops, sorry!" the woman said, a trickle of sweat dangling on the tip of her nose.

Sadie bumbled to regain synchronization with the instructor who was now moving onto some sort of side step combination. Step, step, shoulder press. She dragged her body through the motions, then yawned as her weights touched together above her head. Tap.

She really needed to *tap* into some meditation to clear her mind before bed. Nights of restless sleep were catching up to her. She recalled reading once how sleep affects all bodily functions. Come to think of it, her appetite had been funky too. *Jesus*, Sadie thought, nothing like falling apart at one of the worst possible times—the Miami Pro was only ten days away. Her mind and body couldn't fail her now.

When the class ended, Sadie bent to grab her towel from the floor but was so exhausted she couldn't even stand back up, so instead let her knees buckle and took a seat, wiping her forehead with the smooth terrycloth.

"Nice work, folks!" the instructor called. "See you next week."

Sadie smiled and stayed put, taking long pulls from her water bottle, until she finally talked herself into getting up and headed to the locker room. Each step felt like work. Maybe she'd go home and take a nap—the idea sounded glorious.

A few women lingered among the locker bays, chatting about things like husbands and kids and that really good Italian restaurant that just opened. *You have to try the eggplant parmesan—literally to* die *for.*

On one of the benches, Sadie stripped off her sweaty tank top and changed into a clean sports bra. It felt tighter than usual, and she tried to recall if it had just come from the dryer. The women nearby droned on. Just as Sadie was stepping into new shorts, she caught a piece of a conversation that grabbed her attention enough to make her freeze.

"...and I look like an absolute whale when I'm on my period. Look at me. Look how bloated I am. I swear, men have it so easy. How is it even fair, right?" A chorus of agreement.

A chill traveled up Sadie's spine, like someone had just walked over her grave. That word, it struck her dumb. *Period.* It wasn't something she thought much of, the annoying monthly visitor. Hers had been regular since that damn day at the junior race, despite the heavy training schedule that sometimes granted reprieve from menstruation for some athletes. All those gymnasts and runners whose bodies still lived in pre-adolescence. Not for her. Her period showed up like clockwork each month, so much so that she could almost predict the hour.

Except...

Sadie counted in her head. And then the blood drained from her face. She was late. Not just by a day or two, but—she counted again—over a week.

No way, she thought. It would be impossible. They'd hardly even hugged lately, let alone—

But then she remembered that night with the champagne. Celebrating her win after the MasterCraft event. The night she tried to fall back in love with her husband but didn't. The sex hadn't solved anything. In a surprising plot twist, Sadie now feared it might have actually *created* something.

Sadie finished changing with shaking hands and a knot in her stomach. As she walked toward the locker room door, she caught a glimpse of herself in the full-length mirror opposite a row of sinks, stopping her mid-stride. She paused, taking in her reflection, eyes instinctively drawn to her abdomen. She placed a hand on her belly, wondering. The exhaustion, the loss of appetite, the missing period. Could it be? And if so...then what?

She imagined telling her parents. Her family reacting with shouts of joy. A new generation of Norcross! The public would eat it up. There'd be a new round of headlines, only this time they'd be happy ones. A baby would fix everything. At least on the outside. All would be right in the world.

But Sadie felt none of those things, not only for the sheer shock coursing through her, but for the fact that she'd been struck with déjà vu.

She'd been here before.

Chapter 39

THEN
Summer 2010

By the time the California Pro rolled around at the end of August, Sadie and Baz were officially a couple. It was hard to tell who loved them more: the media or Sadie's parents. For an overbearing individual like Deb Norcross, you'd think her daughter having a boyfriend would have been a hard no. Too much risk of distraction. But because being linked with Baz only amped up Sadie's star power, Deb and Mark were fully on board. Alone, their daughter was great. But with Baz, Sadie was even better. Who wouldn't root for a gorgeous young couple? Forget the fact that they were only sixteen and barely knew how to parallel park a car. Or that Sadie still slept with a ratty stuffed animal at night. To everyone else, they were the darlings of the waterski world.

The media quickly gave them a nickname: Bazie. They were portrayed as the picture of innocence and purity, fluttering around competitions, rooting each other on and holding hands—nothing more. Dating Baz came with one clear expectation from the Norcrosses: abstinence. They even had Jed highlight a few Bible passages about the importance of virtue and honor. She read them with the attention one would expect. That is, very little. *Yes, yes, sure, of course. Blah, blah, blah.* Couldn't she just get back to snuggling up to Baz with googly eyes?

Sadie's image, that wholesome girl next door with a lengthy family lineage, was something her sponsors liked. She was the face of junior waterskiing for so many years. Girls looked up to her. She wouldn't want to let them down, would she? After all, the family had ties to the Church, and God had a hand in blessing Sadie with such a talent. All that money floating around, the potential for it to grow exponentially. That, above all else, was not something the Norcross family was willing to risk.

If only it were that easy. If only girls didn't grow into young women. If only hormones didn't exist.

If only...

***

Willa sipped peppermint tea from her travel mug and wondered where Sadie was. The Malibu Open in Tuscaloosa was one of the biggest of the season, which meant more athletes milling around.

"Another tournament in California?" her dad had asked, to which Willa explained that Malibu was the sponsoring boat brand, not the city, and that she'd be in Alabama, not California. These were things most parents of a sixteen-year-old would know if they really cared.

Another sip. The peppermint warmed and cooled her throat at the same time.

Willa smoothed the new Billabong tank top she'd just received in the mail—her first freebie from a sponsor. It felt like being in the cool kid's club. Now, if anyone asked who repped her, she'd have an answer just like

Sadie. Maybe it wasn't as big of a deal—not yet—but it was something. And she wanted to show it off.

Willa looked around, coming up empty. Disappointment swirled. Sadie was probably off with Baz somewhere, drinking her Red Bull with him instead. Now that they were officially dating, Willa didn't see as much of them at the events—they were always off somewhere canoodling together, leaving her out. So much for the Three Musketeers.

Willa stood, raised her arms above her head, and gave a good stretch, willing the envy to stay at bay. She finished the last sip of her tea, no longer hot, but equally soothing. She'd have to hit the restroom at least once before her run and then pee again in the water, but the tea was a ritual she couldn't break. When she did a couple of jumping jacks in place, her bladder answered back. Yep, time to go. She walked to the pavilion. Thank goodness this venue had restrooms, she thought, remembering Sadie's unfortunate tampon situation.

Willa pulled open the door, expecting silence so early in the morning. Only the competitors and over-eager fans had shown up so far. But, instead of an empty bathroom, she was met with the distinct sound of vomit hitting the toilet bowl. She stopped mid-step, considering whether she should turn around and leave, give this person privacy—and wait for the stench to dissipate—when the stall swung open and out stumbled Sadie, pale and shaken.

"Sadie?" Willa took a step forward. "That was you? Are you all right?"

That's all it took. Sadie crumbled into Willa's arms, taking the stunned girl by surprise.

"What is it?" Willa said.

Who knows what makes a person come clean? Maybe it's a gesture of care from another, or maybe the truth simply gets more and more rotten the longer one keeps it in. Either way, Sadie spilled the secret she'd been keeping for two weeks. She sobbed as she spoke, and Willa listened, paralyzed. When Sadie finished, the girls stared at each other.

"You have to tell your parents," Willa said. "Look at you, you can barely stand up. You can't ski like this."

And it was true—Sadie's morning sickness was far more than throwing up once and getting on with her day. She couldn't keep anything down, and not eating meant she'd already lost weight on a frame that didn't have weight to lose. How her mother hadn't noticed would never be clear. Or, Sadie would later think, perhaps Deb did suspect something and spent her days praying the obvious wasn't really the truth. It couldn't be. Not her good little Sadie.

* * *

"You're *what?*" Deb's eyes were like saucers, the confession all but smacking her in the face, and Sadie saw it in her mother's aghast expression—she hadn't suspected. They were at the car where Sadie had dragged her mom away from earshot. "Oh god, no. Sadie, how could you be so stupid? This will ruin us!"

"Us?"

"You know what I mean. It will ruin everything you've worked for. Everything!" Deb's hands flew frantically to her temples.

Sadie expected the blow, which was why she'd been torturing herself with what to do for fourteen long days. At times, she'd convinced herself it wasn't true. Denial cast a thick cloud in front of her eyes. It wasn't until she finally confessed to Willa that the reality sunk in. Pregnant. But not just any teenage pregnancy—America's virgin with thousands of dollars of sponsorships on the line and generations of conservative legacy to uphold.

"I'm sorry." A salty tear rolled into the corner of her mouth, and she licked it, letting the taste momentarily zap her back to life.

"Does he know?" Deb couldn't even say Baz's name, as though impregnating her daughter kicked him off the pedestal on which he had been firmly planted. The horny little bastard had ruined her daughter's life.

"No, I haven't told him."

"Good." She paced in a small circle. "Keep it that way, at least for now. We'll get this sorted out and—"

"Willa knows."

Deb came to a halt. "Willa?"

"She saw me getting sick in the bathroom, and I—"

"Great. Just what we need." Deb dropped her head into her hands. She took several deep breaths and Sadie waited for what was to come. Her instructions. Her marching orders. After a long pause, Deb looked back up, resolute, mouth set. "Okay, listen. Here's what we're going to do. We're going to withdraw from today's event. You're clearly sick. We'll say it's the flu. I'm calling my doctor and we'll get you an appointment as soon as possible to have this taken care of."

Sadie's mouth dropped. "What do you mean, taken care of?" She immediately thought of the pro-life pamphlets on the coffee table outside the church office. Something she knew about on only an obscure level.

Her mother reached for Sadie's hands. "Sadie, you're sixteen years old. This isn't what you want for your life. You have the world ahead of you. Think about it. We'll just pretend this never happened, okay? We can...we can go somewhere else. No one will know. In a few days, it'll be all over, and you can go on like normal. You'll be better in time for Miami."

Better in time for Miami. But Sadie didn't want to think about skiing right now. She wanted someone to hug her and tell her it was okay to make mistakes, to give her time, and talk through options. The Norcross family didn't work that way. Problems were dealt with swiftly and covertly. After all, they couldn't forget about that shiny reputation.

For the next twenty-four hours, Sadie withdrew into herself. Back at home, she holed up in her room, and Deb let herself believe they'd be able to pull off a discreet fix. There was just one problem: Sadie was only one part of the equation. The other part—the part Deb had hoped wouldn't even be included in the discussion—came into play the following morning.

"I told Baz," Sadie confessed to her parents.

Deb smacked her forehead in frustration. "What? Why? Sadie, I told you to keep this between us. You didn't need to bring him into this."

"It's only fair for him to know," Sadie argued. Then, softer, "I was sad. I felt alone. It felt right to tell him. Dad, you agree, right?"

Mark went to speak, but Deb sliced a hand through the air at him. "Mark, don't."

Deb stewed for a minute, pacing in their custom-designed kitchen. She placed both hands on the granite counter with purpose and gave an exaggerated exhale. "We need to have a conversation with Baz and his parents."

Mark crossed his arms. "I don't see why—"

"Baz knows, Mark. And if he knows, there's no telling how fast this could spread. You know how kids talk. We *cannot* let my father find out. This would absolutely crush him. Can you imagine the church..." Her voice hitched like the sky were falling.

"Baz won't tell anyone," Sadie said.

"You don't know that. We need to get this taken care of. And now that it's not just us—now that he's in the loop—we need to be sure the Tanners are on board. We need to be sure they...understand."

And so, because Deb typically got what Deb wanted, the families came together for dinner after an event the following week. A fish and chips joint on the water—as if they didn't get enough water every other day of the year.

"We have something we want to talk to you all about," Deb said, taking the lead. Even Mark was there, a rarity, but that day it was important to show unity. "Sadie is pregnant."

Sadie had hung her head, embarrassed to look at Baz's parents. Deb's announcement was met with a small gasp, deep sigh, and the shaking of heads. Baz sunk in his chair.

"Don't worry," Deb said, speaking softly. "We're taking care of it. This doesn't need to ruin anything. Baz, we're not angry with you. In fact, we think you two are a great couple. But this—this little piece of information—it needs to stay within this circle." She drew her finger around at all of them.

Baz's father tried to speak. "Deb, I...we..."

"Carl, say no more. Really, it's fine. Sadie and I have talked. She's made a decision. We all agree this is for the best." She nodded to Mark, who joined her. "Baz and Sadie will remain pure in the public eye. No one needs to know. Nothing has to change."

There was no opportunity for the Tanners to object. No asking how they felt, what Baz preferred to do. It was a done deal, signed and sealed and presented for no reason other than to ensure loyalty. Deb didn't have to say it outright. If the Tanners wanted their son to retain his clean reputation, for their family to be attached to the great Norcrosses, they'd go along with her plan. It was what was best for their son.

That's exactly what they did.

Which is how Sadie ended up in an exam room six days later with her feet in stirrups and a small suction tube inserted through her cervix. The numbing medicine took away most of the discomfort, but that didn't replace the cement in her stomach or the crack in her heart. When they vacuumed out any and all pregnancy tissue, Sadie felt a part of her soul being sucked away too.

"We'll keep this between us. Us and the Tanners," her mother said, stroking her hand.

"And Willa," Sadie squeaked.

"Yes, and Willa. I'll need to have a talk with her."

"She won't say anything."

"Let's hope not."

Willa spilling Sadie's secret pregnancy and what it would do to her career was the last thing on Sadie's mind, because if truth be told, in that moment, Sadie couldn't have cared less about water skiing. But like the good girl she was, she took three days to recover and heal before hitting the water again, grandfather behind the wheel. And sure enough, when the Miami Pro came in early November—the last comp of the season—Sadie put on a show. No one could have guessed the trauma she'd endured or the brokenness inside her. All anyone saw was the beautiful, up-and-coming skier ready to take over the sport. The girl with endless possibilities, zero problems, and a boyfriend clearly enamored by her.

That's what everyone saw. Everyone but Willa.

"Are you...okay?" Willa asked when she caught Sadie in a rare moment alone in Miami. "I mean, how are you, you know, feeling?"

"What? Oh, that! Yeah, I'm fine. Everything's...fine." Sadie smiled, but it fell short of ringing true. She averted her gaze.

Willa stepped closer, her voice quiet. "So everything's okay with the baby? Your family, they were okay with everything?" She hadn't seen Sadie since that last tournament when Sadie had been sick in the bathroom. As far as Willa knew, Sadie had told her parents and life moved on. While she imagined the Norcrosses had been less than thrilled, they must have come to accept it, because here Sadie was, seemingly happy and skiing again. Her stomach was as flat as ever, and Willa wondered when Sadie would begin to show.

A shadow cast over Sadie's face. "There is no baby."

Willa's breath hitched. She must have misheard. "No baby? But you said you were—"

"And now I'm not."

Heat met Willa's face. "Oh, I thought...I mean...I'm sorry." She didn't understand. Did the baby die? That happened sometimes, she thought. Miscarriages. She remembered her mother's friend crying at the kitchen table, Autumn draping an arm around her shoulders. *Some babies just aren't meant to be*, her mom explained to her later. Maybe that's what happened with Sadie's baby. Maybe it was all the skiing. Willa scrambled to find some words of comfort. "It's not your fault."

Four quick words and Sadie folded forward, dropping her chin to her chest. Even though no sound came out, her shaking shoulders told Willa that Sadie was crying. Willa leaned in, put a hand on Sadie's back. The touch was like a release button, allowing Sadie to fall into Willa's arms. They stood there in that surprising embrace, and Willa was reminded of the last time she'd held Sadie, only a few weeks earlier. Eerily similar, and yet completely different.

A man walked past, giving the girls a look of concern. Willa's better sense kicked in. Sadie was a mess, and there were too many people around to witness such a private moment. She dragged Sadie behind a pop-up vendor tent, hidden away from any onlookers.

"It's okay," Willa soothed. What could she say? It wasn't like she'd ever known anyone her age who'd gotten pregnant. She didn't know what Sadie needed, what would be the most comfort, but silence felt dumb, and so she said the only thing that came to mind. "Some babies just aren't meant to be."

Sadie sniffed. "You don't understand."

"You're right, I don't know what it's like to be pregnant, and I don't know what it's like to have a miscarriage. I'm just trying to—"

"I didn't have a miscarriage." Sadie's face hardened, like part of her youth and beauty had been stolen.

Willa furrowed her brow. "I don't underst—"

"I didn't have a choice." Sadie's voice shook. "They never would have let me keep the baby. It was impossible."

Everything suddenly made sense. "Wait, you had an abortion?"

"Like I said, I didn't have a choice." Sadie looked to the ground, and then crumbled forward again, as if speaking it aloud brought back the physical pain. Willa could almost see the awful memories trickling into Sadie's mind, crawling through her ears and seizing her brain.

Willa shivered picturing it all. Sadie must have been so scared. Did it hurt? It had to. She imagined a doctor reaching inside with a tool like an ice-cream scoop, scraping at the sides to get every last bit. "Sadie, I'm so, so sorry." It felt like an inadequate response, like people who sent *thoughts and prayers* in the face of tragedy when everyone knew those things wouldn't do a damn thing.

Sadie righted herself, wiping her eyes with the back of her hand. "I just want to forget about it, but it's like it's following me. Every time I close my eyes, I see that room, feel that needle."

What was Willa supposed to say? She wasn't a counselor; she was a teenager. As bad as she felt for Sadie, this was beyond her scope. "Maybe you should talk to someone?"

Sadie's eyes snapped wide. She grabbed Willa's shoulders, staring her square in the face. "No. I can't tell anyone, and neither can you. Do you understand? This cannot get out."

"Of course, of course," Willa bumbled.

"You can't say a word. Do you promise?"

The gravity with which Sadie spoke was like that of someone revealing sensitive government information. The code to nuclear weapons. As though if Willa didn't immediately comply, Sadie might go off the deep end. And so Willa nodded vehemently. "I promise. I won't say anything."

Only then did Sadie take a deep breath. She looked skyward and dried any remaining water from the corners of her eyes. Returning her gaze to Willa, she reached out and squeezed Willa's hand. "Thank you."

With that, Sadie strode away. Willa watched her go, momentarily struck by the amazement that someone could carry such a dark secret and pretend it didn't exist. But that thought didn't last long. If anyone knew about the ability to hold secrets, it was Willa.

Chapter 40

NOW

Pregnancy tests don't lie very often, but Sadie took four just to be sure.

All four were positive.

Sadie sat back against the bathroom vanity, knees pulled into her chest, staring at the line of tests before her like little plastic soldiers. And that's when the memories flooded in, bringing with them a rainbow of emotions from a time she thought she'd buried down deep. She remembered that time so clearly. The fear, the shame. The anger she snuffed out like a candle at the end of the day. At that time, she'd been torn apart with such fluctuating emotions, it felt like whiplash.

When they'd sat with Baz's family, she hadn't eaten a single bite of her meal. Nausea made it impossible—not sickness caused by the baby inside her, but by the conversation being held with the people at the table.

She'd been taught to obey her parents. What they said was right and true. She trusted them. Only sitting there, it all felt so...wrong. Something icky nagged at her that day when they'd gotten up from the table at the restaurant, the dads shaking hands, the moms giving each other a knowing look, and only she and Baz standing there without touching.

Sadie cringed at the memory of what followed. That sterile room. The smell of blood leaking from her for days. The hollowness, both physically and mentally. She had entered that room one person and left it another.

They'd agreed never to speak of it again, and for over twenty years, they'd kept that promise. But like so many promises, it had been made under the veil of secrecy. How would the world react if they knew sweet, young Sadie had gotten pregnant at sixteen? The family's values would be called into question. The church under fire. Absolutely not. Leather would never stand for it.

And so they'd swept it under the rug, along with any emotion Sadie or Baz tied to it. Deb had a special way of hanging it over their heads, making subtle references that kept Baz from ever leaving. *You owe her.* The guilt made him stay.

For so long, Sadie operated as though it had been a dream, something she'd seen in a movie, not her real life. But now, with the pregnancy sticks in front of her, the past came barreling back. Sadie placed a hand on her chest and counted to ten with each inhale. She couldn't hide. She was no longer a child needing protection. This time, she could make her own choices.

If only she knew what she wanted.

Chapter 41

Travers Grand Prix
Groveland, FL
October 8

The Travers Grand Prix was unlike any other event in the season. It was a team event, where one pro skier would be paired with two amateur participants to compete in three events: water skiing, go-karting, and skeet shooting. If one thought this was a random combination, they'd be right. But that's what made Travers so different. The competition element was still there, but more than that, athletes were encouraged to have fun. Try something new. For many, it was the entertainment highlight of the year. Where else would such seemingly unrelated activities fuse into one giant competition?

Being back in tournament mode felt different for Willa. It was the first race since her dad's death, and even though her parents never came to events anyway, she liked to imagine them at home watching the live stream and cheering her on. Call it wishful thinking, fool's paradise—whatever it was, it had always been a false assurance, just something she could pretend to hold onto. Now, Willa knew it was absurd. Her parents were gone. Any delusions she'd carried with her as a kid were now impossible.

When she hopped into the water, it embraced her like a long-lost friend. *Welcome home.* A true Scorpio, being a water sign was more than just semantics. She lived and breathed for the vitality water brought her, almost as though the universe knew her destiny long before she did.

For Willa, arriving at Travers would usually mark the nearing of the season's end. A chance to unwind a little before the final big event the first weekend of November. But this year, things felt different. The pressure mounted higher than any year before. Lines had been drawn in the sand, especially after Sadie's wild accusation of Willa tampering with the tow rope. Things were on a new level. You couldn't just go around throwing out those kinds of charges. Willa wouldn't let her name be dragged down when she'd done nothing wrong.

And so the fun of Travers was diluted by the reinstated need to win. Willa would go on to ski her personal best on that October morning. She never looked stronger, more focused. Simply put, she nailed the course— and the crowd loved it. Only then did she let herself come down enough to enjoy the other contests. She laughed at the go-karts taking the inner turns too hard and spinning out of control. Sipped from a can of beer as her teammate yelled, "Pull!" and followed the clay pigeon into the air with the end of her rifle. *Bang!* The disc exploded into dust. Who knew skiers were so multi-talented?

* * *

Sadie's performance wasn't so hot.

After a trip to the doctor and a blood test to confirm the pregnancy, Sadie had been given the go-ahead to keep skiing for the next month before she'd have to hang it up temporarily. For now, it was safe to continue.

She still hadn't told anyone—not even Baz—about the baby. It was still so new in her brain, and aside from sore breasts and feeling sluggish, she sometimes forgot altogether. Perhaps it was a coping mechanism—if she didn't think about being pregnant, she wasn't actually pregnant. She could pretend things were okay. That her marriage wasn't in trouble. That she wasn't living someone else's dream.

But pretending only went so far in the world of water skiing. You either performed well or you crashed and burned. And that October day at the Travers Grand Prix, Sadie did the opposite of what she'd hoped. She missed balls that she never missed. It was a terrible showing, and her team suffered for it.

The audience hummed with confusion, as though they weren't watching Sadie Norcross at all. *Who is this imposter and what did she do with the real Sadie?* Not even good work in the go-kart or skeet shooting events could lift her team from the grave. The two amateurs who'd been paired with her initially thought they'd hit the jackpot—fucking yes!—only to be served a giant slice of humble pie. Evidently, queens could be dethroned.

Sadie waded back to shore through the marshy perimeter of the lake, ski out in front as a false defense against any gators that might have slipped in unnoticed. Her head hung, feet sinking heavy into the muck at the bottom.

The results were crushing. Somehow, Sadie trailed Willa not just that day, but in overall season points. And with only one event left to finish the year, Sadie found herself in a very unfamiliar position. Behind.

She didn't like it.

* * *

As Willa stood atop the podium in front of a white backdrop splashed with black and red sponsor logos, she processed the rarity of the moment. She looked to her left and right. No Sadie. Sadie hadn't even made the podium. Willa couldn't recall a time—ever—when this had happened. Her posture swelled.

"Bet on Betts!" the crowd chanted. Willa raised the prized gold plate above her head as cameras clicked away. She beamed, flushed from both ends of the emotional spectrum. It felt like an unimaginable milestone, one that came with the bittersweet realization that for all the people celebrating her win, there were two who couldn't—even if they never would have.

Forget about them.

Willa hopped down from the top step and grinned at the coach walking toward her.

"I'm so freaking proud of you," Roxanne said, giving Willa a hug. The two mingled with fans for a few minutes, signing autographs on posters and towels and t-shirts. A little girl held up her hand to show Willa a temporary tattoo in the shape of a water ski. The men's teams slapped each other's backs with rounds of *Yo, bro, you killed it today*. Another walked around filming what would be a compilation of clips for his sponsor's YouTube channel.

After the crowd thinned, Willa packed her things into her bag and grabbed her ski. "Ya did good," she said to the board speckled with logos, giving it a pat.

As they walked from the lake, Willa was on a high. She'd go home, take a dip in the hot tub for some muscle recovery, and post a video to Instagram, announcing her big win. The sun beat down, drying her hair into beachy waves. Everything had gone better than planned, and nothing could burst her spirits.

Or so she thought.

Willa stopped in her tracks. A few yards away, she spotted Deb Norcross near the Radar tent.

"Why's Deb Norcross talking to Jimmy Ponce?" she said to Roxanne, who followed Willa's gaze. "Radar is my sponsor. Sadie uses Goode."

Before Roxanne could answer, Willa was tromping in the direction of the tent. "Hi," she said cheerily, like someone catching their spouse cheating. Whatever this was—this little *meeting*—it wouldn't get past her.

"Willa," Jimmy said, surprised. "Hey...uh...great race today."

"Thanks." She put on an overly dramatic smile.

Roxanne caught up. She stood next to Willa, arms crossed, eyebrows arched. "You guys dropping Goode?" she said to Deb.

"Friendly conversation is all," Deb replied.

"I don't know why else you'd be talking with a competing sponsor to your own."

Deb mimicked Willa's smile, though neither was genuine. "Just doing my due diligence as manager. Always on the lookout for what's best for Sadie."

"I'm pretty sure Radar likes to represent winners," Roxanne said, as though the rep wasn't standing there with a dumb look on his face.

Jimmy blubbered. "I, uh..."

Willa snorted. They hadn't even *tried* to conceal their conversation, for goodness' sake. She met Deb's eyes. "Stay away from my sponsor." It suddenly became more than Willa versus Sadie. More than who repped who. This was her income they were messing with.

Deb raised her hands in surrender. "There's no rule against chit-chat." She looked back to the panicked rep. "Feel free to give me a call, Jimmy. You have my number." And then she walked away. Jimmy quickly darted from the hot zone.

Alone again, Willa gaped at Roxanne. "What the hell?"

"She's just trying to get to you," Roxanne said, leading Willa to their car. "Don't let her. There's no way Sadie's leaving Goode. It's all a ruse. Probably payback for that whole rope bullshit."

Steam blew from Willa's ears. "Why can't that family give someone else a chance in the spotlight? It's like they're obsessed. Like they don't know how to stay in their own lane. I swear, if Sadie steals my sponsorship, I'll kill her."

"She won't. Radar would be crazy. Wills, you just won Travers and Sadie didn't even place."

Willa told herself to calm down. Roxanne was right. But the feeling still lingered the whole drive home and into the night. Sadie got everything Willa wanted. Wins. Followers. Sponsors.

Even Baz.

Chapter 42

CrimeWatch Blog

BREAKING: "Tragedy on the Water: What Really Happened?"
posted November 5, 4:38 p.m.

A thrilling day on the water ended in devastation at the Miami Pro waterski event today, and questions still swirl about the deadly explosion that left one dead and several others injured. Official reports have confirmed that the explosion was no accident, but the details of what happened and why remain shrouded in mystery.

Let's break down what we know so far—and what we don't.

The identity of the person killed has been withheld out of respect for the family, but sources close to the investigation describe them as a prominent figure in the sport. Some claim it was a beloved insider, while others suggest the individual may have known too much about the business's shadowy underbelly. Was the victim simply in the wrong place at the wrong time? Or were they the intended target?

Here's where things get murky. Multiple theories have emerged:

1. Rivalries Run Deep: The waterskiing world, glamorous as it may seem, is no stranger to fierce rivalries. It's not just the athletes competing—coaches, sponsors, and families are all deeply invested in the outcomes. Could a grudge between competitors have boiled over?
2. Financial Corruption: Rumors have long swirled about questionable dealings behind the scenes—sponsorship deals, illicit substances, and even rigged results. Could the explosion be tied to an effort to silence someone who knew too much?
3. A Personal Vendetta: Some insiders hint that the victim may have been caught in a personal conflict. A lover's quarrel? Family drama? Or perhaps someone seeking revenge for a perceived betrayal?

What's next?

The waterskiing community remains shaken by the tragedy, and the investigation continues. Sources suggest that more answers—and perhaps more shocking revelations—could surface. But for now, this story remains one of tragedy and unanswered questions.

As more details emerge, we'll be watching closely. Stay tuned for updates, and be sure to follow us for all the latest breaking crime news.

Chapter 43

Willa wore a dress about one night a year, and this was it—the IWWF Awards Dinner. She stood back from the bathroom mirror to take in her reflection. The little red dress hugged her in all the right spots, hitting at mid-thigh to show off her toned legs. The halter style accentuated her shoulders, which poked out from behind the thick, dark hair she'd spent forty minutes curling.

She looked like a doll on display, all shiny and new, full makeup and even heels for the finishing touch. The look couldn't have been more opposite from her real-life approach to appearances, but it was also one of the biggest nights of the year for her sport. The Oscars of water skiing, if you will. The athletes took it seriously. Willa wanted to stand out, and red was just the color to do so. She hoped the little Marc Jacobs number would turn heads—a particular head—just enough before she needed to return it to the designer website from which she'd rented it. Sort of like Cinderella's stagecoach turning back into a pumpkin at midnight, Willa would return home and strip out of the form-fitting dress and into sweats.

But not now. Not yet. First, she had some awards to win.

The dinner was held in the ballroom of a hotel in Gainsville, for reasons the federation attributed to the venue's scenery and renowned menu, but what Willa could only guess was because Gainsville sat equidistant from where both she and Sadie lived. It would be a disaster if one of them didn't show up—the IWWF didn't want to risk that—so it had chosen a mid-point, a comfortable hour and a half drive for each of them.

Willa picked up Roxanne—her plus-one—on the way out of Orlando. The coach opened the passenger door. "These Spanx are crawling up my ass," she said, and both women cackled. Roxanne shimmied in her black dress. The sheer mesh sleeves gave a hint at the strong arms underneath. It was so true—the getup might be fun for an evening, but nothing beat a relaxed t-shirt and shorts.

"Look at you," Roxanne continued, as Willa pulled back onto the road. "Very Jessica Rabbit."

"She gets the guy doesn't she?"

"Honey, she's married to a rabbit."

"Whatever," Willa laughed.

On their drive, Roxanne flipped through social media, landing on IWWF's Instagram page. "Tonight's the night!" she read from the caption on the latest post. "Still time to vote!" Turning to Willa she said, "Think I should vote too? Hmmm...Who is my favorite female athlete?"

Willa gave her a punch in the arm. "Very funny."

To outsiders, the awards might have seemed silly, but to Willa, being named Fans' Choice was a big deal. It was the first year for this new category, a way for the association to engage with the public, to encourage interaction with the fans. Points and scores were one thing, but being the most popular—that was something Willa had little experience with. One too many memories of childhood bullies and always feeling less than made tonight more than a dumb trophy.

* * *

The ballroom glittered with the soft shimmer of chandeliers. Organizers had set up a red carpet leading into the wide open space, along which several event photographers snapped pictures of incoming attendees.

"Willa! Over here!"

She posed, one hand on her hip, the other dangling down, clutching a small, ridiculous bag that held no more than her phone. She'd even forgotten the lipstick for reapplication after dinner.

"Great! Now one with Roxanne?" the photographer said.

The women stood together, smiling. A round of clicks from the cameras. Willa was just about to shift into another pose—didn't Angelina Jolie always stick a leg out?—when everyone's attention turned.

"Sadie! Sadie!" the photographers called. "Sadie! Baz!"

Willa looked over her shoulder, and sure enough, the golden couple had arrived. Sadie had gone for the ethereal look, it seemed, with a thin layer of the palest pink chiffon flowing out behind her. Her hair was blown out, so slick and blond it practically glowed. One arm reached back behind her, and Willa realized that hand was interlocked with Baz's. He came up behind her, and the two cemented themselves on the red carpet like perfect smiling statues.

"Beautiful, you two!"

"Another one, right here!"

"How about a kiss?"

Willa's stomach turned. She should carry on down the carpet and find her seat amongst the dozen round tables set with china. But like a train wreck you can't help but stare at—that horrible cliché—she didn't look away. Instead, she watched as Baz leaned in and pressed his lip to his wife's. A small peck that told a far bigger story.

"Come on," Roxanne said, shepherding Willa away. After circling tables and reading name tags, they found their seats near the front. The table was set with six settings. Willa peered to see the other names, who they'd be sitting with.

She gasped. Her mouth went slack. This had to be a joke.

Sadie and Baz were among the other four at the table.

"Are you kidding me?" she said louder than intended.

"What?" Roxanne said, and Willa pointed. "No. Are these people really that thick in the head?"

Willa rolled her neck. She'd been looking forward to the evening, and this put a massive damper on it. Now she'd have to sit across from Sadie and Baz and watch them interact all night. Nuzzling noses. Holding hands. No amount of alcohol would make it tolerable.

"I'm not doing this," Willa said, all but ready to take her stupid mini purse and leave.

Roxanne placed a hand on her knee. "An hour. Let's just get through dinner, then it will be awards, then we can go. Okay? This is a big deal. I know you don't want to miss it."

Willa swallowed hard. She looked around the room and found a server with a bottle of champagne. She waved him over and held out her glass.

"Fill 'er up."

Chapter 44

Sadie noticed Willa and Roxanne sitting at one of the front tables, and she prayed her seat would be on the opposite side of the room. As she and Baz mingled with other athletes—everyone looked so nice!—she discreetly peeked at name tags for her own. Nothing yet. The further into the room they went, the more Sadie's throat began to tighten. Now there were only two tables left, the one where Willa sat, and another with a few empty chairs.

Please be that one.

Sadie casually approached, only to read the names Harper Cruz and Christina Bear. Her heart dropped. That meant...

She glanced at Willa's table and the two rivals locked eyes, both with deadpan expressions like, *I don't like this any more than you do.*

"I'm not sitting with her," Sadie hissed at Baz. "Why would they do that? It's just fucking mean."

Baz's cheeks burned. Sitting at the same table between Sadie and Willa was the last thing he wanted either. And yet, they couldn't just leave...could they? It was a big event. He imagined the tongue-lashing they'd get from Sadie's mother and grandfather. *Everything is about appearances.*

"It's just for appearances," he found himself saying, though he didn't believe it himself. "Let's just get this over with." He led the way, practically dragging Sadie. "IWWF sure has a twisted sense of humor," he said when they reached the table. The joke landed flat. Not one of the women cracked as much as a smirk.

Baz pulled out a chair for Sadie and she sat. She took a sip from the water goblet.

"You might want something stronger than that," Willa said.

Sure enough, as though she'd magically materialized him herself, the server appeared with a fresh bottle. "Champagne, anyone?"

Baz nodded, and the server filled his flute. Moving onto Sadie, he extended the bottle, but she blocked him with her hand.

"None for me, thanks."

Willa eyed her. Sadie's cheeks were rosy. She exuded a quiet vibrancy, a radiance. What makeup did she use?

Before long, the room had filled with athletes. Around the tables, people chattered and clinked glasses, laughed, and told stories. Another season almost complete. Only one event left—the biggest. Sadie needed no reminding that it would be the last chance for her to earn enough points to surpass Willa. But those concerns were for another day. Right now, she needed nothing more than to survive the next few hours sitting in close proximity to the woman she suspected her husband secretly still loved.

Torture, in a word.

The whole of dinner, Baz and Sadie kept up those tight appearances that had been preached upon them. "Marriage is a divine institution," Jed had said in a recent meeting. "Your husband is your leader and protector. You should always look upon him with tenderness and love."

Tenderness and love. It was easy enough to keep up the façade. Baz reached for the bread basket for Sadie. Sadie, in turn, rested her hand on his in between courses. Very little conversation happened during that tense meal. The other skiers at the table tried their best to carry a dialogue, but after a while, gave up, hoping it would soon be time for awards.

The entire time, Willa caught herself looking at Baz. His deep blue suit complemented his skin tone, bringing out his eyes and hair in a way she wasn't used to. Was this the same man who had kissed her in the hospital lobby? She studied his lips, trying to remember. It all felt like an alternate life. She couldn't place the man before her—the man with a glowing wife on his arm—to the man she'd pined over for years.

Suddenly, just as small plates of cherry cheesecake were placed in front of them, a shift rocked Willa to her core. Disruption bubbled inside her, and she felt lightheaded. What was this feeling? She stared at Baz again, scanning herself from head to toe, searching and analyzing. Something felt different. In short, Willa was utterly tired.

"Check, check."

They turned to find the IWWF president tapping on the microphone. His patent leather shoes were so shiny they were practically blinding, and Willa wondered if he'd bought them new just for the evening.

"Welcome everyone," he said. "I'd like to start by thanking you all for being here, and to the lovely staff for pulling off such a gorgeous event." Everyone clapped. "The yearly awards dinner is one of the highlights of the season, a chance for all of us to come together to celebrate this sport we love so much and to honor the best of the best. You're all here tonight because you represent the highest talent in professional water skiing. And that is quite an accomplishment."

Another round of applause. Someone whistled.

"As you know, the culmination of tonight's festivities is the awards." He lowered his voice and smirked. "Let's not pretend to hide the competitiveness in this room."

Willa folded her hands in her lap. Her red nails matched her dress. Dammit, why did she try so hard?

Three other officials stepped out onto the stage, each holding an engraved plaque. From where she sat, Willa could almost squint and see the names. If hers wasn't there, she should just get up and leave. Spare herself any further humiliation. But she couldn't get a good enough view, and so, she remained.

"We'll start with Best Male Athlete," the president continued. "After a total of four thousand, six hundred and fifty-seven votes, our winner is...Rocky Cobb!"

Rocky, arguably the most skilled male skier in the pack stood from his table and took the stage, accepting his award to loud cheers. He stepped up to the microphone. "Thank you so much..." His voice drowned out, as Sadie and Willa both imagined what they'd say if their name was announced next.

When he finished, the president resumed his position. "Next is Best Female Athlete. If you think the votes were impressive on the men's side, wait until you hear this. Almost seven thousand votes were cast, and only two hundred separate the winner from the runner-up."

A collective *ooooh* traveled around the room. Sadie sat up straighter. Willa bit the inside of her cheek.

"This year's winner is...Sadie Norcross!"

Sadie pushed her chair back and stood, a closed-lip smile on her face. As she stepped away from the table, she caught a glimpse of Willa, whose eyes were daggers. Splotches crawled up her neck, as red as her dress, as though they'd color-coordinated.

Sadie climbed the three steps to the stage, past Rocky Cobb, who stood off to the side, and accepted her award. "I'm so honored," she said into the microphone, looking out over the room packed with her peers. In the back, a red light indicated a camera was filming. She was probably live on the internet. She imagined her parents jumping up and down in their living room. Leather, somewhere in the church—he always attended Saturday evening service when he was home—probably grinned from wrinkly ear to wrinkly ear.

The world would expect some deep, heartfelt acceptance speech, but Sadie didn't have the stomach for it. Was she proud? Yes. But did it stop short of being truly fulfilling? Also yes. She thanked her family, the water skiing community, and all her fans, quickly adding in Baz at the last second. With a final smile and nod, she stepped back next to Rocky. There was one final award to be given.

From where she stood, she had a clear line of vision to Willa, front and center. But Willa wasn't staring back at Sadie anymore; she was looking at Baz. Without Sadie at the table, it was as if the two were alone, no more protective buffer in the middle. Sadie was slapped with the urge to return to the table immediately.

"Two very deserving recipients," the president said. "And now, we'll move onto the final award of the night. As you likely know, this is a new category this year, voted completely by the fans without any input from the organization." He leaned even further into the microphone. "Without further ado, I'm pleased to announce this year's Fan Choice Award to..."

Sadie glanced at Willa. She appeared to be holding her breath. Would this be Willa's moment? The crowds undoubtedly loved her. She'd really connected with her online audience in recent months. Then again, Sadie's star power had never been higher. And after the scandal with Willa and Baz, public opinion of Sadie had only gone up.

It was a complete toss up, and yet something in Sadie's gut prayed Willa would win. Sadie couldn't manage another speech full of false gratitudes. Willa could take this one. Sadie simply didn't care anymore.

But then the room was applauding again. Wait, what just happened? Did she tune out so much she hadn't heard the winner? Her eyes ping-ponged from the president to Willa. Willa remained seated. The president was looking at Sadie with a toothy grin. Her breath hitched. She'd won? She'd taken home *both* awards? Oh, now her family would *really* be celebrating.

Sadie stepped forward again, taking the second award in her other hand, cradling them like twin babies.

"Go ahead," the president said, a hand on Sadie's back, "the floor is yours."

But she couldn't possibly manage a sentence. What was she supposed to say? *Thank you for loving me so much, I wish my husband felt the same?* Or, *Thank you for giving me an award, but I wish I could quit?*

In the end, Sadie left the crowd with a few short words, and stepped off the stage. Everyone clapped and clapped. *Overcome with so much happiness she can't even speak*, they must have thought. Let them. Let them think whatever they wanted.

Witness #5 Statement

I grew up racing against Sadie and Willa. The only times I had a chance at silver were when one of them wasn't there for whatever reason. Never gold though—that was always for them. They switched on and off who'd be in the top spot. And I have to tell you, no matter which one won, the other always seemed happy for them. I mean, not like *thrilled* happy of course—those girls were fiercely competitive—but they were friends, and friends celebrate each other's successes, right? I knew there was always a bit of rivalry between them, but I thought it was more media hype than anything.

Guess I was wrong.

Chapter 45

November 5
Miami Pro
Miami, FL

The morning sun cast a golden gleam over the lake. It was seven a.m. and already seventy-one degrees—cooler than the mid-summer events that baked in heat and humidity. To Willa, November in Florida was perfection.

Skiers began arriving to the Greater Miami Ski Club where event volunteers had set up tents along the grassy banks. Spectators already had chairs positioned for the best views along the narrow strip of water. Under the broadcast tent, a table and cameras had been erected with a clear shot of the race course. Each lake was different, with its unique shape and characteristics. Like people, bodies of water had personalities, flavors. Some were known to be more cooperative than others. Miami felt exotic, lush with palm trees and drifting ocean breeze.

Willa carried her ski under her arm, backpack slung over her other shoulder. Despite the letdown of the IWWF awards, she was confident coming off her win at Traverse. Not receiving the Fan's Choice Award had stung, and she'd put on a brave face for the few remaining minutes she sat at that table before scurrying out.

The torment of watching Sadie on stage had bitten her like a venomous snake, and later, after the sting wore off, made her question whether she held as much of a place in the fans' hearts as she'd originally thought. She drowned herself in a pint of ice cream that night, throwing herself a pity party. The following morning came with clarity. Of course she wanted the public to like her, but skiing was about so much more than that. It was her lifeline. She didn't need to win a vote to feel validated.

Maybe not a vote. But a hard-earned victory in the water was another story.

Now, they'd made it to the final event of the season, and Willa was at the top of the leaderboard. Six measly points separated her from Sadie. She should have come into this tournament with brash impotence—when had anyone but Sadie been leading going into Miami? And yet, Willa walked with an unsteady stride. It was a big day, and she knew it. So much at stake. So much had happened this season; gone was the typical levity in the pre-race hours. The air felt charged.

Within minutes, Sadie arrived. Willa watched her get out of the passenger side of the SUV, followed by Baz on the other side. Willa's eyes met Baz's for the briefest second before looking away. The familiar belly flutter felt different. She flashed back to the awards dinner, the confusing swirl of thoughts as she sat at the same table with him. Since then, they hadn't spoken. She hadn't even pulled up his Instagram.

What did it mean?

Concentrate, Willa told herself. *You have a job to do.* She sat on the ground and extended her leg, stretching, nose to knee.

"Willa, hi." She looked up. It was Greg Redding, retired pro-turned-sportscaster. He wore a flat-billed baseball cap that made his shaggy hair puff out the sides.

"Hey, Greg."

"I was hoping I could snag you for a pre-race interview?"

Willa switched legs. "Sure, no problem."

"Awesome, thanks. Give me ten to finish setting up my equipment. I'll be just over there." He pointed to the broadcast tent twenty yards away.

Willa nodded. She moved onto her arms, bending one behind her head and pulling on her elbow. The stretch felt incredible.

* * *

When she came around the corner of the tent, Willa stopped in her tracks. Greg was at the table, microphone in hand, but he wasn't alone. Sadie sat to his right, chunky blonde braid draped over her shoulder. Her tank top had the Goode logo in the center, and Willa wanted to sneer, *See? Radar never wanted you anyway.*

Greg waved Willa over. "Sadie was available too, so I figured we'd just do a joint interview. You don't mind, do you?"

Fucking hell. Willa clenched her teeth. Saying no would look catty. Only feed into the narrative.

"Yeah, sure," Willa said. She took a seat beside Sadie, who—Willa swore—scooted a few inches in the other direction, as though they were children and Willa had cooties.

"Okay," Greg said. "We're going live in two." He signaled to the cameraman, who gave a nod.

Willa cleared her throat, and sat up straighter. Sadie did the same. Willa stretched even higher.

The cameraman pointed at Greg, and the livestream started.

"Ladies and gentlemen, welcome to this special pre-race interview. Today, we have two remarkable athletes who I have a sneaky suspicion you'll recognize." Both Willa and Sadie smiled. "Willa Betts and Sadie

Norcross, thank you for joining me here this morning as we get ready for the Miami Pro.

"It's no secret the two of you have been one-upping each other all season. Sadie, you're the reigning champ here in Miami, but Willa had a personal best a few weeks ago at Travers. How do you feel about facing off in such a high-stakes final race and defending your title against such a formidable competitor?"

If it was possible for Willa to grow any taller, she did. Nothing like a little dig live on air. She hoped Sadie felt flustered.

"Thanks, Greg," Sadie said. "You know, I'm feeling really good coming into Miami. I thrive on competition. It's what makes our sport so exciting. Willa has been exceptional this season...but I look forward to the challenge."

Was that a...compliment?

"Willa, what does it mean to you to take on Sadie, who has won here two years in a row?"

Ah, the perfect setup, like Greg handed it to her on a silver platter. Willa leaned closer to the microphone. "Yeah, I mean, there are a lot of great skiers here today. I guess I'm just gonna channel that Swiss Pro energy."

Greg's eyebrows raised playfully at the comment. Willa didn't need to elaborate—anyone watching would know she was referring to the first event of the season where Willa crushed Sadie's seven-year winning streak at the Swiss Pro Slalom event in Clermont. The one where Willa had stolen the purple race bib.

"So you're saying it's time for a new champion?" Greg said, keeping it light. Willa sensed Sadie stiffen, the energy getting cooler.

"I think so, yes."

As he pulled the microphone back toward himself, Sadie quickly grabbed it. "We'll see," she said.

Greg laughed and addressed the camera. "As you can tell, folks, competition is fierce around here." He returned to the women. "Both of you have a history that goes beyond the sport. How do you manage to separate personal tensions from your professional rivalry?"

Willa twisted in her seat. Was he really going there? The whole Baz thing? This was supposed to be about the tournament, nothing else. Willa went to speak, but Sadie beat her to it.

"We're professionals. When we're on the water, our focus is the sport and the race. Off the water, we respect each other. That's what keeps this rivalry healthy." Sadie's smile held a hint of steel as she answered.

"And you agree?" he addressed Willa. "I mean, you guys have been skiing together a long time."

Willa nodded. "We may have our differences, but the competition pushes us to excel. Our personal history stays off the ski course."

It was all diplomatic and restrained, exactly as professionals were taught to be. Scripted questions and scripted answers. But anyone—Greg included—could feel the tension between the women. You'd have to be dead not to.

"There you have it," he said into the camera. "You've heard it from the champions themselves. Today, we'll see an epic showdown that promises excitement and thrill. Stick around for complete coverage of each round, including both men's and women's events, and for all live updates on standings."

Sadie and Willa smiled once more for the camera, then got up and exited the tent. A few feet and they split in separate directions, but not without first a quiet exchange.

"Good luck," Sadie said.

"You too," Willa replied, the comment catching her off guard after all that had transpired.

As they went on their ways, both mumbled the same thing: *I will* not *let her win.*

Chapter 46

arper Cruz killed it in the first round.

"Damn," Sadie said to herself. The pressure was huge. Everyone was on their game. She couldn't let Harper surpass her. They were friends and all, but an underdog victory would put Sadie even further behind.

As second seed, Sadie was up next. She stood on the dock and gave a final stretch skyward, loosening up her arms. While Harper swam into shore, Sadie bent and buckled her feet into the boots.

Harper climbed out of the water.

"Nice run, girl," Sadie said.

"Thanks." Then quieter, "Don't let Willa beat you." She smiled as she said it, using the pretense of shared hatred to bring her closer to the best.

"Oh, she won't," Sadie said, though her stomach said otherwise. Morning sickness had officially kicked in—same as last time—and the normal nerves that came with race days didn't help. Good thing her vest didn't feel tight yet. She was thankful this was the last event of the season before her belly began to grow.

If she let it grow.

She still hadn't decided. But that would have to happen soon—pushing twelve weeks meant she wouldn't be able to hide it much longer. Wasn't there a cut-off point for termination? Tears came to her eyes. What kind of person has two abortions?

Those stormy thoughts had to wait. She couldn't think about babies and secret pregnancies now. She needed to get through this last tournament. If Serena Williams could win the Australian Open while pregnant, surely Sadie could manage less than thirty seconds of skiing. *Suck it up.* She packed it all up and tucked it away in her mind. Later. She'd reveal it all to Baz later.

Sadie hopped into the water. The boat went into gear. Laser-focused, Sadie mentally ran through the course, only barely hearing the announcer's voice booming through the loud speakers. The crowd cheered as the boat idled forward and then flew into speed.

This is it. This is your moment.

If she scored well enough, she could bump Willa from the overall season lead. It was possible—if only she focused and didn't let her mind get in the way.

She soared out to the one ball and rounded it. On to the second and third—yes and yes. Halfway. Each time her ski bounced across the wake, her stomach bounced with it, and Sadie had to actively concentrate not to vomit right there in the middle of her run. The force on her body as she made the turns made her woozy. So many bumps, so many jerks.

When she reached the sixth and final ball, she was barely hanging on. She pulled and leaned. *Come on, come on.* She squinted, extending with all her might. Her ski clipped the edge of the buoy, failing to completely circle it. A sharp gasp came from the crowd.

Sadie let her head fall as she exited the course. Fully and wholly exhausted, every ounce of mental and physical stamina sucked from her. She gracefully dropped into the water. It had been the first run on the longest rope and she'd struggled to finish. Her body was telling her something: it didn't want to be skiing.

Oh, but she had to. There was no other choice.

Or was there?

Something firm settled into her gut. It was time to take matters into her own hands.

Chapter 47

When Sadie missed the last ball at twelve meters, Willa's breath caught in her throat. What the hell happened? A miss like that was so out of character. They'd been skiing at that length and speed since they were kids.

Willa sat in the grass cross-legged, doing her pre-race run-through. She watched as the boat towed Sadie back to shore. Watched Deb at the edge of the dock, one hand on her hip, the other holding the same tumbler with straw. Deb peered down at Sadie below, exchanging indecipherable words.

Willa looked around for the rest of them—the Norcross crew. Leather had to be displeased with that showing. Where was Baz? That family traveled like a pack.

She didn't find them, and instead of reading into it, Willa stood and stripped off her shirt. She was up next. She put on her vest and tucked her mother's sapphire necklace inside. Adjusted the blue race bib. *Time to shine.* She reached up and tightened her ponytail, then grabbed her ski and headed toward the dock. On the way, she passed a dripping wet Sadie, breathing hard. They exchanged no words, not even a glance. Deb followed her daughter, a disgruntled look on her face.

Willa placed her ski down on the wooden dock.

"Let's hear it for our next competitor, currently in first place, Willa Betts!" the announcer hollered into the microphone. A round of applause followed, and Willa gave a quick wave. Her chest was tight, something pecking at her like an incessant beetle. She was the leader, so why didn't she feel better about it?

She knew exactly why.

Willa got her feet into the bindings and took a deep inhale. She looked around, nerves piling on top of nerves. She shook her gloved hands, trying to release the toxic energy. But the nagging continued. Something in the back of her mind. She looked for Sadie. There, a few yards away on the bank, and now Baz was there too. But wait, were they arguing? Their expressions looked tight, body language tense. Sadie spun and stormed off. Willa kept her eyes glued on her. Was this part of the plan?

No time to wonder. She had to ski.

Chapter 48

Thin blades of grass stuck to Sadie's feet as she left the dock area. Her chest rose and fell rapidly with each heavy breath. What a disappointing run. She wasn't hurt outwardly, but the crash wedged a sliver of panic in her mind. There was another life to think about other than her own.

Sadie saw Baz standing not far away, and her body naturally directed her toward him as a habitual source of comfort.

"You okay?" he said.

"Not my best run." Annoyed, she wiped her feet on a towel then slipped them into flip-flops. She crossed her arms.

Baz studied her. "What happened with the six ball?"

Her temper flared. She was just about to snap back something about how not everyone could be perfect all the time—*everyone has bad runs, I don't need your criticism, thankyouverymuch*—when her face changed, eyes popping like the look of someone who just realized something.

"I have to go," she said abruptly, and spun away.

* * *

Baz blinked, his mouth hanging open. *What?* "Sadie, wait," he called. "I didn't mean to— Can't we talk?"

"Just give me a minute," she called over her shoulder. "I... I need to do something. I'll be right back."

Baz watched her hurry away like a woman on a mission. When he turned back to the dock, Willa was sitting on the edge, about to drop in. Her thick ponytail blew in the breeze. He thought of the awards dinner and how incredible she'd looked. Sadie too—they were both beautifully different women.

Reflection pulled him in. He got so lost staring at her that he didn't realize Sadie never returned.

Chapter 49

Where was Roxanne? Willa's coach always gave her the final high-five before each run, but now she was nowhere to be seen. In fact, everyone seemed out of place today. Was it some sort of unseen astrological shift? It made Willa even more on edge. Her senses stood on high alert—for what?

She looked around for Roxanne again. Nothing. And despite all reason, she couldn't help but remember those old feelings of abandonment she wrestled with as a kid.

Something was weird. Roxanne had been off all morning. Short, quiet. Had she slept poorly? Was she not feeling well? Or was it something else? And what was the deal with Sadie and Baz? Sure, Sadie had a bad run, but the way she walked off indicated more. It was the face that gave her away— something registered. Something had hit Sadie like a lightning bolt.

If Willa had the time to contemplate, maybe she could figure it all out. But not now. Now, there was no time.

Willa sat down at the edge of the dock and let her ski drop into the water. The coolness brought goosebumps to her legs. One last event, and then a much-needed break from everything. The year had come with far too much drama. She looked forward to a respite.

"You've got this, Wills!"

Willa turned. Bursting through the line of people on the shore came Roxanne. She shouted, clapping her hands above her head. Her face was red, like she'd been running. From where? Why hadn't she been here on the dock the whole time?

"All set?" the driver said.

All Willa could do was give a quick nod in reply, her mind in a million places. What happened next unfolded in the span of seconds.

The boat engine revved to life and slowly pulled away. Willa gripped the dock's edge, ready to hop into the water, but then there were footsteps behind her. Fast, close. Too late, she'd already pushed off. Willa turned her head as her body left the dock.

Deb was coming toward her. Reaching. What? No, not to her. To something. Something on the dock. Willa followed Deb's gaze. The white tumbler.

"Sorry, I forgot my—"

But Deb didn't get to finish her sentence. Just as Willa's head went under, a sound like she'd never heard pierced her ears, and the dock went up in flames.

Chapter 50

In the immediate aftermath, people thought it was the boat that had exploded. They didn't realize it was actually the dock. Having moved itself just far enough away, the boat suffered damage from flying debris, but the driver and spotter were unharmed. Only one received a few lacerations that required stitches.

As for Willa, the water had saved her. Just as the dock blasted into shards, her head slipped under the surface. It all happened in a flash: Willa pushing off the dock, hearing footsteps, turning, Deb reaching for her tumbler.

A series of simultaneous events. Then, BOOM.

The dock erupted skyward, sending wooden shrapnel in all directions. Willa felt the vibration of the blast, the heat from the surge, but it wasn't until she popped back up from the surface that scraps of wood fell around her. The shockwave had pushed her out farther than where she would have originally landed.

Dust and smoke filled the air, making it hard to see. Her lungs filled with dark air, and she coughed, waving a hand in front of her as if she could wipe away the fog. Her ears buzzed, feeling like they were filled with cotton, and then slowly, sound made its way back. The air began to clear. All around her, people were screaming. Arms flailed, legs sprinted away from the water. Willa kicked off her ski underwater to free her feet. She frantically treaded backward.

"Get out of there!" someone yelled. Willa recognized the voice as Roxanne's, but where was she? Water splashed in her face from her flapping arms. There, she spotted her. Knee-deep in the lake, Roxanne waved Willa toward her with giant swoops. Her face read pure terror. "Willa! Willa, are you okay? Get out of the water!"

Willa swam, but it was as if her limbs didn't work. Shock rendered her paralyzed, an infant unable to make her arms and legs move how she wanted. The screams pierced her ears. She clumsily paddled her way to shore, where Roxanne pulled her out. She staggered to her feet.

"Oh my god, are you okay?" Roxanne cried, wrapping her arms around Willa's neck. Her face scrunched into an ugly cry.

"Wha— what happened?" Willa said, dazed, still looking around, desperate for answers.

"The dock. It blew up! And you were..."

It hit Willa then. "I was on it."

Roxanne's face drained of color. She nodded shakily. Willa's hands went numb. She had been sitting on the dock seconds before it exploded. How close had she just come to a major injury? Or worse—death?

Willa's heart rate hit the roof, and she fought to catch her breath. She braced herself against Roxanne, legs suddenly unable to hold her. The last few minutes replayed in her mind, a million what-ifs. She'd been ready to hop in the water. The boat idled away. Scooted to the edge, pushed off.

Willa's body tingled with a million goosebumps. She was so lucky. If she'd still been on the dock, she could have been—

Willa froze. There *had* been someone on the dock.

Willa whipped her head to where the dock once stood, now a jumble of jagged planks and debris scattered across the surface of the water. Smoke wafted, and a chemical smell that reminded Willa of plastic burning in a campfire hung in the air. The dock—completely gone in a matter of a second. Willa struggled to comprehend.

Her attention drifted. Several people were splashing through the water toward something a few feet from where the edge of the dock used to be. They reached it. Willa squinted. So much commotion. It looked like... No! Willa gasped.

"Oh my god," she cried. "Mrs. Norcross!"

"What?" Roxanne said, following Willa's line of vision.

"Deb!" It all came back into focus. "She was... she was on the dock. Right as I was getting in the water. She forgot her drink."

"Oh my god," Roxanne echoed, bringing a hand to her mouth. They both stood on shaky legs and watched in horror as two men hauled Deb out of the water and laid her on the grass. One of her legs was gone, completely blown off. A stream of bright red blood formed a path from where she'd been dragged. A cry caught in Willa's throat. She strained to look closer, horrified at what she saw. Deb's neck and face bore a criss-cross of gashes. Her eyes were closed, her body limp.

Just then, an on-scene paramedic rushed in, leaned over Deb and began CPR. All around, people screamed orders.

"Call 911!"

"Someone check for a pulse!"

"We need a tourniquet!"

"What happened? Did anyone see anything?"

Willa couldn't even think. Everything whirled around her like she were in a tornado. Only minutes ago, she'd been getting ready to ski, and now a terrible accident changed everything.

But was it an accident? What exactly had happened? The details still weren't clear. All anyone knew was the frantic pulse of panic.

Willa and Roxanne ran closer to where more people had gathered around Deb.

"She's not breathing," someone said. "I think she's..."

Anyone with a brain could see Deb was gone. Her lips were already turning blue. The paramedic desperately patted Deb's face. "Come on, stay with me." Zero response. Just a limp head and a body's worth of blood draining from a gaping hole that should have held a leg.

"Let me through!" came a man's voice, a voice Willa knew instantly. Baz pushed his way through the onlookers, falling on his knees beside his mother-in-law. "Oh my god, Deb!" He visibly shook, and Willa ached at his pain. She couldn't help herself. She flung down next to him, wrapping him in her arms. Tears poured from her eyes, as her body processed the shock. Still, the whole time she wondered, *where is Sadie?*

"I'm so sorry," someone said. Willa couldn't be sure who. The paramedic fell back, exhausted from so much exertion in vain. Around the circle, people were all crying and shaking their heads, hands to their mouths.

No, Willa thought. *No, she can't be...*

The sound of sirens cut through the air, gradually getting louder. But the sirens were nothing compared to the scream that came next.

"MOM!"

Sadie barreled in with superhuman speed. She kept saying it over and over. *Mom! Mom! Mom!* A cry of pure and primal fear. A sound altogether unholy. She fell on top of Deb, face to face, shaking her mother's lifeless body, willing her to wake up. "No!" she howled.

It was a scene no person should have to witness. Something Willa wouldn't wish on her worst enemy.

Baz laid a hand on his wife's shoulder. "Sadie," he said.

And that's when Sadie turned and saw them: Baz and Willa, her arm around him, their bodies too close.

"You did this!" Sadie hurled at Willa, finger pointed like a dagger.

Willa recoiled. "What? No!"

"You killed her. You did it to hurt me." People gasped.

"Sadie, no! I would never!"

"You couldn't stand the thought of losing to me again. Just like you can't stand that Baz is with me and not you."

"You're crazy! I was on the dock too, remember? Just a second before. Your mom... she came back. She wasn't even supposed to be there."

When she said it, her body went cold. *She wasn't supposed to be there.* Deb wasn't supposed to be on the dock. She'd only come back because she'd forgotten her tumbler. Only one person should have been on the dock when it exploded.

Her.

Chapter 51

Sadie hadn't been by the water at the time of the explosion for a reason only she knew. She'd hurried off after a tense conversation with Baz. Eyes forward, one thing on her mind. Some people might have wondered why. What was with the snippy exchange? The curious moment where her face had lost all expression and gone ghost pale. Did Sadie know something was about to happen? Was she running away to avoid being at the scene—or worse, to somehow...cause it?

None of those.

Sure, Sadie was agitated after her ski run. And yeah, she wasn't in the mood to rehash the whole thing with Baz. But that moment when something struck her, it wasn't some sinister realization or premeditated plan.

In that moment, she'd felt a warm trickle between her legs. Not lake water. A sensation much like the times her period came out of nowhere when she wasn't prepared. Only, it couldn't be her period. Pregnant women didn't get their periods.

Her insides had frozen, her neck stiffened.

The crash. The baby.

No. Please no.

And then she'd left a perplexed Baz and dashed to the bathroom, where she discovered a squishy blood clot inside her suit. It was as she was wiping the stain with a wad of toilet paper that she heard the boom.

Chapter 52

When the ambulance carrying Deb's body pulled away, Sadie and Baz followed in their car, leaving behind a stunned group of athletes and spectators. The few who remained wore tear stains down their cheeks, smudged mascara that was no match for its waterproof claims. An indescribable layer of shock and confusion blanketed the entire lake, and now with police already examining the area, a general sense of realization hit. This hadn't been an accident. Docks don't just explode on their own. This had been a targeted attack.

Willa sat at a picnic table across from a police officer in a short-sleeve black uniform. A dark tattoo peeked out on his upper arm. He wore a stern, determined expression.

Willa hugged her middle, unable to stop the trembling of her body, like aftershocks hours post-earthquake.

"Did you see anything? Anything at all?" the officer said.

Willa shook her head. "I was just getting ready to ski."

"So, nothing out of the ordinary."

"No."

It had been less than an hour since the explosion, and already the pieces were coming together. Willa caught snippets of conversations, heard words like *IED, metal cylinder, fuse.* But the why and the who—those remained unanswered.

"Was it really a bomb?" Willa said. The word made her shudder. Who would do such a thing? These people, this community, she'd known them her whole life.

"All signs point to yes. We've found pieces that appear to be from a homemade explosive device."

Willa's pulse pounded. "And it just happened to go off?"

The detective's eyes flicked down then back to Willa's face. "No. It was remotely detonated."

"Someone purposely exploded it at that very second?"

"That's what it looks like."

"But... but that means whoever did it knew I was on the dock. And...and..." She couldn't catch her breath. Her body shook. Someone draped a towel over her wet shoulders.

"I'm sorry," the detective said. "I know how disturbing this must be. That's why we need to find out who is responsible. You weren't the only one on the dock at the time, as we know. Mrs. Norcross..." his voice trailed off.

Yes, Deb had been on the dock, but she wasn't supposed to be. Or was she? Nothing made sense. Too many circumstances. Too much chaos. And yet, the primary question lingered: if the bomb was triggered, had it been intended for Deb or for Willa?

***

"Ms. Hill, we understand you and Mrs. Norcross had a bit of a contentious history." A new detective sat with Roxanne now. Sweat left rings in the underarms of his button-down shirt. He flipped his notepad to a clean page.

"I'm not sure what you mean." Roxanne's usually calm demeanor rattled. The sun arched in the sky, bumping the temperature into the eighties at only ten in the morning. Perspiration speckled her forehead. She felt light-headed.

"You were, how should I say it, rivals?"

"Deb and I skied against each other for twenty years, yes."

"And you weren't exactly friends during that time."

Roxanne set her jaw, defenses rising. There was no way around it. "No, we aren't—I mean, weren't—friends." Switching to past tense made her ill.

"Ms. Hill, where were you in the moments before the bomb went off? If I'm not mistaken, coaches are typically on or near the dock when their athlete is getting ready to ski. When we spoke to Willa, she said she had been looking for you, but you were nowhere to be found."

He made it sound far more dramatic than need be. "I was down the lake a bit, getting a picture for Willa's Instagram. I didn't realize she was already up, but when I heard her name announced, I hurried back." The detective eyed her, then wrote something on the notepad. "Why are you asking me this?"

"We're just trying to figure out who would want to hurt Mrs. Norcross."

"Listen," Roxanne said, pumping her hands. "Deb and I had our issues, but I would never, *never*, try to kill her. What reason would I have?"

"I'm not accusing you, Ms. Hill."

"Well, it feels like it. And don't you think you should be more concerned about Willa being the target? She was the one sitting on the dock directly above whatever exploded. Deb's being there was pure coincidence."

"We're looking into all angles. But since you brought it up, do you have an idea of someone who would want to hurt Willa? Does Willa have any enemies?"

Roxanne stared at him like he was an idiot. This was a professional sport they were talking about. Maybe "enemy" was too strong a word, but did Willa have opponents? People who would love to see her fail?

Absolutely.

***

The police couldn't question Sadie or Baz at the scene because the two weren't there. Instead, they held each other in the basement of the hospital, where Deb's body laid on a cold metal table.

Distraught and disoriented, a kind doctor led them to a small conference room where police gathered, offering condolences that did nothing. Sadie had phoned her father with the news—the hardest call she'd ever made. They'd wailed and wept. Mark was now on his way, but until then, Sadie found needed comfort in her husband's arms.

"I don't understand," she repeated over and over. "Why? Why?"

"My deepest sympathies," the same detective said. His face was sober, and yet his expression hinted that he was there for more than condolences. This wasn't a small mishap—it was murder. "I'm afraid I need to ask you both some questions. I realize given the circumstances it's the last thing you probably feel like doing, and I'm sorry for that, but time is of the essence for our investigation."

"My mother just died," Sadie hurled at him.

"And that's precisely why we need to figure out who did it and why."

"You think it was planned?" Baz asked.

"Planned?" Sadie said. "Of course it was planned. That bitch Willa and her pathetic coach." Spit gathered in the corners of her mouth.

The detective cleared his throat. "Actually, we think your mother happened to be in the wrong place at the wrong time."

Sadie's face scrunched into a question mark. "I'm not following."

"We don't think she was the target. We think it was Willa Betts."

"Willa?" Baz breathed, and Sadie looked to him, seeing the way his face twisted in agony at her name, and something inside her broke. Her eyes quickly turned sad.

"Ms. Norcross, it's become clear to us that you and Willa have somewhat of a complicated history. And given the headlines this summer..."

"What are you saying?" Sadie said.

The detective stared at her, and it became clear what he was getting at. The kiss at the hospital. The media frenzy and all the speculation that followed. What wife wouldn't be hell-bent on revenge?

"Are you accusing me of trying to kill Willa?" Sadie spat. "I wasn't even near the dock!"

"Where were you?"

Her mouth clamped shut. It struck her right then. Not only had she just lost her mother, but she was also losing her baby. Her belly cramped. "The bathroom."

"The bathroom?"

"Yes. I...I wasn't feeling well." The detective narrowed his eyes. Sadie thought about blurting it out—*I'm pretty sure I'm having a miscarriage, okay?*—but held back. It wasn't his business, and she couldn't wrap her head around it in the moment anyway.

"Did anyone see you?"

Baz spoke up. "I saw her heading in that direction. We were talking and she said she had to pee."

Sadie looked at her husband, trying to recall the exact wording of their conversation. She'd been short with him, and then she'd felt the blood. Had she said she was going to the bathroom? No, not specifically. So why was Baz covering for her? Did he think she was somehow involved in all of this?

"Okay," the detective said, taking notes. "Your father, he wasn't at the event, correct?"

"He had to work. He doesn't come to every tournament."

"And would you say that he and your mom had a healthy marriage?"

Sadie blinked. If she knew anything about marriage, it was that what you saw on the outside wasn't always a realistic picture. She found herself suddenly curious, re-examining her parents through snapshots like a film reel in fast forward. What she saw was mostly happy, smiling people. But was that the truth?

Thinking of her father as anything but a good person made her sick. There was no way she could reconcile anything else. She shook her head. "My parents love each other. Plus, like I said, my dad wasn't even there."

"It doesn't mean he wasn't involved."

Sadie gaped at the impossibility, but before she could come to his defense, the detective was already moving on.

"Now, tell us about Willa's coach, Roxanne Hill. We understand she and your mother were competitors for many years."

"Yes," Sadie said.

"Ms. Hill admitted to us that she and your mother were not friends. Do you know anything about this? Do you think Roxanne would have some sort of vendetta against your mom?"

Sadie shrugged, mind whirling trying to keep up with the direction of the conversation. "I... I have no idea." The truth was, she didn't know much about Roxanne at all, aside from her being Willa's coach and the less-than-sunny things Deb said. Sure, she'd witnessed the women being frosty toward one another, but that didn't prove anything more than the fact that some people just didn't get along. Period.

"I thought you said my mom wasn't the target," Sadie said, confused. "Why are you asking me about Roxanne? She obviously wouldn't have wanted to hurt Willa."

The detective folded his hands on the table. "True. But we're just trying to get a sense of all dynamics involved. The full picture. So, as we see it, witnesses saw you, Baz, on the shore. Sadie, you were in the bathroom. Your father wasn't present at the event. Correct?"

Sadie nodded. "Yes, I already said that. He wasn't there. But the rest of us were." At that, her body seized and a tingling spread from her core out to the tips of her fingers. *The rest of us.* The Norcrosses were a group. She, Baz, her parents, and... one other person. The one she hadn't yet spoken to. The one she had forgotten about in the pandemonium of the last hour.

Her grandfather.

Chapter 53

They found him exactly where Sadie said he'd be—at the church. Less than five hours had passed since the blast, and yet for Sadie, time dragged in slow motion.

"We're looking for Bill Norcross," the detective said to a woman behind the welcome desk. When she didn't immediately respond, he added, "Leather."

The woman's eyes darted, cheeks flushed. "Um, I'm afraid...I'm not sure if—" She shuffled papers, heat visibly rising above her pretty floral top.

"It's alright, Denise," a man's voice said. "I'll take it from here." The detective, Sadie, and Baz turned to find Pastor Jed. He approached them, polished as ever, cane aiding his slow steps. "Sadie," he said, "I'm so sorry to hear about your mom. We're all shocked. Truly devastated. What a senseless, senseless tragedy."

How had he heard so fast? A flare went off in Sadie's chest.

"And you are...?" the detective said.

Jed extended a hand. Age spots covered his twisted knuckles. "Jedidiah Abraham. I'm the pastor of this church."

"We're looking for Bill Norcross," the detective repeated. "His granddaughter seemed to think we might find him here."

"Hmmm." Jed scratched his chin. "I haven't—"

Maybe it was the smug look on Jed's face, too soon and too repulsing after her mother had just been killed, but Sadie couldn't stand it.

"Cut the crap, Jed," she said. "He has to be here. He's always here." Her hands trembled at her side, shocked by her own brazenness. She'd never spoken to Jed this way—her grandfather would have been appalled. Her brain played tug-of-war between loyalty and justice. How could she go against the people she'd been taught to obey? And yet, how could she not do what was right?

Jed blinked several times. "Well, what exactly do you want with him?"

The detective cocked his head, clearly irritated. "We need to ask him some questions."

"This is a place of worship, sir, and I don't think you can just—"

Sadie gave a loud exhale. "Follow me," she said, storming past Jed. Baz and the detective followed.

She knew the church like the back of her hand. It had been her playground as a child. So many Sunday school classes, so many retreats and camps. Enough group prayer to last a lifetime.

Sadie wasn't sure what led her to the sanctuary, but it was as if her feet knew where to go. The lights were off—strange for the middle of the day, even outside service times—but a faint glow seeped in from the large windows near the ceiling. Countless rows of seats in every direction all faced a large stage at the front, where a projection screen was flanked by elaborate lighting and sound equipment. She'd always thought it felt more like a concert hall than a church. This was nothing like the chapels she read about in books. This was something else altogether.

Her eyes scanned left and right, up and down. Empty and quiet, it didn't take long for Sadie to see him. When she did, her heart clenched. Leather sat in the second row, arms braced on the chair in front of him, head down, as though in prayer...or repentance?

Chills overtook her, and all at once an incredible sadness descended. Without any proof, she knew. Something very tragic had happened at her grandfather's hand.

They approached quietly, until a few feet away, he spoke, stopping them in their tracks. His head remained down, like he foresaw their arrival.

"I didn't mean to," Leather said, voice shaky. "It wasn't supposed to... Not her..."

Sadie and Baz exchanged horrified looks. Tears welled in her eyes, spilling over. She winced as though in physical pain.

"Mr. Norcross," the detective said, stepping forward. "We're here to—"

Leather lifted his head like he hadn't heard a word the detective said. His eyes were bloodshot, skin sallow. Deep regret, palpable and unforgivable. "I killed my daughter."

The detective fumbled, clearly stunned by such a sudden confession. He looked to Sadie like, *is this for real?* "Mr. Norcross, are you admitting you planted the bomb?"

"I never thought... she wasn't supposed to be on the dock..."

"Sir?"

"It was only supposed to injure...too much explosive..."

Sadie grabbed onto the back of a chair to brace herself. The room spun, and she had to remind herself to breathe. This couldn't be possible. She left her body, traveled up to the ceiling, peering down at the scene. They were all just specks. Tiny dots in the house of the Lord. How could something so evil live here?

Sadie returned to her body, trembling, tears pouring in rivers. "Pops," she said, her voice barely a squeak.

Leather met her eyes, and it was like she didn't recognize him. The man she'd known and admired her whole life. The one who started it all. So many long days together in the sun, where little Sadie would crawl up under the driver's seat of the boat and fall asleep to the sound of a humming engine. It was always her grandfather's smile she looked for after those early races. She'd so badly wanted to please him. She'd have done anything. She *had* done everything.

And now... now, he said things she couldn't comprehend. Couldn't match to the man she thought she knew. He was old and dull, a fragment of his lustrous self. Who was this person?

Leather slowly stood then, and Sadie instinctively took a step back, like he was a dangerous criminal, instead of an aging soul of seventy-five. But their eyes remained locked, and finally, after a stretch of silence that seemed to last forever, his lips parted, and he uttered words that broke her heart. "I was doing it for you, champ."

Epilogue

Six months later

It was hard to believe a new ski season was upon them already, but time had a funny way of rolling on even in the midst of tragedy. Spring brought with it the Swiss Pro Slalom, the first event of the season, and the one that had set everything in motion the previous year. Willa often wondered if she hadn't won that first race, hadn't crushed Sadie's seven-year winning streak, if things would still have unfolded like they did. For many weeks she suffered chilling nightmares, and even as months passed, the choices made on that terrible day followed her. The guilt she carried was inescapable. How could she not blame herself? For pushing so hard to win. For not putting an end to the rivalry.

For not accepting second best.

No, her therapist reminded her on repeat. What Leather Norcross did was not Willa's fault, and she shouldn't harbor any guilt for the natural talent she possessed. After nearly six months in therapy, Willa still struggled to accept it. But like the long list of other baggage she unpacked in her weekly sessions, coming to terms with the events of her life was a work in progress.

Willa waded into the water until it reached her chest. She plunged her ski under and reached down to stick her feet in the boots. It wasn't as easy to put a ski on underwater as it was on the dock, but she had a thing about docks now. She preferred to keep her distance.

Ski on, Willa grabbed the tow rope handle and let the boat gently pull her away from shore. Through her concentration, she heard the announcer over the loudspeaker. "And in the first seed position, ladies and gentlemen, let's hear it for Willa Betts!" A round of applause echoed off the water. Willa let it permeate her skin, feeling it on a cellular level.

The boat roared to life and pulled Willa up out of the water. Wind whipped in her face, sending her dark braid back off her shoulder. She adjusted her grip, took a breath, then cruised out over the wake.

* * *

Willa easily smoked the competition that day, largely in part because her number one competitor wasn't there. Sadie Norcross, the water ski princess, no longer took to the water. Sadie's ski, at one time more familiar to her than her own feet, now lived in the front closet of her apartment, next to a yoga mat and a pile of sneakers. If anyone checked, they'd have found a thin layer of dust on the bindings.

Sadie hadn't been back in the water since the day her mother was killed. As though a light switch had finally turned on in her brain, she made a decision that day, unbeknownst at the time, but slowly coming into focus. She wouldn't live for anyone else. Moving forward, she'd chart a new path—one that wasn't carved out for her.

It started with the baby growing inside her.

* * *

"Sounds perfect," the doctor said, pressing the fetal doppler monitor against Sadie's belly. "What's your guess?"

"Girl," Sadie said.

"And you, Baz?"

Baz's mouth tipped up into a smile. "Girl."

"Two guesses for a girl. I guess I'll say boy just to balance the scales a little. Only six more weeks until we find out." The doctor helped Sadie sit up and handed her a wad of paper towels to wipe the gel from her stomach. "Everything looks great. Keep doing what you're doing. I'll see you in two weeks for your next appointment."

Sadie and Baz thanked the doctor, and she left the room. Sadie wiggled her shirt down over her swollen stomach and hobbled off the table. Everything was a challenge at this point in her pregnancy, but Sadie regularly reminded herself to be grateful. Things could have taken a different route. All those months ago when she'd seen the blood in her suit, she'd been convinced she was losing the baby. What had been such a scary moment turned out to be nothing more than a false alarm. Both Sadie and the growing life inside her were fine—at least in that regard.

"Do you want to go grab lunch or something?" Baz said, hands in his pockets.

Sadie's eyes flashed to his, but quickly darted away. She stuffed her appointment paperwork into her bag. "Sorry, I... I have to get back. Class at one."

"Okay." His posture deflated a bit, but he didn't push. Didn't have the right to.

Such was the new dynamic between them—committed co-parents and nothing more. When she'd broken down after her mother's funeral and told Baz about the baby, he'd wrapped Sadie in his arms and they'd both cried.

Cried for the grandmother this baby would never know.

Cried for the stained legacy left behind by its great-grandfather.

Cried for the marriage they'd tried to make work for too long, the one that was only held together by the pressure of outside forces.

Baz knew it was over. Guilt was the only thing that had made him stay. He'd contributed to their teenage circumstances, and so he needed to see it through. Only that was naïve thinking. No marriage could survive under false pretenses.

Sadie accepted the unspoken understanding that things would be very different for them moving forward. What once was love hadn't been love for quite some time—not in the way it took to keep a marriage afloat. And so they made the decision and put out a statement to the public the following week—this time, one they crafted themselves and that spoke the truth. Resentment, it turned out for Sadie, only hurt one person—and it wasn't the one she was resenting.

After much thought and consideration, we have decided to amicably end our marriage. We arrived at this decision with gratitude for the twelve loving years we spent together. Doing so is, of course, painful and difficult, and so we kindly ask for privacy and respect as we navigate our new chapter as friends and co-parents.

The past six months had been anything but easy for Sadie. Burying a mother, seeing a grandfather put away for the rest of his life. The things she'd learned about Leather's dark past were hard to reconcile. His thirst to win, his capacity to skirt the rules to get there. In the aftermath of his arrest, Leather admitted to slashing the tow rope at the MasterCraft Pro, mistakenly thinking Willa would be skiing first. He'd hoped she'd take a fall, maybe tear a rotator cuff or an ACL. Clear a wider path for Sadie. As horrifying as this revelation was, however, it couldn't compare to the next confession: the doping, the homemade bomb that was a little too powerful and hit the wrong target. Suddenly, Sadie questioned everything. This bloodline of gifted athletes—was it all a sham? One thing was for sure: honesty didn't always pay, but dishonesty sure cost a lot.

She'd fallen under a cloud of darkness for weeks after that, and it wasn't until the internet algorithm gods started sending targeted college admissions ads for interior design programs that the weight began to lift. She knew what she needed to do. Going back to school to discover her true passions took guts. There were times she had serious doubts—could she be anything other than a water skier? Could she make a name for herself outside her family's shadow?

One thing was for certain: she was sure going to try.

Succeed was more like it. Sadie would go on to graduate top of her class from Florida State. At her graduation, Baz would hold four-year-old Nora so the little girl could see her mommy cross the stage. Next to him, Sadie's father would watch with pride. She'd leave behind the water for the business world and be just as dominant, growing a small design shop into a full-fledged tourist destination. Product lines and design services, a full-blown lifestyle brand. She'd have a future she never could have dreamed of. It wouldn't be perfect—nothing ever was—but it would be beautifully imperfect. Just her and Nora.

Loves would come and go for both Sadie and Baz, but they'd find solace in every relationship that came their way. And then finally, when Nora would reach high school, Sadie would meet someone who would light up her heart—a man with a history of his own and what some might call baggage, but what she simply would call bonus kids. They'd marry, and she'd take his last name, leaving Norcross behind.

* * *

"Kicking the season off with a whopping score of 5@10.25, your first place winner...Willa Betts!" Willa stepped onto the podium and waved to the crowd. "Willa, anything you'd like to say?" The announcer extended the microphone to her. Willa cautiously accepted it, pulse steady despite her expanding chest.

"Thank you so much," she began. She hadn't prepared anything. Sometimes there were live post-race interviews, and sometimes there weren't. Being the first event of the season, she should have come ready with a few words. This was a big moment, so many eyes on her. Instead, she spoke off the cuff with one thing in mind: the only way to end a rivalry was for someone to rise above it.

"I'd like to dedicate today's event to the memory of Deb Norcross, a phenomenal skier who paved the way for girls like me." She caught Roxanne's eye from the sideline. Roxanne gave a gentle nod of approval. Willa returned to the camera. "And to Sadie. It wasn't the same without you here today. Thanks for always pushing me to be my best. We miss you."

Everyone clapped. Several onlookers wiped at misty eyes. Willa handed the mic back to the announcer, who wrapped up with a reminder about the next tournament's dates. Life moved on.

As she headed to her car, Willa's phone buzzed with an incoming text. Her chest warmed. One word, from Sadie: **Thanks**.

Willa left it at that. Everything else was understood.

Thinking of Sadie, however, didn't come without strings. She could no more conjure Sadie's face without seeing Baz's right next to it. Even though Willa knew the two had split, it did little to mend the hole in her heart she knew would always belong to him. But stories didn't always have happy endings, and for Willa and Baz, their pasts were too complicated for anything feasible to make sense. The lines between lust and love and friendship blurred, so that neither of them could see straight. So when Willa read the news of Sadie and Baz's impending divorce, it didn't jumpstart her lust like she once thought it would. She used to imagine running into his arms, everything finally perfect, exactly how it was always meant to be. But that sentiment didn't come—not anymore. In its place was perhaps the first sense of contentment she'd ever felt.

She sent a text on a cold December morning, a month after the attack.

I'm sorry to hear about you and Sadie.

ya, been a long time coming

You'll be a great dad.

thx I'm gonna try

I guess I just wanted to let you know I'm going to disconnect for a while, clear my head.

i get it. what would they call us? a rebound

You know I always loved you.

i loved you too

Maybe, Willa told herself, their stars would align when the time was right. But for now, she needed space to see through the cobwebs.

They weren't friends, they weren't enemies. Just strangers with memories.

What she didn't know and couldn't predict was the arrival of a new man in her life—someone outside the waterskiing world who knew so very little about her past, but who would listen to every detail as she told him her story over cups of coffee, lakeside picnics, and later, curled up skin-to-skin beneath the sheets. He'd become all that she hoped to find, and the two of them would bring three children into the world. Children who found happiness in the water like their mother, and who would grow up hearing stories about Willa and her friends, Sadie and Baz—their adventures, their secrets, their triumphs and their tragedies. Willa would tuck them into bed every night until the day they left home, each kiss on the forehead sewing up another of her childhood wounds.

She would go on to become the winningest female slalom skier, hanging up her beloved ski at the age of forty-five when her body said it was enough. But she'd never abandon the water completely. Each time her body sank under the cool surface, she would remember why she loved it so much, how it wrote her history—and the people that came along for the ride. Each time water rushed over her scar, she would remind herself: There are two types of pain. One that hurts you, and the other that changes you.

Acknowledgments

I'd be remiss not to begin these acknowledgments by thanking the person who not only taught me to ski, but who gave me so many wonderful childhood memories on the water. Dad, whether or not you knew it at the time, getting us kids on skis, in inner tubes, and splashing in the water created life-long memories I'll always cherish. I may be a baby when it comes to hopping off the platform into a chilly morning lake, and I'm sorry I'm so afraid of seaweed ("Jenny, it's literally just *grass!*"), but I hope you know how fondly I look back on all the time spent on the boat. Now, I couldn't be happier to watch *my* kids discover the joy of the lake, boating, and skiing.

Despite spending a good portion of my childhood on the lake and learning to ski when I was six, I'm far from a professional skier. In fact, every time I yell *Hit it!* nowadays, I pray I'll get up (I almost always do). With that, I had to do a great deal of research while writing this book. Way back when I was in the earliest stages of drafting, I did a simple Google search for "professional women water skiers," and came across a list of names. I found many on social media, and after browsing some profiles, sent an Instagram message to Chelsea Mills, explaining the premise of my book and asking if she'd be willing to answer a few questions. To my surprise, she responded almost immediately with a friendly *Sure!* and her phone number. This was my first clue into the culture of the water ski community: welcoming and generous.

We got on the phone that day. And to my great fortune, Chelsea happened to be coming off a morning training session with another skier, Whitney McClintock-Rini. Both women said they'd be happy for me to email additional questions. That was October 2022. It wasn't until over a year later—January 2024—when I reached back out to Whitney again with a big ask: would she be willing to read my now-completed manuscript? Her response: "I'm in!"

Whitney, your feedback and insight helped me fine-tune key aspects of the book, particularly the race scenes, and I feel so fortunate to have had your eyes on my early draft. Thank you for your time and thoughtful comments—they were truly invaluable.

To my other early readers—Maggie Giles, Jenn Bouchard, Kerry Chaput and Caitlin Weaver—my books wouldn't be anything without your priceless input (no really, they'd be half the length). I'm so grateful for the brainstorming sessions, manuscript comments that made me laugh, and help when I wasn't quite sure if certain parts were working.

An author is nothing without her community, and so I must give a shoutout to my fellow authors at The Eleventh Chapter, whom I adore and who have become not only my dear friends, but my biggest support in the rollercoaster that is writing and publishing. HOWARD!

Thank you to my friends and family, especially DJ and my three kids, who are the best cheerleaders. My local and extended community of bookstores and booksellers have always supported me, and for that I'm eternally thankful.

Finally, I want to give credit where credit is due...and that's to the incredible athletes in the world of professional waterskiing. It's a little-known sport—one that receives far less fanfare than others (hint: there's

ACKNOWLEDGMENTS

no paparazzi)—but the men and women at the helm are world-class athletes who travel around the world to compete. Thank you, especially the women (sorry guys, this book is largely about the ladies), for kicking ass. You all have a new fan in me.

If my book scratched an itch and you're interested in learning more about the world of waterskiing, there's a fabulous documentary on YouTube, produced by the Waterski Broadcasting Company, called *The Unknown Sport of Waterskiing*. So great...check it out!

About the Author

Jen Craven is the author of commercial fiction, both indie and traditionally published. Her contemporary debut, *Best Years of Your Life* was inspired from over a decade teaching at a small liberal arts university. She later signed with Bookouture where she publishes domestic suspense: *The Baby Left Behind*, *Her Daughter*, and *The Day She Vanished*.

Jen writes from northwestern Pennsylvania, where she lives with her husband and three children. When not working on her books, she can be found thrift shopping, running (reluctantly), and attending a myriad of youth sports.

Learn more at www.jencraven.com or by following her on Facebook and Instagram at @jencravenauthor.